I0575143

SAVE THE WORLD

SAVE THE HUMANS | BOOK 3

AVERY BLAKE

JOHNNY B. TRUANT

STERLING & STONE

Copyright © 2019 by Johnny B. Truant & Sean Platt

All rights reserved.

No part of this book may be reproduced in any form or by any electronic or mechanical means, including information storage and retrieval systems, without written permission from the author, except for the use of brief quotations in a book review.

SAVE THE WORLD

1

Now

With flames starting to spread through the flammable parts of the Fortress, Hollis realized he'd made a mistake. Fortunately, Mia was there to point it out, lest it go unmentioned.

"I see," she said as he found her in the Barbie room. "Now we're going to die in here."

They were surrounded — not just by the mindless others, but by the fences as well. Where they were was as much backyard as Fortress, as much Fortress as it was backyard. The support members of the ramshackle structure were all unknown materials, the whole structure questionably sound. The major value of the place wasn't its architecture, though that was impressive. No, what set it apart was the nostalgia of everything that had gone into it — which, he supposed, was the whole reason they'd come here in the first place, and also why the hordes had come as well.

Hollis had seen a Hobie surfboard, just like the one he'd

ridden during a summer spent with a bunch of do-nothings in San Diego, now turned into the door of a bedroom. One entire wall of the main sitting area was wallpapered with discarded license plates in the old style, before so many of the states had changed their look. The creator had lined one corridor in action figures, most of their faces rubbed raw, broken, or corroded by acids at the dump, from back when they'd first been tossed, before they'd been rescued and turned into art here.

It was a shame to let it burn, with all the memories that Hollis — who hadn't even grown up in San Antonio — felt from even the clearly-local doodads that made up the ramshackle structure. The artist was brilliant. Somehow, he'd made something that evoked memory in all who visited.

Again: the entire point, and the reason the Fortress had to go — regrettable though it was.

"You set the fire?" Mia said. "We talked about thinking first, Hollis. Remember? You set it too close!"

"Yeah? How the hell am I supposed to set a fire without being close to it?"

Now the hordes of dead-eyed humans were all around them. Not really attacking; more just causing congestion. And that caused another problem. Hollis and Mia hadn't wanted to kill them. They'd set the blaze to break whatever force kept drawing people here.

"I was going to make a molotov cocktail," Mia said, holding up a vodka bottle, already stuffed with a wad of fabric.

"Can we just drink it instead?" He smiled wider, now reaching for her, their inside joke percolating. He could play this. He could spin it to his favor. "You still owe me one, remember. Because: *'I never ...'*"

She shook her head. And in her rolled eyes, he could almost hear her chide him: *Just like you, to ruin something that should have been sweet.*

"Not now, Hollis," she said, retreating and heading for the door. "Of *all* times, not now."

"Hang on, now. What did I—"

But she was gone, out the door.

With Mia in the lead and Hollis behind like a puppy, they rushed out just as the stairway was consumed behind them. The Fortress, being such an unconventional structure, was falling apart in an unconventional manner. Hollis had expected it to go up in one big pyre and to do so slowly given all the metal inside, but already the blaze was growing — and, to Mia's *going to die in here* point — had begun to spit sparks and drop flaming members all over the fenced-in yard. The Fortress itself wasn't large, but its halo, it turned out, was impressive. From a firefighting sense, anyway.

But at least the fire was doing what it was supposed to do. The fences were covered with dead-eyed zombies who, if they didn't walk away right now, were going to go up like human torches. They weren't very smart and weren't at all aggressive; they'd proven both when they'd parted to let Mia and Hollis enter the grounds, then stayed outside because they couldn't figure out the gate.

The gate that Hollis went to now, with all those moaning, fucked-up people beyond. Getting out would be like exiting a house without the cats escaping.

He unlatched it, knowing from frustrating experience that once they pushed it out with the car's grille, it'd just swing closed again. Finally, that might work in their favor. The damn dead-brained people shaking the fences wouldn't be able to figure that out, wouldn't get inside — and with luck, wouldn't burn.

With the gate unlatched but still leaning closed, Hollis returned to the car, almost spearing himself on the action figures glued to the front fins. Mia was already behind the wheel, the engine running. She'd put on sunglasses, possibly against the glare of the spreading flame. Or maybe just because she was a badass bitch.

"I should drive," Hollis said.

And Mia, depressing the accelerator as the Fortress burned behind them, said, "No, you should not."

"Look out!"

But Mia had seen. She jockeyed the wheel, avoiding the falling kayak that struck the ground in front of them. Then, wordlessly, she threaded through the gate, pushing the dead-eyed people away, metal on flesh.

Then she parked, looked back at the burning Fortress, and glared at Hollis.

"Why are you stopping?"

"I thought you might want to stop and admire what you did without thinking" Mia said. She glanced back; she'd clearly stopped to ensure the gate fully closed. But that's not what her eyes said right now.

The thing was burning. More debris was falling. It had gone up in minutes — all that highly flammable junk.

Then something new happened.

Instead of continuing to try and bash through what would soon be a very hot fence, the people around the Fortress of Refuse turned and began to advance on the car.

"What are they doing?" Mia asked, her anger evaporated.

"Looks like they don't like us burning down their temple."

They were surrounding the car. Banging on the windshield: metaphorical zombies doing their best to impersonate real ones. Good thing the top was up, but under this assault, that half-shattered driver-side window wouldn't last long.

"Still want to stick around?" Hollis asked. "Because right now I want to *get the fuck out of dodge!*"

Mia swapped brake for gas and dropped the clutch.

Rubber burnt and Hollis looked over his shoulder, disbelieving how quickly the fire had spread since just—

2
———

Ten Minutes Ago

"WHAT ARE THEY DOING NOW?" Mia yelled out the window.

Hollis, on the outside of the structure, was surveying the fences. The people here had been docile when they'd arrived. Mia still wasn't sure she understood exactly what had happened to them — ahem, what the Fortress of Refuse had *done* to them — but she had a pretty good idea of the basics. In theory, some of those folks could recover. But it was hard to become who you were (or, perhaps anyone at all) once all that had made you *YOU* was gone.

Again she wondered at them, not waiting for Hollis to answer, going to the window instead. The window had no glass, and the frame was discarded golf clubs. It was strange: the roadside monument, for being made of trash, should stink more. But it was all "clean" trash, for whatever that was worth — stuff the builder had scrubbed clean before going about his insanity.

All around the room: Barbie dream houses, Barbies,

assorted girl toys. Some were very old, a few were somewhat late-model, but many were about as old as Mia — the right age, essentially, that Mia might have played with these exact same sets when she'd been little. She hadn't; Mia had been more of a tomboy who'd found dolls stupid. Her cousin Leslie, though, had had the full set, and she and Leslie had been close. Just being here — zombies or no zombies — was tugging something from deep inside her.

She felt the tug, like a part of her wanted to leave and go away forever. It was heavy, like an emotional weight. How could something so heavy float away? And yet it had, for the people of San Antonio, over what Theo had guessed were just days. That right there made Mia not want to stay long. A man had built this place, but the aliens were the ones who'd made it holy — who'd made San Antonio quietly famous for something entirely new. *Remember the Alamo?* Not around here, anymore.

Hollis hadn't heard her. She shouted to him again. He'd been too lost watching the people. Maybe even worried about them. When they'd discovered this place, those milling around it had been so passive as to be nonexistent. Sad, really. If a zombie movie could make you cry, it'd be these zombies starring in it. Being in the Barbie room, Mia could feel both sides of what they must have felt before they'd come up empty. Mia and Hollis, at least, knew they had to act fast. They'd come, seen, left, analyzed, and decided to come back for this ugly solution to a big problem, unsure if it'd even work. They knew most of all that no matter what, they had to get in and out, spending as little time at the Fortress of Refuse as possible. There were too many thoughts around this place. Too many memories once closely held, yet eager, here, to be stolen away.

That's why Theo and Carol weren't here with them,

obviously. Only four people in the world knew the whole story of what the aliens were doing with the all the data the Astral app had gathered. Only they knew the connection between the data once accessible via Thomas's attache case, the Fortress in San Antonio, and the mothership. If this place scooped out what Hollis and Mia knew, at least Theo and Carol, miles distant, would still remember. But even the fact that they'd planned for a failsafe gave Mia the chills.

She remembered these toys. She remembered her sweet cousin Leslie. She didn't want to forget.

"Everyone out here seems cool," Hollis said.

Mia looked. They very much weren't cool. They were dead, wanting only to get inside, to touch the old items so recently in their memories. They weren't humans, so much as husks of humans.

She had a plan, just like she'd had a plan back at Brendan's compound weeks ago. The only difference was that this time, Hollis wouldn't screw it up with some dumbass plan of his own.

Mia picked up the bottle of vodka she'd found, conveniently half-full, just asking to become a bomb. They'd found fliers in the abandoned house beside the Fortress. The owner — and builder of the monstrosity in which Mia found herself — was gone, possibly dead, possibly run off to hide when the ships arrived on Astral day and the bug-things started to patrol the towns. But the fliers said he'd built the place as if obsessed, scavenging junkyards to build first one room, then another and another with last year's trash. Mia, judging by the vodka, was willing to bet that his obsession had caught up with him. The empty-brained people couldn't figure out how to pass the fence, so he'd probably just come into the Fortress as the end days came, drinking himself into oblivion while watching out the exact same window Mia was standing at now. Thinking it made her feel sad. But then again, even the best of this place made her sad — which was, she knew, why the aliens had chosen it as their skimming net.

Mia ripped a line of fabric from her worse-for-wear jacket, then stuffed it into the bottle's mouth. The fences weren't far from the Fortress. After some analysis on exactly how best to burn the place down, throwing a molotov cocktail seemed like the best option. They could hit the thing from past the fence, ensuring that they were clear and the humans stayed out. There was enough in here, despite the steel and aluminum, that would quickly burn.

Outside, the people who'd been so docile began to shout and claw at the fence. Some clawed at their own faces, or at each other. It was a sudden and undifferentiated frenzy, shocking after the two days they'd spent watching these people, Theo and Carol both offered theories as to how exactly it all worked and why the people of San Antonio had become the way they now were. They sagged about, morose, just shells of conscious beings. You could murder one slowly, if you wanted, and it wouldn't protest.

But now, they were protesting.

Why?

That's when Mia smelled smoke, and yet she hadn't thrown her molotov.

She looked. Flames were spreading fast, seemingly from another room inside the structure.

Hollis. God dammit, Hollis.

Because they'd talked about this. Destroying the Fortress of Refuse had to be done like a controlled implosion. When demolitionists wanted to take down a building, they didn't just toss C4 in the basement and go to town. It was considered, measured, every plan made and precaution taken.

And yet Hollis, despite their talks about conferring before acting, appeared to have just thrown a match.

He rushed into the room while the people outside began to clamber all over one another, shouting in pain and sorrow, losing their minds even further than they were already lost. The flames seemed to double every fifteen seconds and already Mia felt herself being surrounded. They could make it out. Maybe. If they hurried, and didn't do any of that pre-sabotage thinking they talked about after all.

When Hollis popped through her room's entrance (hockey-stick frame and a diner sign for a door), he was smiling like he had a coat hanger between his gums and teeth. Like a big old dumb asshole, in other words.

"I see," Mia said. "Now we're going to die in here."

They ran for the car. And all the while Mia kept thinking how stupid Hollis was to have already forgotten the things they'd *just* talked about—

3

———

In an abandoned dry cleaner building, Theo sat atop a shutdown hydraulic pressing machine like the King of Clean. Carol was in a rolling chair she'd taken from the office, tapping her finger against her chin, rolling as she tried to think. The rolling was distracting for Hollis, but he tried to remember that so much of what he did was distracting to others. It was part of the personal growth program he'd silently gone on after nearly dying. The quack they'd found had been good enough to patch his cuts and yank a few dislocations back into place, but he hadn't been able to fix Hollis's head. Not that he'd thought it needed fixing, but he pissed Mia off often enough that he figured he might as well try. Every time he was spontaneous, something went wrong. Maybe it wasn't defeat to actually work with others to create a plan, then follow it.

After much contemplation, Theo said, "Honestly, I wonder if the best thing to do is to just burn it down."

"It's metal," Carol said. "It won't burn."

But Hollis, unlike Carol, had been there. For obvious reasons, half of their party had stayed behind, but Hollis and Mia had actually *seen* the Fortress of Refuse. They'd gone inside, briefly, to walk its halls. They'd found the mindless people around it exactly the same as they'd found in the surrounding areas, the worst of it well into downtown San Antonio. There'd been a lot more people around the Fortress, drawn there just as they'd predicted. But they hadn't resisted when he and Mia had opened the gate to sneak inside. And inside, despite the metal and fiberglass and plastic that made the place's best features, there was also plenty of wood and cloth to burn.

"It'll go," Hollis said. "All we need is a match."

"What about the people around it?" Mia asked.

Theo shrugged. "What *about* them? I think we've decided that everything the aliens used the Fortress to suck out of them is gone for good."

"I don't mean, 'What will happen to their minds if we destroy the Fortress?' Seems to me you guys are right; their minds are probably not coming back no matter what happens."

"Which is why I'm so excited to go back," Hollis said. "Devil knows I'm too smart already."

"If you move fast, the damage it does to you will be minimal," Theo said. "Remember what I showed you? Exponential decay the farther out you go, like a magnetic—"

Hollis flapped a hand to shut him up.

"What I *meant*," Mia said, grabbing back the conversational baton that Hollis (*of course,* her eyes said) had once again stolen, "was, 'Won't they be in danger when the Fortress burns?'"

"Why would they?" Carol asked.

"Because they're mindless. Because all the ones around it seem to be able to do is to try and get as close to it as possible, like an insect being drawn toward a light. Or, once we light it up, toward a bug zapper."

"And you think that if the Fortress burns, they'll try to get at it. To rush into the flames?"

"They can't get past the fence," Hollis said.

Theo shifted, uncomfortable. "Look, I hate to be the one to say it, but it hardly matters. What quality of life can those people have anyway? Even if they can still form new memories once the Fortress is no longer siphoning off of them, they'll be completely different people. Their childhoods will be blank. We've already seen serious psychological problems in them, because they're all instinct — all id. That won't stop if they're as empty as they seem. Even without the Fortress drawing on them, the best they can hope is to become some horrible breed of feral."

"So we should just kill them," Mia said. "Is that the idea?"

"If it means stopping it," Carol said from Hollis's side, "yes."

Mia crossed her arms. For as hard as she could sometimes be, some things turned her curiously soft. She wasn't great at facing unpleasant truths, and didn't like this one even though it'd fallen into their laps, and their laps alone.

"Look," Theo said, leaning forward. "We can't shut whatever the aliens are doing down, because we don't know enough about it — even after going through *everything* that was in the attache case. There's just so much atop even the complexities Thomas's people had documented off the back of the Astral app data, and even then, the way the aliens tethered the datacenter in Austin all the way to this pile of garbage up here is far beyond me. We all agree what will happen if it's not shut down, though, and that means we have to shut it down any way we can. I don't know how to reprogram it, so the only option left is a system reset." He settled back. "In this case, that means destroying it. The best way to destroy it completely is the most primal way nature settles things: with fire."

Mia didn't like that, and it was apparent to Hollis at the time, in the little dry cleaner far from the Fortress that they'd commandeered as temporary group HQ during their time in town — which, to forestall brainlessness, Hollis intended to be as short a time as possible. It was also apparent to Hollis as they got back in the car, leaving Carol and Theo behind again so their superior brains would stay maximally intact. It was apparent during the drive to the opposite side of San Antonio, out into the suburbs, out to the weird little plot of land where Lawrence Brayburn had built his ridiculous roadside attraction over (according to the fliers) the past fifteen years.

Had he known? Hollis wondered. Had Brayburn had any idea, while he was scavenging car bumpers and foosball table parts and the remains of a million broken toys from the dump, that he was building the world's most base temple to nostalgia ... and that an unknown force, years later, might come along and turn it into a beacon for human memory and emotion?

They got through the crowd, sneaking themselves and the car inside so it'd be ready when they had to bolt, careful to let none of the dead-headed citizens enter the small back-yard in which the Fortress had been built.

This time, things were somehow easier — for Hollis, yes, but also for Mia. He could see the difference on her face. Where last time she'd been pale, this time she seemed determined. Where last time she'd looked unsettled, this time she was focused, because they had a job to do.

But it wasn't *all* focus, he was starting to see. She'd driven the car; Sonny's now-absurd classic hadn't been built with autodrive. Hollis had been watching her on and off the whole way, trying to riddle her mood. After last night, everything between them was a little different. Some bridge had been crossed out in that barren land, behind the hill, around the fire. And after this morning, things were even *more* different — complicated by this strange place. Hollis remembered the feeling of her hand seeking his. He wouldn't be getting that, this time.

"How do you feel?" Hollis asked.

"I'm fine."

"Being back here, I mean."

"I know what we came here to do. That's what matters."

"I'm just asking because last time—"

"Let's just get it over with, Hollis."

Mia put the car in park, but left the engine running. Hollis's eyes strayed to the fence, beyond which he saw a structure he'd seen before: One wall of the Fortress's outer ring was made entirely of old aluminum lunchboxes. There was even one in there like the lunchbox he used to have, with G.I. Joe on the front.

Of course.

Looking at it felt too close to home. One more thing their predictor had seen coming. It freaked him right the fuck out, so he turned away.

But still a voice inside said,

It was old when I got it. Dad picked it up at a garage sale.

The rubber band. The warm coatroom. The illness, which hobbled him for hours.

Hollis pushed it away. He made himself remember this

morning. Neither of them wanted that feeling again, so he tightened something inside. Then it was just the two of them again in the car's cab, ridiculous add-ons beyond the windshield, hot-glued to the hood.

Mia turned to face him.

"It's going to be a controlled burn. You understand?" she said, waving a finger. Hollis had known a lecture was coming; he'd gotten that much from her silence during the half-hour drive. So he was all ready to nod first and ask questions later, as he was doing now.

Mia went on: "Like when they need to clear overgrown areas in a national park, but don't want it to devolve into a raging wildfire. *A controlled burn.* We'll scope it out, see what might burn best and how to burn it most safely, then get back together and make a plan."

"I hear you," Hollis said. "But honestly, it ain't hard to burn something."

"I'm not talking about ease. I'm talking about safety."

"C'mon, Mia. Every boy was a little bit pyro growing up. I used to set things on fire all the time — just little stuff, 'round the burn pit near our barn — and it never got out of hand. We don't want to be here any longer than we gotta." He put a finger to his temple, smiled in a way that was supposed to be engaging, and said, "Rots the brain worse than TV usedt'a."

Mia's eyebrows didn't part. Her face didn't relax. Hollis wondered what was wrong. His face had mostly healed after all the beatings. He should be able to charm her now, and it wasn't working.

"We make a plan," Mia said. "That's how it's going to go. So that we can be safe, and *they* can be safe." She swung her hand toward the babbling, mindless idiots pressing against the fence. They weren't even using their hands. Many were just pressing their faces into the wire. Would it really be such a tragedy if a big fire got them all?

"Fine," Hollis said. But it wasn't fine at all. He could already feel his brain getting softer, and he knew damn well how to set a simple blaze.

Mia regarded him for another few seconds, as if to see if he meant to flinch, then went inside. He heard her rattling around, taking unnecessary measure of the situation. But mama, you didn't need to analyze a cockroach before killing it. Analyzed or not, a boot squished them just the same.

Play along, Hollis said. *It's easier than arguing.*

He had a lighter in his pocket — a big silver Zippo he'd snatched from some old house as they'd made their pit stops on the trip here. Nice thing about Zippos was, you didn't need to hold anything down to keep them burning. You could light them, then toss them at whatever you wanted aflame. That's why all the guys in the movies used them. They were perfect for starting shit so you could walk dramatically away while something blew up behind you.

Hollis thought this as he bided his time, not caring to analyze anything, knowing exactly what he meant to burn. It was so simple. There were hoarded newspapers in one of the lower rooms. It didn't take a rocket scientist to figure out that's where this should begin, and doing so wouldn't take more than ten seconds.

Mia was already in one of the rooms high up, putzing around, wasting time. He could see and hear her, but kept his eyes on the Fortress instead.

He made a circuit of the place, killing time. The builder had planted a garbage garden full of spinning plastic sunflowers and tacky ornaments. There was a wing made only of road signs, and another made only of crushed soda cans, nailed together to form an impervious sheet. And as he concluded his circuit, he came again to the lunchbox wall. To the G.I. Joe lunchbox, front and center as if put there just for him.

It brought back shame. Humility.

Walk away, Hollis, he told himself.

But even now he could feel the memory tugged from somewhere, trying to leave on its own. He wouldn't need to forget about it, as he'd been trying to force himself to do. If he waited here long enough, the forgetting would happen all by itself.

Walk away. Walk a—

"What are they doing now?"

Hollis blinked. That was Mia, shouting from inside the Fortress. He didn't, for some reason, feel up to responding. But it broke his gaze at the lunchbox wall, and for that he was nonspecifically grateful.

He moved away from the Fortress, now walking the fence. People-watching ... in this case literally.

They were glassy-eyed, all of them. Nothing at all behind the windows. They weren't smart enough to be crazy. The alien machine network had (through some magic Theo and Carol seemed to understand, but Hollis didn't) sucked all the memories out of their heads. Memories brought forth through nostalgia for the stuff in this shit-pile, apparently. But in Hollis's opinion, if all it took to rattle your cage was a junkyard, then it was no big loss when you finally left the planet.

"*Hollis?*" Mia yelled from above.

He glanced up.

"Everyone out here seems cool."

That seemed to satisfy her, but nothing about the way they were approaching this errand was cool. It was, in fact, stupid. When you found a nest of something bad, you eradicated it without hesitating. All Mia was demanding, by her over-inspection of this hole, would only get them stung by wasps from the hive they'd come here to destroy.

When he saw her back away from the window from the corner of his eye, Hollis pulled the lighter from his pocket, flicked it, and watched the flame. Really, he should just do it. Once the flames were burning, she'd have to stop figuring and start their asses running. He'd known what needed to be done from the very first time he'd set eyes on this place, which according to his watch had happened just about—

4

"Holy shit."

"Holy shit," Mia agreed, though her thoughts about the place were more complex than she imagined Hollis's being. Hollis's reaction was mission-driven. They'd come here to figure out what significance a certain set of geographic coordinates (or network coordinates; she wasn't sure what Carol had done to triangulate this place from which the Astral database was receiving a crapload of data) had to the alien machine, then shut it down. Hollis, surely, was looking at the massive treehouse made of trash and seeing it as a strange target, but a target nonetheless. But for Mia, there was also a feeling. The second they'd gotten close to San Antonio, they'd seen how people were being drawn to this place — and so, it was, for Mia.

As Hollis drew the car to a stop, she heard echoes from the past that only she could hear. It wasn't unlike the mental congress she'd shared with the reptar back at Banks's place, or with unknown others through the lines of massive alien telepathy stones, or even Hollis, that one time. It felt ephemeral. Transitory. Even more so than the understanding she'd once had with the mind of that alien beast, and even that was more or less forgotten.

What comes here, dies here.

It was Mia's own thought, but she knew it was true. Not of the people, though. As they could see in the eyes of the lost souls clotting around what nearby signs called "The Fortress of Refuse," there was certainly a lot of figurative death here. But Mia's thought, rather, was of things no longer here. Of whispers from the past — things deep in her mind that she held close and precious. She wanted to hold her nostalgia close, the more this place somehow made her feel it — because if she relaxed her grip, it'd die, and be gone forever.

It felt like a hollow place. A place that had once been, but now nothing was left.

Mia shivered.

"You cold?"

She looked over. Funnily enough, Hollis's cluelessness made her feel better.

"I'm fine."

"This place is nuts. Just the sort of thing aliens would make, if they were out of their fucking E.T. minds."

Mia watched the scene for as long as her mind could handle it. Something was askew here, and it wasn't just the odd structure itself, or all the droolers trying to reach it. It was an itch Mia couldn't scratch, and staring at it all through a windshield with slopped-on paint at the corners and past toys glued all over the hood just made it too surreal to take.

She got out, minding the flagpole on the passenger side they hadn't taken the time to remove. There were people all around them, milling like pigeons. They'd seen people like this on the way — had stopped, surveyed, and realized they were harmless. What had happened to them, they hadn't known at first. But Mia, combining Theo and Carol's theories, her own mental experiences with the aliens, and a sense in her gut, thought she'd figured it out. They shouldn't fear these beings. They should pity them.

There were pieces of paper all over the ground, as if some unseen office had exploded. Mia stooped to pick one up. She read, while Hollis approached the jammed fence surrounding the thing.

"This says a man built it."

"Under alien influence?"

She shook her head. "Says he started it fifteen years ago and has been adding scraps to it ever since. 'Lawrence Brayburn.'" She flipped the paper over. "Look. There's a picture."

Hollis leaned to see the photo of Brayburn, but didn't take the paper. He returned his attention to the bizarre structure, which from here looked like a madman's cathedral, his back to Mia.

"I was expecting something more industrial," Hollis said.

They hadn't known what would be at the coordinates Theo had given them, carefully marking a map because GPS was so scattered as to be unreliable. On the drive up from Austin, they'd been playing a game: *What will we find?* Neither had any clue, but Mia herself had been expecting something alien, if what this place did was to harvest human thoughts for processing by the Austin datacenter. But they hadn't known for sure. All they'd known was that there was a lot of incoming data, and it was coming from here.

"Like a factory?" Mia asked.

"Like a computer place. You know. With antennas every-where. This is ... Well. I don't *know* what it is."

"I think it is an antenna," Mia said. "Or at least, part of it is. It's broadcasting to Austin. But look at these people, Hollis. I think it's drawing them in, so there's something to harvest."

Hollis looked from the structure to the people, then back again.

'Theo said the aliens were harvesting memories," Mia said.

"I guess it's zero sum," Hollis said, "because I don't think a copy of whatever was 'harvested' stayed inside these folks."

One of them ran into Hollis's unseen side, deflected without notice or incident, then began to play with the life-size He-Man head bolted to the Chevelle's front bumper. And why not? Judging by what they could see from here and what Mia had read on the flier, the Fortress of Refuse was full of toys and memorabilia just like it. All that mattered was evocation, and Lawrence Brayburn had hit on a formula that the aliens seem to have piggybacked right on top of. Forget about working hard to evoke human emotion. This place *was* evocation. This ridiculous thing before them, cobbled from the detritus of ages, was memory incarnate.

They approached the fence, carefully nudging aside vacant citizens to do so. They went gently, but once the brain-dead surrounded them, Mia's sense of emotional bottomlessness trebled. It was like being afloat in a bound-less sea, and knowing there was a chance Theo and Carol might not even make it to town wasn't helping tether her.

Once they stood side by side, Hollis did a curious thing — something he'd never have done, if not for the night they'd spent before. He took her hand, and gently at that.

She looked over, feeling strange. Lost. Dangling in a void, honestly unsure which direction was up.

"I never," Hollis said, "saw some weirdo's hobby get turned into an alien brain scoop."

"I guess I can't drink to that."

"Well then," Hollis said. "I never drove a car that looked like *that*." He pointed.

"That's cheating."

"Yeah. Well."

"I don't have a drink to take. And you'd have to drink, too, seeing as you drove most of the way here."

"Maybe I rigged it. Maybe I'd like a drink right around now."

That's when she realized: He was as freaked-out and scared as she was. There was nothing overtly threatening about the Fortress of Refuse, but there was something in the air that both of them could feel. On the surface, they'd seen much more frightening things and been in much more dangerous situations — both before the aliens arrived and after.

But still, this was worse. It was like a subtle vortex. If they stood where they were for long enough, they'd slowly lose their minds. They'd go empty and never even see it was coming. Mia had heard, in a high school chemistry class, about why strong bases could be more dangerous than strong acids. It was because with bases, you didn't always feel your flesh being corroded away. Her teacher told a story about a factory worker who spilled concentrated sodium hydroxide into his boot, but didn't notice until the end of the day when he took the boot off and his foot came with it.

That's what this place would do to them. It'd take what they had, a bit at a time. Soon they'd forget what it was doing, and why it was bad, and why they'd want it to stop.

And so it would go until they were like the rest. Until they made to take themselves from the boot, only to realize that they, themselves, were no longer there.

They went through the gate, leaving the car idling outside. The zombies stayed behind. The tour was quick. Mia couldn't take being inside the place, but felt a curious duality about it. On one hand, it was something unholy that, true to expectations, needed to be shut down. But on the other hand, it was something precious that should be protected forever. The mix of both was disarming. It was like something deadly hidden inside a childhood keepsake.

They only spent a few minutes. After that, they were beyond the gate again, looking in at it again, spellbound again, and for some reason unable to leave.

Hollis cleared his throat, then spoke in his *Let's-make-sure-I've-got-this-right* voice.

"So people are *feeling feelings* about all the shit here, thanks to whatever the aliens did to this guy's backyard monument to pop history," he said, "and as they *feel*, it's sucking those feelings away?"

"And, apparently, sending them to the database containing the Astral app data," Mia finished. Then she corrected herself: "To whatever the aliens have built *using* the Astral app data."

"How do you send memories over the air?"

"I don't know."

"Why send them anywhere, let alone all the way down to Austin?"

"You heard Carol's theory. Didn't it make sense?"

"No," Hollis said.

Mia watched the structure. Drawn to it far more than she liked.

"Me either," she said.

"I never understood what some lady said about decoding memories," Hollis said. "But on that one, I guess nobody drinks."

The cuteness was wearing off. She knew he was just trying to make her feel better, but she felt too numb, now, to appreciate it.

She slipped her hand from his. Hollis looked over as she kept her gaze forward — just a shape in the corner of her eye.

"You okay, Sparkles?"

"No."

"Theo wants us to destroy it."

"When Theo said that, he didn't know what it was."

"I say we burn it."

"We can't just burn it without understanding it," Mia said.

"You heard what they said. This thing, right here, is the center of the problem. And according to what Carol thinks, it's spreading."

"We just need a little time."

"I don't want to stay here anymore. I can feel myself forgetting math."

"Not time *here*," Mia said. "We go away. Take time to think and assess. *Then* we come back and act."

"Go away where?"

"We meet up with Carol and Theo as planned."

"We don't even know that the dry cleaner Theo remembered is even still there, let alone that some gang hasn't claimed it. And what about Carol and Theo? We don't know they'll show up today, or tomorrow. They could get held up. *We* sure got held up."

"Just a while," she said. "Let's go there and just see. See if they're there. And if they are, we tell them what we found, and see what they have to say. It's just ... It's not what I expected to find. Is it for you?"

"Obviously not."

She shook her head. Lips pressed together. It was hard to find the antecedent of whatever she was feeling, whatever it was.

"*Please,* Hollis," she said, turning to face him.

So they went. And thank God, Theo and Carol had already arrived. If they hadn't, Mia would have felt even more lost. She could talk to Hollis about what they'd seen inside the monument to human culture, and now that they were farther away from it, she thought she could talk with some amount of objectivity. But still she was relieved for the others — relieved, in some strange way, to have the comforting anchor of someone who hadn't seen it, who'd *never* see it, who'd never be polluted by its strange energy. Someone who, from a distance and using only the flier as recon, could imagine the thing for what it had been rather than what the aliens had somehow made it today.

They went over it and over it. Mia felt herself torn, but less so as she spent more time away from the Fortress's lure. She started to feel less kinship with the thing and more anger at what, again from a distance, suddenly struck her as manipulation. Whatever siren song the Fortress was putting out to call people to it — whatever it was doing once it had the people close, like doomed ships approaching the rocks — began to feel like something squeezed from its victims rather than something genuine.

Inside one of the rooms in particular, she'd spent one very long minute recalling fond memories of her cousin Leslie — and, almost immediately, felt those memories wanting to drift away. But in retrospect those memories struck Mia as false. They were *like* her real feelings about her past, but not the real thing. And yet she felt sure that if she'd let her attention slip and the first of those memories — fake as they were — had begun to drift away, they'd all start to go. If she'd stayed there long enough, she might not even remember Leslie. Her precious moments would have become part of something hideous: a monster cobbled from not just her memory but all memories, no less Frankenstein than the Fortress itself.

Finally, with all sides reporting in and all arguments discussed throughout most of an afternoon, Carol thought deep and Theo, sitting atop a steam press, rendered his verdict.

"Honestly," he said, "I wonder if the best thing to do is to just burn it down."

Hollis was already nodding along, and Mia was of split feeling about that, about Hollis's conviction. He'd been as strange around the Fortress as she'd felt, like when he'd taken her hand by the gate, as she'd been mired in emotion she didn't understand, strangely kind for Hollis, just like he'd done—

5

———

"You come over here," he said. "You will look into this with me. Ha ha ha ha." The four "ha's" came out mechanical, as if produced by a machine. It was possible, Mia thought as she listened, that their man had only said two sentences, and the laughter had actually been his vacuum cleaner with something caught in the brushes — not a human sound, but perfectly timed.

But no, that's how Torchy Banner talked. It was just one more reason atop the rather large pile that kept Hollis from taking him seriously.

He gave Mia a look now. She rolled her eyes, because they'd been through this and through it. He'd had his reservations about coming here, okay. But if he was going to be a dick now that they'd come, why hadn't he waited in the car?

This guy is a joke, Hollis's eyes told her.

I don't want to hear it, Mia's eyes tried to tell him back.

Then she turned her head, refusing to look in Hollis's

direction. Torchy had already risen and was walking away, so Mia mentally blocked out her so-called partner and went with him. She could feel Hollis's annoyed energy behind her. But really: *What the hell?* She hadn't asked, on a whim, to go to have her palm read just for something to do. No. This was something they'd all agreed was worth checking out — the most analytical members of their party included.

Torchy, of course, led them to a crystal ball. Despite no longer looking at Hollis, she could feel him rolling his eyes from the shift in gravity.

"Look into it. Look!"

Mia looked, because this was a pretty clear order. Torchy had long black hair, pocked skin, a highly abnormal social compass, and wore a suit tethered by four belts. It was a look somewhere between elegant professional and what the fuck.

She saw nothing in the ball, though. It was a fortune-teller's parlor trick. There even seemed to be a light embedded in the bottom, to fool the rubes. She could see the wires.

Torchy waited, then spoke.

"What do you think? I think it is in the future you see, is that right?"

He was beside her, not looking into the ball himself, his hair dangling, his face (there was no other word for it) weird. It was impossible to tell how old he was. It was easier to tell how big of a joke he was. That one was actually pretty clear.

She heard Hollis sigh behind her.

"I kid, I kid!" Torchy said, all of a sudden, very pleased with himself. He laughed some more mechanical laughs: the machine back at work, not human at all. For the first time, Mia wondered if Torchy was, in fact, an alien. He'd been an Austin feature for years before the ships came, but maybe he'd been planted ahead of time, like a spy. That could happen, right?

"It is a gag," Torchy said. "You see?" he grabbed a cord from under the table, then rolled a rotary switch on its length to turn the ball on and off, on and off. "I like it as a light for my nighttime. I also have cut glass lamps. Very expensive. Thousands of dollars. We will talk about that later." He clapped his hands together. "Now, we play!"

"Play what?"

Torchy waved a hand. "I have many games."

"Uh-huh," Hollis said. "Have a lot of people up here to the player's lounge, Skippy?"

"Torchy."

"Whatever."

"No," Torchy said. "I do not have many visitors. There are many bad people out. *Mostly* bad. It will become worse. There is not much good left."

"You sound like my friend Dave," Hollis said.

"I should like to meet this Dave."

"Actually," Mia said, interrupting, "I was hoping you could tell us about the signal we discussed."

Torchy raised his hands to the heavens, but since they were inside his apartment, he really just raised his hands to a plaster fresco. The apartment was (and there was no other word for this, either) stunning. Mia didn't know much about Austin real estate, but she did know that pre-arrival, it hadn't stopped booming for decades. When, after approaching Torchy for information, he'd suggested going back to his apartment, she and Hollis had both steeled themselves for a craptastic flophouse with roaches tossed about for artistic flair. What they found instead was in one of the city's best buildings, on the very top floor, looking out across Ladybird Lake. The state lines were still closed, but the city borders had been opened. That had cleared a lot of downtown, and the armies had moved elsewhere to hate (but apparently not fight) each other, and Torchy's penthouse, somehow, remained unlooted and untouched.

When Hollis had commented on this — first disbelieving that this was really Torchy's place, until they saw all the photos and artifacts that made clear that it was — Torchy's reply had been, "I have many guns. And also traps. Ha ha ha ha." And then he ran his hands through his hair, which he seemed to find elegant and worthy of a magazine cover. Like Fabio. Remember Fabio?

"The signal," he said. "You mean to the sky."

"You say in your sermons that the energy is from south by southwest."

"This is stupid," he said. "I do the sermons for fun. Do you want a fun pop? You want a fun pop."

Mia wasn't sure what that meant, but Torchy returned with candy. They both refused, Hollis now insufferable.

"Torchy ..."

"My name is *Torchy*," he said. "Everyone says I own Torchy's Tacos. I do not. I do not. I do *naaaaaaht*."

"*Is* your name really 'Torchy,' Sport?" Hollis asked, looking shamelessly through papers on Torchy's desk. Hard to believe the crazy street preacher had a desk, Mia thought. Hard to believe he had papers.

"I do not want to answer this. It is stupid. We want to talk about energy from south by southwest. And not the festival!" Strange laughs followed this. Then he was immediately stern again. "No. The direction." He held out a hand, roughly in the direction he'd named. "I can hear it. There. Can you?"

"No," said Hollis. Again he looked at Mia.

"It is like the past. I hear many people in their childhoods. When I was a boy I had a skateboard. I fell and skinned both my legs, and after that I had bandages, and they came in a special dispenser."

Hollis came close enough to Mia to whisper. "This guy's nuts. We should go."

But Mia held up a finger and put some distance between them. On one hand, she had her own knowledge of Torchy Banner as an Austin street preacher of some note, and all the wacko baggage that came with it. Right now, he was talking the way he did on his soapbox, while people gathered around him — a few listening for real, as crazy as he was, but most chuckling and taking pictures. But on the other hand, she had Carol and Theo's blessing and the accounts of almost fifty people who'd heard Torchy, in the months before the arrival, predict exactly what had happened, when and how it'd happened. While nobody had been listening, it seemed that Torchy had told the city that silver ships were coming and then issued a countdown. While the world had been ignoring Torchy, he'd preached that Moscow would burn and that a bomb would be dropped into downtown Austin but would not detonate. He'd described both kinds of aliens before they'd shown up: black beasts that walked on many legs and had blue fire inside, and tall white-skinned creatures that looked like muscular, hairless humans.

And these days, apparently, Torchy kept talking about a great human force from the south by southwest direction. He described it as a "flood of feeling" that the aliens were stealing away. And while that description had been interesting when Mia had first heard that Torchy was selling it, what made them all sit up and take notice was his speechifying about the "artificial brain" the creatures had made in town and the "beam sent from out of town to feed it."

Which lined up perfectly with what Theo was seeing, as he dug deeper into whatever the aliens were doing with the Astral app databank.

"Torchy," Mia said, following the street preacher as he crossed what had to be one of the most expensive apartments in town. "Some friends of ours are able to get inside the database for the Astral app. Do you know the Astral app?"

"Of course! I am not stupid. Why do you ask this thing? Sit. You make me nervous."

They sat. On a couch that looked like it might cost five thousand dollars.

Torchy crossed one leg over the other at the ankle, throwing an arm along the back of the couch. Then he waited, seemingly for Mia to go on.

"The datacenter for the Astral app is here in Austin. We think the aliens are using it. But not because the app has anything to do with outer space, the way the app let the world watch their arrival, or anything like that. We think they want it because the app interfaces with so much social media and — not entirely legally — pulls behavioral information about its users from all over the web."

There was more, too. After they'd gotten Hollis's phone with all the briefcase photos on it, Carol and Theo had dug in and delved deep. They learned all sorts of things about the Astral app, like how it was a trojan horse for skimming behavioral data in the real world, too — not just online. Turned out that even when a user's settings were supposed to prevent it, the app was always running in the background. It kept the microphone and camera covertly on at pretty much all times, recording as much of a user's life and doings as possible. *No wonder it can predict so well,* Carol had said.

It's gathered so much information, it's become an algorithm for human behavior.

Or, as Theo had put it: *Literally nobody or nothing, anywhere, understands humanity better right now than Astral.*

Mia paused to see if what she'd said was making sense to Crazy Torchy Banner, but he was making circular *get-on-with-it gestures* with one finger.

"One of our people thinks that the aliens have taken all that data and made a kind of machine from it. Or a brain."

"I know this. Keep going. I am bored with this."

"But the brain needs 'something to think about,' if that makes sense. And that's why we wanted to ask you about the energy from the southwest."

"South by southwest," Torchy corrected.

"Our friends say that there's a whole lot of information coming into the Astral datacenter in Austin, but they don't know what it is. It's like the brain has found something to think about after all. The problem is, we don't know where all that stuff is, or where it's coming from. But we do know that it's coming from the same direction as the energy you talk about."

Theo had given them a lot more complexity there, too, but Torchy didn't need to hear it. Or didn't want to, it seemed.

He suddenly said, "This is dog shit."

"I'm sorry?"

"It is not energy, or electricity or computer things like you say. It is memory."

"*Oookay,*" Hollis said, making to stand. Mia put an arm out, holding him down, and addressed Torchy.

"What do you mean, 'Memory'?"

"What I said. Memory." He put all of his fingers to his head, under his hair, and looked dramatically down at the couch before responding. "Like I think. And you think. You walk up stairs to your grandmother's house every day when you are little, and you remember those stairs. You have a lunchbox with Snoopy on it, and you remember the lunchbox. From south by southwest, this is what is coming."

"I don't understand."

"You not hear it? It is so loud."

"Say ... *Torchy*," Hollis said. "How did you know the aliens were coming?"

"Because they always come."

"All right ... " he said, shifting on the couch and giving Mia another of those *Why the fuck are we here?* looks. "So how did you know when they'd come ... *this time*, I guess."

"Because there are doors. When you take the medicines, you can see them. Sometimes, they can see you."

"You mean drugs."

"Medicines."

To Mia, Hollis said, "I understand now. When our boy here takes drugs, he sees aliens. And remembers lunchboxes." Then to Torchy: "Thanks for your time."

"We're not leaving," Mia said. Theo and Carol were out of ideas; they knew only that a vast power source from the southwest (based on the location of IP routers or something Mia didn't understand) was lighting up whatever the aliens had done to the Astral data like a Christmas tree. At first, they'd thought it was a local problem, able to be addressed locally. But, Carol said, the Astral datacenter was now only part of the problem. If they couldn't find this other power source, anything they did with the local databank would be pointless. But it wasn't normal data; it came somehow through the air without the aid of electricity or internet. And they'd had no idea how to find it until Mia, on a whim, had read the right thing at the right time and suggested finding Torchy Banner. Not that Hollis planned to let her hear the end of it.

"Yes," Hollis said. "We are."

He was halfway to standing when Torchy said, "You had a lunchbox, too."

"Come on, Mia." Hand out, but Mia wasn't budging. He was so infuriating. If they didn't have it out soon — or make peace, which never really felt possible — she might just have to kill him.

"It had an army man on it," Torchy went on, ignoring their power struggle. "The clasp was broken, so you wrapped it with a rubber band — one of those big ones, from your father's work. You told him, 'I want a new box. They are making fun of me. I want the one with the cartoon robots — one that actually works.' But you were poor and he did not buy it, and so you walked to school every day with your army man lunchbox with the rubber band on it, and every day you put it in the cloak room instead of the cooler because you wanted nobody to see. But one day there was no ice pack and it was warm and in the morning time, the mayo on your sandwich went bad. When you ate it you were throwing up for days. They made fun of you more for that, and after school you took that lunchbox and threw it into the river and told your family you lost it. After that it was only leftover shopping bags to carry your lunch, which was worse. So you went to the river again, thinking you might be able to find it. But of course you could not."

Hollis had never fully straightened. He was looking at Torchy like something that'd crawled from under a rock.

"How the hell did you know that?"

Mia looked from one man to the other. She asked Hollis, "Is ... Is it true? Just like he said?"

"Nobody knows about that. I was alone. I never told anyone."

Torchy still had his arm across the back of the couch, still with his legs crossed. He looked at Mia. "You do not know this?" he asked. "It is so *loud,* from south by southwest."

"I'm right here, Freak Show," Hollis said, suddenly angry. "I'm not at the bottom of your weird southern memory stream. Tell me how the hell you hear my memory coming from there if I'm right the fuck in front of you."

"Maybe you went there," Torchy said, "or maybe you will."

"Where?"

"San Antonio."

"WHERE?"

But Mia didn't like Hollis's tone, and was fascinated by the way Torchy had, somehow, nailed him. She pulled out a notebook and said, "Torchy. Do you know where exactly? San Antonio isn't small."

He waved both hands. "Give me a map."

"Do you have a map?"

"In the map room."

Which, of course, the luxury penthouse had in spades. It looked like a room on a trans-oceanic boat from the last century, when sailors had to navigate using transits to measure the stars. She found a Texas atlas quickly, hurrying so that Hollis wouldn't pop Torchy's head off while she was out of the room. Twice she heard Torchy say something and conclude with "Ha ha ha ha." She worked faster. Hollis, hearing that laugh, might just go to murder.

"South," Torchy said, waving Mia through page after page. "Southwest."

Torchy stopped her on a page showing a zoom of San

Antonio, hovered his hands mystically above the page, then stabbed at a spot.

Mia and Hollis looked. If his prediction was accurate, it meant the missing piece in the alien machine — source of all the power Theo and Carol saw streaming into the data-center through technologies unknown — was about ten miles outside of town, at the intersection of two rather ordinary semi-rural streets. A destination, Theo had said, that he should be able to verify or deny once he knew where to look and what triangulations to try.

"Vine Street," Hollis said, "reading the map. *That's* where you say you 'hear' my private memories somehow coming from, even though I've never been anywhere near it in my life?"

"Is easy," Torchy told him, smiling, missing all the ire in Hollis's stare. Then he stood. "You would like some Fresca?"

6

Theo set the phone on the table. He said, "The information here helps, of course, but it still doesn't explain that second source. All I can tell is it's somewhere south, and somewhere outside the city."

Hollis, listening, thought, *Second source?*

Even after finally getting past what should have been an impossible hurdle, Theo didn't look to Hollis like he felt anything was solved. Apparently this was more complicated than Hollis and Mia had thought even over this past week of bullshit, and there were still a lot of hurdles ahead.

A few minutes ago, Theo and Carol had been uploading photos from the phone to Carol's MacBook, which so far she'd kept operational by charging it off the car's engine. The power came on and off and was in no way reliable. Soon, they'd all have to switch to diesel generators, and then the road warriors would come.

Carol replied to Theo, and the two of them began chattering back and forth. Some was geographic in nature, some was geek-speak, and some seemed to be snippets of pre-existing conversations. Hollis tried to follow, but soon realized that while his mind had been wandering, he'd missed something vital. Rather than admitting it, he just kept nodding along. Eventually things would circle and they'd say something that would help him figure out what they were talking about. But just as he was trying to catch up, he saw Mia glance his way. And that's when he realized that Theo and Carol were the eccentric ones, and that what Theo had said wasn't something she'd seen coming, either.

"Wait," Hollis said. "Help me understand."

"Help *us* understand," Mia clarified.

"We've been talking about this thing in Austin. This big data place."

Carol nodded. "The datacenter for the Astral app."

"So what's this about something outside the city?"

"Well, there seems to be a power source," Theo told her.

"Not just a power source," Carol said.

"You can *think* of it like a power source," Theo countered.

"Like an electrical plant?"

"Different kind of power."

"'Fuel' is better," Carol said.

"Fine. Fuel, power ... *something*." He tapped the screen of Carol's computer, indicating something unknown and undiscussed. "The point is, there's a second part to this. It's pulling data from somewhere."

"*Lots* of data," Carol said.

"But not internet-type data. Not like we know data."

"Of course not," Carol said.

Hollis raised his hands. "Hang on. You're saying there's a second database? Also for the Astral app?"

"Oh, no," Theo said. "There's only *one* databank for the Astral app."

"This is more like a massive pool of *external* data," Carol says. "Stuff the Astral database wants to assimilate."

"Is that the way it works? Databases get all hungry, wanting more data?"

"Ordinarily, no. But in this case, yes."

"It's semi-sentient," Theo blurted.

"Maybe," Carol said, narrowing her eyes at him. This seemed to be an unresolved debate, and Theo was advancing his theory out of turn. "All we know is that data is coming in huge waves, not really the will or intention behind it."

"Either way, it means the same thing."

Hollis, frustrated by the constant techo-banter he didn't understand since they'd delved into the phone's bounty, said, "How about you *tell* us what it means."

"All right," Theo said, moving away from the computer. "What we think's going on is this: At first, the aliens were just interested in the Astral database, here in Austin. Both of us reached that conclusion early on, when we saw their access footprints. Remember how we told you it looked like they were training an AI? Or 'building a brain' they could then use to understand human thought better?"

"I remember," Mia said. It jibed with what she'd told them about her psychic experiences around the stones and the aliens — that sense of *wanting to understand* from the aliens above all else. Hollis had felt some of that too, maybe, when his mind had somehow reached out to Mia's. He hadn't gone as deep and Mia couldn't do any of it anymore, but the alignment felt right.

"Well, at first we thought that was all there was to it. The Astral app has a ton of data, and Thomas's papers showed us that even its enormous amount of declared data isn't all there is. The app violates a lot of privacy laws, when you dig deep enough. Since so many people have it, it's harvested an ungodly amount of personal information from a broad sample of tech-enabled humanity. We know this because now, we can see all sorts of hidden places it's pulling from, and we can make sense of them all. Except for one particular channel."

"One of the incoming data streams is much larger than the others," Theo said, taking the ball from Carol. "It's also unauthorized, even by the program's architects. We think it was added later, using the same methodology. It's like the aliens studied the database and the app, saw what it was doing, and did it better."

"Where are the aliens pulling information from, then?"

"That's the problem. We don't know. There's some routing data in there, but it's like nothing I've seen before. All I can tell is that the source is somewhere outside the city and that it's probably south of us."

"We think they got what they needed from the original Astral databank," Carol said, "but that it wasn't really what they were looking for. So what they did — and this was why it looked like training an AI — was they used it to create a codex to help them understand *other* data, like this new stream. The Austin center looks more like a decoder wheel now. They're pulling information from somewhere outside the city — some unknown power source or collection facility — and funneling it here, to the decoder wheel. They basically run the new stuff through their 'big brain' so they can make sense of it, then pass that information on to the Austin mothership."

"We *think*," Theo said.

"Okay," Mia said. "So why does it matter?"

"Well, it complicates things," Theo said. "We started this with the belief that the aliens were causing trouble — that what they were up to wasn't good for any of us. Carol and I think that more now than ever, but now it seems the real problem isn't even in town. The real problem is ... whatever this new thing is."

"Is the new thing another database, *like* the Astral database?"

"I don't think so. It's something else."

"What?"

"That's where we're coming up short. We don't know. And we don't know how we *can* know."

"Is it in Mexico?" Hollis asked. "That's south."

"We're not sure."

"Houston?"

"No idea, Hollis. All we know is that if we don't find that source and shut it down somehow—"

"Or destroy it," Carol interrupted.

"—or destroy it, then there's nothing we can do."

"What if we just destroy the Austin center? Break the decoder wheel?"

"Without at least some understanding of what's going into the decoder wheel, that feels both ineffective and dangerous," Carol said.

"Not to mention the fact that if we do that, we'll never find this new power source. We'll never figure out what's going on down south somewhere."

"See," Carol said, nodding to Theo, "we don't really know what's going on, but given the 'brain' nature of what they've built here, we think that what's coming from outside the city is some sort of 'mental power.'"

"And?" Hollis said, sensing a catch.

"And there's a good chance — given how much data is

coming and how unfettered it seems — that whatever the aliens are doing to the south, it's some sort of mental manipulation of the people there. It can't be good for them. We've seen, with those big stones and from Mia's experience with the reptar, that the aliens are interested in collecting human thoughts and emotion. So what if that's what this is? What if they made some kind of beacon somewhere out there, and it's drawing people to it so that it can ... sample their minds?"

"Scoop them out and leave them empty, is more like it," Theo said.

"We don't know that," Carol said.

"But we can guess." He sat forward, addressing Mia and Hollis. "Look. It's all just hunches. But if you ask me, I think they've built some sort of a machine that's making people think and feel, then stealing those feelings and thoughts. It's sending them here, to Austin, to the Astral database, which is 'decoding' them like Carol said, so that the aliens can make sense of it all. But the problem is, it's a really brute-force way to understand anything. Wherever this *thing* is, the people close enough to it are suffering. I'd bet on it. And what's worse is that if we don't find it and shut it down, I think it'll spread. They aliens are just too hungry for human experiences for things to be otherwise."

"Spread where?" Mia asked.

"Who knows? Given scale and time, it might cover the whole world. A year from now, the entire population could be mindless zombies."

Hollis sat back. That was bad. Even in selfish mode, that struck Hollis as something worth stopping ... if, in the end, it'd get him too.

"How do we find it?" Mia asked.

Theo sighed, turning up his hands. "All I know is that it's

kind of in that direction." He pointed. "I can't even say how far away it is. It could be in Houston, or it could be in Argentina."

"I doubt it's in Argentina," Carol said. "Curvature of the earth. Line of sight stuff. They'd need a whole satellite network."

"Even if it's close, though," Theo said. "If we say it's … say … inside the state. That still doesn't help us. And even if we knew where it was, we don't know *what* we're looking for. All I have is a direction. That's all."

"How specific is the direction? Can we just walk or drive the way you think it is, and see what we see?"

"All I can say for sure is that it's to the southwest," Theo said. Then he looked at the screen again and said, "*South by southwest,* actually. Like the festival."

"'*Like the festival,*'" Mia repeated. But the way she said it was strange.

Hollis looked over. So did Theo and Carol.

"'South by southwest,'" she said. "That's where you think it is?"

"Ish," Carol said. "Why?"

"If you wanted to be less technical and look at this in a more religious way," Mia said, "do you think you might call this datastream a 'journey of souls'?"

Hollis wanted to laugh at that, but nobody else broke a smile.

"I … *guess?*" Theo said.

Carol shrugged agreement, but neither struck Hollis as particularly religious, nor inclined to such high-minded ways of thinking.

"Why?" Theo asked.

"This is going to sound strange," Mia said, "but I think I know someone we should talk to."

7

Hollis slipped halfway down, his bad leg giving way. The slope was steep — the kind of thing you have to fancy-step down in choppy little strides, arms out for balance, eyes always on your feet. This was the back side of the fancy development and had no need for landscaping. It was all patchy ground and protruding rocks — many of which Hollis struck as he lost control and began to tumble.

He landed in a shallow creek at its bottom, wet across his back. Gunshots were still coming from above — from car to car maybe, or perhaps both their pursuers thought they were still up there somehow, still reaching into the bottom of an empty bag of goodies.

Mia came over to him. Hand on his shoulders, rolling him over. Her eyes — an intense green — studied him in quick little motions.

"Are you okay?"

"You wanna make out?"

Yes. He seemed to be okay.

"Were those the Flesh Eaters?"

"Yeah. The one who looked in love with me was Vika."

She looked around, grabbed Hollis's arm, and pulled him up. "Come on."

They moved through a thicket. Hollis, who'd spent a lot of time in such places as a kid, found himself looking out for snakes. They didn't always love the water, but they did love hidey holes. Getting snake-bit right now was all they needed.

An unknown time later, they came out in another subdivision, also high up, seemingly accessible by another long, private drive. If company was still after them, they'd have to get lucky to find them — and, Hollis told himself, they had other things to deal with. Like each other, for instance.

"Now what?" Mia asked after they slid to sitting behind a gray car, out of sight even from the rest of the lot.

"Now we give up?"

"We can't give up."

"Without the phone, I don't know how we can do anything else."

"Where, exactly, was the phone inside the car?"

"I think I tossed it under the seat."

Mia was thinking. Hollis watched, still breathing hard, as she nodded to herself.

"So it might still be in the car."

"Which is helpful why?"

"Because if we can find the car, we might find the phone," she said, as if this wasn't 1) obvious from context but also 2) fucking impossible.

"Okay. *You* go find the car."

"Think, Hollis. We don't have a lot of time."

"You're right. You'd better skip the formalities and take your pants off."

She slapped his chest. Only restraint — and having gotten to know him — kept her from slapping his face. "Be serious."

"What do you want me to say, shit? I told you: the car was stuffed full of bags of cash. It looked like the Monopoly Man's car must look. I didn't think I'd be away from it long; the plan was to head down to the bar at the bottom of the hill and ask around about Brendan and whether he'd been talking about women he wanted to sell. I didn't want to take the keys in case they searched me, but I always planned to come right back. I got into trouble; I took one of their bikes to get away; they took it personally and the rest is history. It's taken me ... what ... a coupla weeks to get back to check on it? Hell, Mia. It was stuffed with cash and the keys were right friggin' there. I didn't know I had to chain it up with a bike lock. Now it's gone, and there's a whole goddamn city out there that might have it. So tell me. I'm serious. I'm listening. What would *you* do?"

Mia sat back, seeing his point but far too frustrated to admit it.

Then she said, "Let's ask at the bar."

Hollis laughed.

"I'm serious. I'll do it. They don't know me; they just know you."

"They saw you just now."

"The people up there did." She pointed across, to where their quest had hit its abbreviated end. "But not the people in the bar. I can go quick." Then she pointed at a rack nearby. "Look. I can even take one of those bikes."

"Mia ..."

But he was hurt and she was fast. She was away before

he could grab her, leaving him to shout and then worry. Within five minutes, Hollis was sure she'd been kidnapped. Within ten, she'd probably been cut to pieces and served on the bar's buffet: the gang's name finally made literal. But at the twelve-minute mark, by Hollis's watch, Mia returned on her bike like a kid coming back from a fun little ride.

"Good news," she said, dismounting.

IN HOLLIS'S OPINION, what Mia brought back wasn't actually very good news. The Flesh Eaters controlled most of the territory around their bar and the Denny's they called HQ, so of course their patrols had located the car in the development's administrative parking lot almost immediately — probably around the time Hollis was waking up to punches in the face inside that sewer grate. As far as Mia could tell, they hadn't connected the car to Hollis, and that *was* good. But they had taken all the cash and sold the thing. It had fetched a nifty price, seeing as it was old enough to run on plain old gas — no sophisticated electronics needed.

"Who'd they sell it to?" Hollis asked.

"I don't know. Either the large gentleman I sweet-talked didn't want to tell me or didn't know."

"So how is this good news?"

"Well, before they sold the car, the crew that found it made some changes."

"What kind of changes?"

"Did I mention they were really, really high at the time?"

And that's how, as they left the second parking lot of the day with no new sign of Flesh Eaters or Beef or any of Hollis's favorite enemies, they found themselves in pursuit of a rather unique Chevelle. Many were beautiful machines with smooth edges and sweeping contours, but only this one had action figures glued all over the hood, roof, and trunk. Only this particular Chevelle had been painted — with brushes — in a sloppy neon green. Only this one, to keep in-theme, had a enormous He-Man head mounted on the front of the grill, a Dixie flagpole welded to the front quarter-panel, and a Dukes of Hazard-style southern flag massacre-painted somehow around it all.

"Is it green, or is it a rebel flag?" Hollis asked.

"It was hard to tell from his description."

"Great."

"It is great," she said. "Around town, they call it the Shit Bomber."

HOLLIS WASN'T BUYING IT. Phone and internet had been almost entirely down in Austin since the EMP, except for the valiant efforts of a few intelligent, Theo-like folks on various sides. Communication happened by walkie-talkie, messengers, and word-of-mouth, and tales of a neon car covered with toys (and, Mia added, a line of doll heads on the rear — looking backward, of course) didn't seem like they'd make the cut. Nobody would know about this car. Nobody would have word of the Shit Bomber. Austin had always been weird, but things had changed. The eccentric seldom merited discussion anymore, now that aliens were on the ground.

But he was wrong.

When they rendezvoused with Carol and Theo back at the coffee shop, Mia told the story and Carol said, "Oh, yeah. The Shit Bomber. I've heard about that." She looked at Hollis. "*That's* the car you drove back from Louisiana?"

"It didn't used to look that way," Hollis said. Because that part was important.

"*You* know about it?" Mia asked.

"Sure. When I went around for parts to fix the generator, it'd just driven by or something. People watch for it. I've never seen it, but they talk about it like kids talk about the ice cream man."

But that was all Carol could tell them, and Theo had heard nothing. So, leaving the nerds to continue discussing the limited information they had about the Astral database and the wacky conspiracy theories surrounding it, Hollis took the circuit Carol had been making over the past few days, orbiting out from the coffee shop they'd been calling home and hitting the other local businesses that other relatively safe groups called home. They'd gotten lucky here; there was as yet no criminal element inside their little community, and everyone seemed more interested in trading than looking and stealing. Hollis felt sure that would change as things got worse (they were still less than a month from the aliens' arrival, after all, and some things had yet to go to shit), but for now, in the little honeymoon period they found themselves in, it was nice. Or as close to nice as the end of the civilized world could be.

He hit all the shops, then returned for Mia. He found her alone, then pulled her aside.

"I think we need to split up," Hollis said.

"But I was just starting to be able to tolerate you!"

"I meant from Carol and Theo. We'll circle back with them later. We'll *need* to circle back with them, if we can find the phone, since neither of us are near smart enough to figure out the stuff that's on it."

"Speak for yourself," Mia told him.

"I talked to some folks. Learned a whole lot about what people say has been going on, while I was sniffin' around about the car. There's a bit of a toss-up lately. Sometime after we left, alien ships destroyed Brendan's estate."

"And Brendan?"

Hollis shook his head. "Just his place. Nobody knows why, but I'm betting it's more of them being morality police. Funny thing for them to do, seeing as they keep abducting and killing us. Brendan's doin' just fine. And that's part of the problem: *He's* sniffing around, too. He doesn't know Carol, really. Probably wouldn't recognize her out of context unless she makes a lot of noise, which I don't really think she's gonna do. He doesn't know Theo at all. He comes through here and finds them, okay. But if we're here, too?"

Mia saw his point.

"Another thing. You seen anyone around here actin' strange?"

"Just everybody," Mia said.

"I mean super strange. Like their brain was scooped out or something."

Mia shook her head.

"The grapevine is all worried about something happening down south. I guess some of it is starting to make its way up here. You know how rumors are, but it's like these folks had their brains fried. Fried all the same way, like someone's doing it on purpose."

"Who?"

"Who knows. Maybe the aliens, maybe someone with a supervillain machine and a mindfuck fetish. I told Theo about it because of what he was saying about those big rocks, the psychic shit ... whatever he thinks we might find is happening with the whole database thing. He was interested in a really specific way."

"What does that mean?"

"It means I got the impression it meant something to him, and he didn't want to tell me why."

"What's this got to do with the car?" Mia asked.

"We've gotta move fast, is what it means. This little Heaven we've got around here, it ain't gonna last. I don't know that we can find that car, but I do want to *figure out* if we can find it so I can make plans. Are we chasing this attache case thing, or are we running to the sticks, starting to build a fortress for whatever's coming?"

Hollis felt his own serious tone, and watched how Mia responded to it. Hollis, bone dry and without sarcasm, was like a klaxon blaring.

"But," he said, "do you want to hear some good news?"

"Is it as good as my last good news?" Mia asked.

"I got a lead from the folks who took over the flower shop." Then he smiled. "I think I might know where to find the car."

But THE CAR wasn't outside the strip club.

"Dammit," Hollis said.

"Don't get discouraged," Mia told him. "We're fast. We're agile. That's why we told Theo to work fast while we're gone — because we'll be back any minute."

But Hollis, looking at the Leg Up club, couldn't help being annoyed. The Shit Bomber, supposedly, came here all the time. There were strippers still inside, according to rumor, though Hollis had to wonder if they were freelance or slaves. All the players came here, including those who liked to drive ostentatious vehicles. Supposedly, in this crowd, owning a car as fine as the Bomber got you extra drinks, extra special treatment.

"Let's ask around," Mia said, walking toward the door.

Fifteen minutes later they came back out, Hollis with a grenade clenched in his fist. He was trying to pay attention to all the people pointing guns at them, but he could barely take his eyes from the bomb in his hands. His hands kept shaking. With his strength still not all the way back, holding the handle down with the pin already pulled required both hands. Mia, holding onto him, kept trying to give advice. She'd held a grenade recently, too. Not a lot of partners could say that.

"Shoot us," Hollis told all the people still inside the Leg Up as they crossed the first few yards of parking lot, "and we all die."

"I'm considering it," said the largest of them, holding something sawed-off.

"The booze will go with it," Mia added, because the club's bar was by the door.

Grumbling, they let them go. A dicey period came when they were far enough from the door that the grenade probably wouldn't have hurt those inside the club much anymore, but nobody fired. Then Hollis faked to throw it at them and that backed them all the way off, door pulled closed. He threw it beside the club instead, ducking and covering, feeling the whiz as shrapnel zipped above them.

"That wasn't helpful," Mia said, looking back at the club.

"It might have been," Hollis said, "if you'd been willing join their stripper crew like they'd wanted."

"I thought about it, but then you saw the grenades."

Yeah. The all-male cast inside hadn't liked that. It'd taken three seconds between when they'd tried to drag the newcomer to the stage and the moment Hollis had pulled the grenade from some guy's bag and yanked the pin. There hadn't been time to think, but it was a rare case where his impulsiveness might just have saved their lives.

"I did learn *something* from this, though," Mia said.

"What?"

She held up a photo she must have snatched from the strip club's wall of fame while he'd been flirting with explosions. It showed a woman with a pink buzz cut in a crop top, leaning cross-armed against the ugliest car Hollis had ever seen.

"And you said this wasn't helpful."

"I was being dramatic," Mia said. "Setting you up for the big reveal."

THE WOMAN, in the photo, was standing just beyond an Arby's with a sign that read, CURLY FIRES ON A SAND- WICH? TRY OUR NEW MEAL TODAY.

"Still not seeing it," Hollis said.

Mia pointed to the Arby's.

"There are Arby's everywhere," Hollis said.

"How many of them serve curly fires?"

"What?"

"Curly *fires*," Mia said, tapping. "Not *fries*."

Now Hollis saw the misspelling. "Oh. So what?"

"My friend's weird son works at an Arby's. He likes to be the one to letter the sign. Last year they brought back the Chicken Cordon Bleu as part of a throwback campaign. The sign was supposed to say 'Chicken Cordon Bleu - Bon Appetit.' Instead he wrote, 'Chicken Cordon Bleu - Bona Drag.'"

"I don't get it."

"My friend thinks he's hilarious. She always texts me what he puts on the signs. I remember thinking that 'curly fires' was pretty uninspired, but he was going for longevity.

Last I heard, nobody noticed and it'd been that way for months."

Now Hollis brightened. "Where's his Arby's?"

"East side. Not far from campus."

"Let's go."

THE ARBY'S WAS, of course, burned down.

"Serves it right," Hollis said. He walked through the ashes, kicking part of (maybe?) a deep-fryer with the toe of his alligator boot. "Do you think the fires were curly?"

Mia had her hands on her hips, exhaling through pursed lips.

"Look. Kids." She pointed.

Hollis looked. A group of teenagers was visible behind a taco truck.

"Ah. A group of kids in an apocalypse. Yes, let's definitely go talk to them. It's not like every movie and book about the end of civilization has painted this exact scenario as one that ends badly, or anything. Oh, and after we're done here, can we maybe go down into a dark basement when a serial killer is on the loose?"

Mia was already moving. Hollis, muttering for her to stop, chased behind. She had the photo in her hand. Once, on a college road trip, Hollis's friend Buddy had driven them right into the ghetto, up to a gas station filled with hard-eyed men in sleeveless shirts with pistols tucked into their belts, and gone to the locked and bulletproof station office to ask for directions without any clue that he might die soon. Mia, right now, reminded Hollis of that.

But the kids were sitting in a circle, heads down over a role-playing card game.

"You take ten hit points of damage," said one of them to another.

They all startled when Mia approached. Maybe because she'd surprised them, maybe because they thought she might mug them, or maybe just because she was a girl and they were all virgins. But no, that couldn't be it; there were girls in the group. Unless *none* of them knew what to do, no matter the gender.

"Nerds," Hollis whispered.

"Our money is in the truck!" blurted the first one to see them.

A solidly built girl beside him hit his arm and hissed, *"Larry!"*

"We actually don't have any money," said another. Not at all convincingly.

Mia waved it all away. She showed them the photo, then indicated the pile of ash that used to be the Arby's. Had this woman come here? Did they know where the car might be?

"That's Becky Bones."

Hollis said, "You're kidding." About the name, not the recognition.

"You know her?"

"Oh, *no,*" said one of the kids. "We'd *never* mess with Becky Bones."

"Does she come around here a lot?"

"She used to, before the Arby's burned down."

"Why? What did she do here?"

The kid who'd spoken first — to give up all their money — replied. "To burn the Arby's. Just a little at a time."

"She came specifically to burn the Arby's?"

"She hated that Arby's," said the girl who'd spoken earlier.

"Why?" Hollis asked. "I mean, other than the obvious."

Mia cut him off.

"Do you know where she might be now?"

And the kid with the dice said, "Graffiti Park."

GRAFFITI PARK, west side, off Lamar just south of Austin Community College. Hollis knew it well. The place used to be an artist-heavy tourist spot, but had degraded into a very colorful criminal lair when the cops had stopped paying attention. Hollis had taken many meetings there over the years, and what he liked about it was that the decor kept changing. During daylight, the graffiti artists — and, sometimes, tourists whose information was out of date — still came.

So they made their way there, but ran into a blockade. An *alien* blockade: four of the little ships that people kept calling shuttles, with the musclebound white aliens standing placidly outside. Hollis was considering going past anyway — they seemed to be observing more than stopping traffic, and the big aliens were as polite as Canadian bouncers. But then Hollis heard a noise that made his bones rattle: that purring sound the insect-like aliens made. He didn't have to see them to decide to find another route.

"Unless you want to try and mind-meld with them," he said to Mia.

But she was already getting back on her motorcycle, turning its wheel the other way.

THEY REACHED the park from an oblique direction — which, given its spot, meant crossing someone's lawn from 10th. They could tell right away that since the arrival, the park's reputation as a gathering place for the underbelly had only deepened. There was a shooting range at one end and in the dimming light of dusk, someone with means had set the place up with generator-mounted spotlights. The spotlights dominated a parking lot filled with cars, most running with their headlights on, lamps pointing inward to illuminate an inner circle. In the circle were a few tables and stations, with people milling between. To Hollis, it looked like a miniature version of the Exchange — fitting, given what two separate people had told him had happened at Brendan's after the alien melee, ending the official Exchange for good.

"They're trading," Mia said, as if she'd read his mind. They were crouched in the bushes. This didn't seem like a place either of them (but especially Hollis) should show his face.

Hollis was thinking of Vika, head of the Flesh Eaters. If she saw him again, after what'd happened this morning, she really would skin him alive. And, as they looked on, Hollis believed she might be here, or might soon arrive if she wasn't. She'd told him that her group had started the Exchange before Brendan had taken it over. Maybe, now that his place was toast, it'd moved here.

"There it is," Mia said.

"Where?"

"Over by the curly fires."

He assumed she was joking, and she was. But only about the fires being curly. There were indeed a few fires along the fence, and there was also ... Oh hell, the car looked so much worse in real life.

Hollis made a mental note: *Never run into Sonny Malone again.* Because if Sonny saw what Hollis had gotten his beautiful little classic car into, he'd hoist Hollis up by the balls.

They crawled forward. They stopped when someone

made a noise something like a bark, drawing the attention of all. Now between the cars with their headlamps on, Hollis rose to look. And there was Becky Bones, in all her glory.

Running the place, by the look of things.

"She's in charge," Hollis said.

"How do you know?"

"I can just tell. I've been in enough of these situations. Enough places like this."

"You sound surprised."

"I've never heard of 'Becky Bones.' I've never seen that woman before in my life. If she's running a gang down here, where did she come from?"

"You're just upset that she's a woman."

"I'm upset that she chose 'Becky Bones' as her nickname. What is she, a deejay?"

"It's this way," Mia said, ignoring Hollis's pondering line of thought. Now that they were amongst the cars and crawling low, they were in a sort of maze. The laughing and chattering of Graffiti Park's criminal element echoed through the maze like small children running laps in a house. It was easy to get lost, even on such a small plot. And, Hollis had to admit, he was a little worried about being seen. They'd managed to be mostly cool since escaping Brendan's, and this morning's toss-up had unsettled him more than he cared to admit.

They arrived at the car. Its paint job was nauseating. Severed Barbie heads were glued to the hubcaps in a circle, like spikes on the wheels of James Bond's car.

"It's unlocked."

Mia eased open the door before Hollis could protest. He would have, though; he'd driven this car through two states and knew very well how loud the driver's side door squealed on its hinges.

Maybe she oiled it, Hollis thought as he waved frantically at Mia, unseen.

But yeah, no, of course she hadn't. The squeal was loud enough to wake the dead. Even over the talking, the shooting, and the low distance, the sound could easily turn heads.

And did.

Which probably wouldn't have been the end of the world, given that Mia was now rushing, seeing how they'd been made, and was frantically searching beneath the seat for the phone — and while she'd been doing that, Hollis had spied something in the center console.

Keys.

Man, were people lazy at the End of Days.

"Get in."

"I'm hurrying!"

"I didn't say hurry. I said *get in.*" Keeping his voice calm, though his insides were already churning. Becky Bones's head was up like a rodent popping above ground on a prairie, noticing them just now. Saying something he couldn't hear in their general direction.

Beside her, because the universe hated Hollis, was Vika of the Flesh Eaters. Which made sense, in a weird way, seeing as Vika had started the first Exchange and Becky seemed to be Lady of this one.

"Hey!" Becky Bones shouted. *"Hey, that's my car!"*

But Hollis wasn't really paying attention to Becky. He'd locked eyes with Vika, who was smiling. He could read her eyes: *I won't miss you this time, Hollis Palmer.*

Reaching behind her. For a gun, surely.

Becky Bones running forward, less cool than she'd seemed moments ago. Now she was somewhere between frantic and angry. And furious. And ready to cut him apart. Because what

Becky Bones came out with, instead of the predictable and tired semiautomatic handgun, was a gigantic hunting knife from a sheath strapped to her leg. It was the offspring of Crocodile Dundee's knife and a bush-cutter's machete.

She was running now, the thing held overhead.

"GET IN!"

He shoved. Hard. Mia went, but she went like a sweater shoved into an already-overstuffed suitcase. Her neck rolled over the console, then her legs above. She ended up almost upside-down. Luckily the top was down, because she'd never have fit otherwise.

He grabbed the keys. Fumbled. Dropped them.

Now others were running at them, too. In the crowd, Hollis saw minor players he'd known before the arrival: two-bit hustlers now full of themselves in the new underground. Many seeing his face, shouting his name.

He got the keys into the ignition. Turned them to start, got nothing, then remembered it was a manual and he needed to depress the clutch. The engine fired loud as anything — that, at least, Becky hadn't made tacky.

Becky struck the hood, big knife up, then moved to cut around.

Hollis jammed the transmission into reverse.

"Hollis!" Mia shouted. "There's—"

But Hollis figured the rest out when, after mashing the gas and releasing the clutch, he hit something hard and bounced halfway over it.

— a shit-ton of motorcycles behind you.

More shouts came. Angrier now. Hollis could see more of his old Flesh Eater friends arriving from behind the graffiti-covered walls: Moose and Fishbone, there to have their fearless leader's back.

"Mother*fucker!*" Fishbone yelled. Then he, too, met Hollis's eyes: *You again.*

Because this was the second time that Hollis had committed an egregious offense against the Flesh Eaters' motorcycles. It was as if he was reckless, or just didn't care.

Hollis slammed into first gear. The car jumped forward as he turned the wheel, colliding with the car that'd been beside them. Then into reverse again, then first, then reverse. Through all of this, Becky Bones, with her crop top and pink buzz cut, seemed caught between leaping at them and trying not to die by aggressive metal compression.

She found her window, came at the side, and almost swiped Hollis with the blade. He did the only thing he could think of. He rolled up the window.

Becky swung, smashing the glass. It remained intact, but took on a starburst. One more hit and it'd explode into a million tiny cubes. But why would she hit it? A good high swing and she could simply reach over the window and scalp him.

The rear was almost clear of the bikes. They had to be pancakes by now, but at least his tires hadn't blown. That, by itself, felt like a miracle.

Open air. Somehow, they'd gotten around. But now the crowd, seeing their chance, rushed at them.

"Go. Go. *GO!*"

As if Mia had to tell him. Hollis slammed into first again, drawing it out until the engine cried. By second gear he was creating distance, and before he hit third they were gone.

A few minutes later, Mia was leaning over, with her head in Hollis's lap. She was going to give him road head, for a job well done.

"Hey. Maybe wait just a few ..."

But Mia wasn't going to blow him, it seemed. She came

up a few seconds later with a device in her hand, a huge smile on her face. She'd been reaching under his seat, and come up with what she'd been seeking.

Ricky's phone, with all those valuable pictures on it.

"Back to the coffee shop," she said. "Let's give Theo and Carol the good news."

But Hollis, in all his confused agitation, had raised a semi-boner that he now had to wait to go down.

"Great," was all he could say.

Mia settled back. She even put on her seat belt. Then, as content as a person could be while speeding off in a stolen car with a He-Man head on the grille, she settled in and woke the phone. The screen lit. It'd been most of a week since Hollis had last touched it, but thanks to the quiescence of sleep mode, it still had power.

"The photos are all here," Mia said, as if she hadn't believed they would be. "Shit, Hollis — there are *thousands* of them. Carol's going to plotz."

"What's plotz?"

"You know," Mia said. "It's what happened this morning, when—"

$$8$$

Four Days And Fifteen Minutes Ago

"Oh, sweet," Hollis said. "This is it. Now we can—"

There was a report. A bullet ricocheted off the stone sign Hollis had been approaching, cocky, trying to smile as best he could — much better, now that the swelling had gone down. Nobody, including Mia, knew where the bullet had actually struck or who had fired it, but they'd all been shot at enough recently to know to duck. Only then did they turn to see the Cadillac.

"You've got to be kidding me," Mia said. Because she'd seen this Cadillac before. It was accented in gold, with tiny chandeliers hung from hooks welded over the headlamps. All the windows were blacked out and it had boomboxes bolted to the hood. Where did a person even *get* boomboxes anymore? Hadn't they stopped making them in 1988?

All the boomboxes — synchronized, somehow — were blasting classic Hip Hop. Snoop Dog, rapping about life in the LBC. The sound had just come on, after the shot. In that instance, the Cadillac went from stealthy to obnoxious. Just like Beef himself: in the passenger seat sipping on gin and juice, never behind the wheel.

More shots came. They were all singles, nothing automatic. Which, for a gangbanger, had to be embarrassing, in Mia's opinion. But based on what they'd heard yesterday, they'd done well to leave Brendan's compound when they had. Alien ships had destroyed it — along with most of the local black market. Beef's crew probably had machine guns, but they were rationing. Hollis Palmer, though a pet target, wasn't worth spraying too many shells in a limited economy.

Hollis shouted something.

"WHAT?"

Snoop was too loud. And also smooth as hell in all that weed smoke he kept rapping about, like Hollis himself.

"I said, '*GET D—!*'"

More gunshots. But Mia had understood. Hollis wanted them all to know that his advised course of action, as the Cadillac slalomed up the wealthy community's driveway, was to get down when bullets started flying. Thanks, genius.

Mia was already down. At first Hollis had barged on ahead and naturally opened distance in their group, but then it was like he had something to prove, waiting for nobody. Now it just meant he was probably the only one who'd die.

Instead of getting down, Hollis ran. At first Mia decided to be smarter and lay low, but Beef's crew had already seen her, and redirected the Caddy's swerving course, putting her right in line with the hood ornament. That was a problem. As much as Beef would want to deal with Hollis, his bigger gripe was with Mia. She'd cost him three bags of Beaver Nuggets that legend said he'd never gotten refunded when things had gone bad, and now he meant to take it out of her skin.

Now they were shooting at her.

Mia ran, too. She couldn't dodge single shots any better than she'd have been able to dodge machine-gun fire, but at least they came less frequently, and the marksman sighting on her had room for improvement.

She ran right into Hollis's back before she saw him. They were both behind another enormous sign for the development, done in landscaping and framed by rocks. *Man*, this place was ritzy. It needed lots of signs to show just how well-off the place's residents were.

"Miss me?" Hollis asked. His lips were still a little swollen, so it came out a little closer to *Mith me?*

"Where's the car?"

"Inside."

"I know *inside*." She wanted to hit him. Now was not the time to be stupid, or slow. "I meant, where inside?"

"The clubhouse? By the pool?"

Mia was exasperated. *"Just point!"*

Hollis did. Mia spied the line between them and the supposed location of Sonny Malone's Chevelle — or where Hollis had left it before running afoul of the gang with all the great hairstyles, at least. She could see the roof of a building, probably the clubhouse he'd mentioned. She could cross land to get there, avoiding the road.

"We both run," she said. "You go that way and I'll go there. Give them two targets to chase. Circle around and meet in the parking lot. They can't know where we're headed, right?"

Hollis didn't answer, but Mia didn't need him to. They'd tried things his way, again and again.

Mia ran. After a moment, she saw Hollis run as well, right where she'd pointed. *Good boy.*

Beef's crew saw her and revved up. The Cadillac's engine should have been drowned out by the rap blasting from its roof, but they'd done something to it — maybe to compensate for electronics that no longer worked, or maybe just to make it more intimidating. The car roared and, without hesitation, bounded across the grass after her.

Mia tried to remember high school track. Tried to summon that energy from a lifetime ago. This was just open space and hurdles. And the Caddy couldn't take the hurdles.

Which it learned, rather noisily, after Mia leapt up a terraced ledge and the Caddy slammed into it.

Then Beef himself was leaning out the window, shouting with his mushmouth.

"You knocked off one my chandeliers, ho!"

All the doors opened. Now there were four guns, taking aim.

But Mia was around landscape trees, over a low hedge, and hauling for the clubhouse. They hadn't followed on foot. If they didn't know this place, they probably wouldn't know that the drive looped around ahead, centering on where Mia was now headed. That had to give her a few minutes' advantage, right?

Fifteen seconds later, panting, Mia arrived at the edge of a rather elaborate pool and a row of tennis courts. The pool had a VW bug at its bottom and one side's black wrought-iron fence had been laid flat. Otherwise, the whole place looked ready for a garden party.

The parking lot.

Already, this was a motherfucker. Hollis, knowing that no matter what happened, separating vehicle and ignition would only complicate things, had tossed the keys beneath a landscaping light when he'd left the car. He didn't remember which one, and Mia hadn't been there. She was going to have a hard time finding them and starting the car with Beef's crew behind them without Hollis to—

But now he was arriving, too. More out of breath than her, she noticed. It was his ribs. He shouldn't be running. In a normal world, he'd still be on a couch, recuperating.

"Where?" Mia demanded.

Hollis went to the parking lot's side to find the keys. But already Mia's present mind was catching up to the panicked mind that only wanted to flee. And as it did, she realized that their search for the keys was at best premature, or at worst totally unnecessary.

"Hollis."

"What?"

"Hollis!"

"What?"

She shoved him. He looked.

The parking lot was totally empty.

"Are you sure this is where you parked it?"

"Of course I'm sure."

"Are you sure?"

"What the hell? Yes! I parked it here, walked that way ... Look, you can see that shitty dive bar from here."

Mia looked. The dive bar, of course, was right where he'd indicated. She'd heard the story enough to know it: Hollis had stashed his car, went on recon, then pissed off the wrong person. The fastest way out had been to steal a motorcycle, seeing as nobody really bothered to pocket their keys anymore and he'd noticed how they were all ready to go, all out front in a shiny chrome line. The plan had always been to come back for the car — for the phone, for the gun, for all the money he said he'd stolen from a Brinks truck, just in case cash still had value. But then so much had happened.

And now here they were.

"Shit," Hollis said.

And Mia agreed: *Shit*.

They'd put themselves in the line of fire for nothing. They'd thought they were clear of Beef (and the others; let's be honest), but leaving cover to find the car had only drawn a target on their backs.

The car was whatever. But *the phone*. They needed that phone, *especially* after all of Carol and Theo's new theories, and it was unfortunately one of a kind.

"Maybe ... Maybe it uploaded the photos," Hollis blubbered, looking at the car that wasn't there. "Phones make backups of your pictures in the cloud, right? Maybe Theo can do some sort of a Fappening."

"What?"

They heard more gunshots. A second engine. Reinforcements, from Beef's crew? No ... because why would they be shooting at each other?

Mia's eye spied activity at the dive bar. Men mounting motorcycles. A line of already-mounted riders sneaked out of sight. She trotted to where she could see the driveway where she'd foiled Beef's fly ride over Hollis's protests and saw. They were no longer alone. Now there was a madcap pickup truck filled with people wearing mohawks and sporting rifles. They were passing just as Beef's guys were getting their Caddy back on the road, both now headed to meet them at the Summit.

Of course. Hollis's problems with the Flesh Eaters gang had started at the bar below, so it wasn't a shock that gunshots were summoning them now.

"Fuck," Hollis said.

The truck crested the rise. A black woman — clearly the leader — was standing in the bed. She locked eyes with Hollis, and her face went sour. Even from a distance, Mia could clearly read her mind: *You.*

"Run," Hollis said as the woman took aim. *"RUN!"*

9

———

"*FINE*," Hollis said with a heavy sigh. "If you're going to be dickheads about it, I guess we can try and save the world."

Mia couldn't help but smile. Hollis was pretty delirious right now, what with all the trauma and blood loss. Their nap earlier had helped, but not enough. She wondered at that, watching him now. He'd been almost sweet. Her hand went to the locket he'd returned safe and sound to her neck. She'd been sure, in that moment, that he was going to kiss her. It would have been okay, if he had. Officially, he was still a big old assface. But he'd been out of his mind and she'd been scarred with fright and anything that had happened in that moment, surely, could be chalked up to temporary insanity.

"Go back to sleep," she said.

But of course he wouldn't. Too much was weird; too much was new. He still looked like death on wheels, but for now, he'd slept enough. There were alien ships overhead; Brendan's compound was far behind, and he'd woken the way few people do: strapped to a travois, discovering he was on a hopeless quest to stop some unknown alien plot. As if he'd have voted for it, if he'd been conscious when they'd discussed it.

Find the car, find the phone.

Find the phone, find the information.

Where it went from there — what they were able to uncover with what they found, once they finally delved deep into the sixty million dollar secret Thomas's case had promised — would be up to Theo and Carol.

"You guys suck," Hollis said.

Mia didn't reply. She wouldn't let Hollis see her smiling at him, but right now, she was just happy he was still alive. He'd be a better man, now that he'd been through this.

"FUCK *ME*?" Mia said. "No, fuck *YOU!*"

Hollis laughed. She wanted to punch him. All that stopped her was an irrational conviction that if she hit him hard enough, she'd knock the flesh off his skull. It was that tenderized.

"You wouldn't have gotten out without me," Hollis said.

"I did *get* out without you. I *was* out, until you got your stupid ass caught."

"What was I doing when Brendan caught me?" Hollis said. "Oh, that's right. I was trying to save you."

"I DIDN'T ASK FOR YOU TO SAVE ME!"

He laughed again. It was a small noise, but it carried so much baggage. Even as beaten as he was, he was still capable of looking smug. With the smugness came all sorts of conclusions with no basis in fact, like the implication that all the good fortune they'd had in escaping was his doing, while all the mistakes had been hers. Objectively, pretty much everything he said wasn't just wrong; it was outright absurd. And yet he had that smirk. Worst of all, it worked. Even though Mia knew the truth (*she'd* gotten out on her own; *she'd* kept the reptar from killing them both; *she'd* dragged him to safety when he'd been too weak to stand; *she'd* spied Beef getting into his Cadillac and told them all to hold back before slipping through the gate, lest he spot them), Hollis's goddamn smirk still got under her skin.

They didn't talk until they reached Zilker Park. They'd gotten a ride to the old Whole Foods on Lamar from a bunch of post-apocalyptic hippies who planned to raid it, hoping the coolers still worked and the kale hadn't had time to go bad. From there, they'd been on foot. Mia had been supporting Hollis most of the way. They'd heard there was a doctor working out of the park, and out of all the aspects of their argument, this one irritated Mia the most: The current quest was to treat *Hollis's* wounds, and he had to lean on *Mia* to get there — and *still* he ran his mouth. She wanted to drop him in the gutter. Kick him before leaving him, for good measure.

"I noticed you keep grabbing my ass," Hollis said. He was trying to smile again, and she wished he'd knock it off. It was creepy, with all the blood.

Mia sighed.

"Theo. Carol."

They looked over. The second they did, she shoved Hollis at them.

"You take this for a while."

Hollis grunted. But Mia didn't want to hear it, so she

walked away before any of the three of them could protest. She was covered in sloughed-off Hollis — fluids of all kinds. She'd done her part, and then some. He could rot behind for all she cared.

Zilker Park was mostly empty. She'd never seen it this way, even when they'd come here during the panic of the arrival.

"Where now?" Carol asked.

"They said he was near the pool."

"He might not be there anymore," Theo said.

"Oh, well. I guess he'll just have to die."

Hollis, wisely, did not respond.

They walked toward Barton Springs Pool, the three-way grunting behind her. Part of Mia wanted to offer to help, but she'd helped enough. She had no grudge with Theo and Carol, but fuck them a little bit if they couldn't carry Hollis for a spell. She'd done it the rest of the way, and she'd done it alone. And that was *after* surviving all she'd survived at the Exchange.

"Inside?" Theo said.

Mia supposed. They went for the gate. Getting past the turnstiles was a trick, but they managed with only a few shrieks of pain. Then there was only the down-sloping lawn, the long and narrow length of the pool itself. Mia had been here before. She enjoyed it, but mainly for the ambiance. The pool itself was too cold for her tastes, spring-fed and supposedly 68 degrees year-round. In reality it was warmer than that, but Mia liked her swimming pools like bathwater.

The space was large and long. It was basically a section of a narrow natural river, blocked off at both ends with concrete added on the sides, for decking. Rocks formed part of the boundary, and there were trails on the far end, and more of the park beyond.

"There," Theo said. The park doctor had put up a Red Cross flag. A small crowd had gathered.

They seemed to be waiting for Mia, but she wasn't particularly interested in going — not with Hollis, not right now. She stared until Theo and Carol got the message, and took him off without her.

At the other end was another gathering. Curious and with time to kill, Mia walked over.

It was Torchy Banner, the city wacko. He was still in the park, still holding court. She strolled over, listened for a while, then sat. He blabbed on behind her, barely registering. But hey — if he could still draw a crowd, good for him. In the coming times, guys like Torchy might finally get their break.

"There is great change," Torchy said. "In a place not far away, a plague is coming."

Then, because he was insane, he said, "Ha ha ha."

Six belts on the guy. Wearing a dress shirt, surely stolen and not yet filthy. Where did he bed down at night, anyway? In the park? Under a bridge?

"It is like a journey of souls. Do you know? We are all like this."

That weird accent of his. Nobody knew how old he was. Nobody knew his real name. It for damn sure wasn't "Torchy."

"You know this city," he said. "There is another south by southwest. Not the festival, ha ha ha. The new south by southwest. Stay away. You should not go there."

Why did people listen to this guy? She glanced over, between glances at the pool. The water was beautiful. It was hard, in this place, to believe there was danger afoot — but from the pool's side, she could see it: the massive Austin mothership, hovering directly over the city. Smaller ships came and went. Even now — *especially* now, with the internet mostly out — nobody knew what they were up to, what was coming next.

"You will feel it," Torchy said. "Do you feel it?" He waited. Mia, for one, felt nothing, but his followers murmured in agreement. "It will try to call you there. To the beacon. To south by southwest. But you must not go. If you go, your memories will leave you. And that is stupid, ha ha ha ha."

She got up, glanced one final time at Torchy, and moved to where his crazy couldn't reach her.

Then, in the quiet, she laid back on the lawn in the sun until sleep found her.

"Two broken ribs, a broken toe, and a hell of a lot of soft tissue damage," Carol reported.

"That's all?" Mia asked. She could express interest and concern, now that Hollis was out of earshot. They'd moved to another section of the park, away from Torchy and all his insanity, and right now Hollis was over by Theo, wrapped in bandages. They'd given him painkillers, from places unknown, and stitched his wounds. She was glad she'd gone off alone. That, she didn't want to see.

"Doctor says he'll heal. As well as can be expected, anyway. There's not a lot he could do for the ribs, but the rest is just down to time."

Two days later, Hollis was in obnoxiously better spirits. He was still in pain, of course, as was to be expected. But he was wearing it as a badge of manly honor, probably enjoying the sympathy he pretended not to like.

"Look," he said, coming to sit beside Mia on a picnic table. "I wanted to say something."

"Is it about your abs?"

He almost laughed, stopped, then tried again. "I wanted to say thank you."

"For what?"

"For what you did back there."

She looked behind them. They'd spent last night in a food truck that had specialized in custom donuts. There'd been nothing particularly thank-worthy.

"I meant back at Brendan's," he said.

Mia looked at him for a good ten seconds, eyes met. It was such a strange thing to hear. The last thing she'd expected. But she knew to take this for what it was, and not to push.

Before she could reply, Hollis seemed to decide she wouldn't and went on.

"I think I'm well enough to travel," he said. "I mean ... to *voluntarily* travel." He chuckled. "Time ain't gettin' any shorter. Theo says he's worried about what might have happened with that alien-brain thing while we were off havin' fun. I think we should head out after we find some food. First thing. Does that sound okay to you?"

Still Mia found it hard to respond. Hollis, asking for her approval? That was new.

She nodded. "You said the place you left it was off of 360, but you've been too loopy to tell us more." It was half true. He'd been plenty cogent after the first day, but they hadn't wanted to split up. She didn't want to admit not wanting to leave him. Not now.

"I can take us there," he said.

.   .   .

AND SO, later that day, he did. Theo and Carol stayed behind in a coffee shop they'd commandeered, working on what data they still had in the history on Carol's MacBook. Most was offline, copied and stored on her hard-drive. They'd only get so far, and things needed to move fast. Meanwhile, Mia and Hollis would go out and retrieve the car. Hollis gave it a 50/50 chance of still being where he'd left it. Apparently he'd stuffed it with cash, but Mia was hoping any comers would take the cash and leave the vehicle.

But Hollis, maybe because he'd been moving fast at the time and so much had happened since, at first couldn't find the development in which he'd parked the car. He took them them up and down 360, peeking into one after another. Then he went down Bee Cave, dangerously near Thomas's house, in case he'd gotten the street wrong.

Rob Roy? No.

Seven Oaks? No.

But then, after what felt like an impossible, demoralizing time, Hollis grabbed her arm.

"Hang on. This looks familiar. Pull over."

Mia did. They'd stolen this car, too, but it was almost out of gas. Without a siphon and an unguarded gas station (those were getting harder to find), it'd be useless anyway.

So she pulled into a gravel lot that seemed to head nowhere and killed the engine.

Hollis got out. She saw where he was headed: toward a ritzy-looking alcove with a sign made of stone. She hadn't pulled in; there was a wreck near the gate. Now she saw that she could probably have gotten around, but Hollis was already off, on foot. He moved well. Most of the damage to his legs, at least, had been tissue, and was healing well.

Then he stopped and shook a finger at the sign just as

she saw something — a pimped-out Cadillac, perhaps — pass the corner of her eye.

"Oh, sweet," Hollis said. "This is it. Now we can—"

10

———

Now, Again

"—*GET THE FUCK OUT OF DODGE!*"

Mia slammed the car (which, even in this panicked moment, Hollis thought fondly of by its new name of Shit Bomber) from first gear to second. She drove well; there was only the slightest pause while she shifted. Moments later they were rumbling up the dirt road with the Fortress of Refuse ablaze behind them.

The zombie-people gave chase for a while, but gave up quickly. All Hollis could hope was that they wouldn't turn around now that their temple was burning and walk right into the blaze. But he didn't think they would. They'd done what they came to San Antonio to do, and now the alien brain Theo and Carol were so worried would "neuro-form" all the way up to Austin and beyond would have nothing to feed it. But Mia, angry all over again now that they were out of danger, seemed not to be seeing the victory.

"Couldn't wait," she gritted. "Couldn't just do what I asked."

"'What you asked' was taking forever. I saw you up there, in the doll room."

"What of it?"

"'*What of it?*'" Hollis repeated. "Mia, you froze for thirty seconds at a time!"

"I was just looking around."

"You know what I think? I think that place had you. I think it was sucking out your brain, same as it sucked out all those people's brains." He put his arm behind Mia's head-rest and turned fully to watch the blaze. It'd gone up like dry tinder in autumn; the pyre, distant now, lit up the whole sky.

"*That,*" he went on, "was a dirty job needing a dirty solu-tion. *You* wanted to pussy-foot, and every second you hesi-tated, it got its hooks into you. Tell me, Mia. Did you find anything up there that took you back in time? Did you find it waking any memories?"

"No," she said.

"Really?"

A pause. Then: "I was just thinking about my cousin, Leslie. No big deal. She had a lot of those toys, was all."

"Which cousin?"

This pause was longer. Only a few more seconds, but Hollis watched panic flit across her eyes for the briefest of moments before vanishing, her next word coming out in a rush of relief.

"Leslie!" she said.

"Almost forgot her name? As if someone sucked it right out of your head?"

"I'm just distracted."

But Hollis didn't think that was true. He kept his mouth shut, trying to make peace. Just last night, things between them, for once, hadn't been angry and loud. And now here were Classic Hollis and Mia again, so predictably at each other's throats.

They didn't speak until, 25 minutes later, Mia pulled the car up in front of the dry cleaner.

"Mia," Hollis said.

She'd been quiet the whole drive, but not because she was mad. Something was — or had recently been — haunting her. When she looked at him, it was like she'd lost track of what speech sounded like.

"It's okay," he said.

"What is?"

"Anything. Everything. Whatever you need to be."

"Are you patronizing me?"

"I'm just trying to help. You let me know how I can help."

He must have come across as sincere — something Mia would probably notice, since he so seldom was. He could feel his eyes too wide, his posture open but tentative, his expression waiting but unsure. She held her defensiveness for another few seconds, then dropped it entirely. It came with a sigh.

"I'm tired," she said.

"We both are." He looked to the dry cleaner, to Theo and Carol presumably waiting inside. "We *all* are."

"You should have let me do it the way we talked about. You should have let me get us outside, then throw the molotov."

"I know."

"But I'm glad it's over. I'm glad we did it."

A big Hollis grin crawled across his face.

"Saved the world tonight, didn't we?" he said.

But they hadn't.

11

———

ALL MIA WANTED WAS to get inside the dry cleaner, give Carol and Theo the briefest of descriptions of what had happened, then pull five of the left-behind comforters from the industrial dryers, make a nest, and sleep for two days.

She was rehearsing her speech to find a version that prompted the fewest number of follow up questions (the current winner was "We destroyed it. More later.") when Hollis said, "Um ..."

"Don't say 'Um.' Say what you actually want to say. I'll bet you're one of those people who texts 'Hi,' then waits for a response before getting down to business."

Hollis paused before responding, probably sensing Mia's edge and how far she could be pushed, and then said, "There's nobody here."

"What do you mean, 'There's nobody here'?"

"How many ways are there to interpret that?"

Mia pushed past him. He'd gone in first, and gone searching for the others while she'd gone first to the driers. Making her nest before engaging would make a point that she didn't particularly want to be bothered. Setting expectations, in a situation like this, made all the difference between getting what you wanted and being bothered by people who hadn't just had their minds fucked a little in the backdoor.

Now, she walked through the dim building. The power in San Antonio was out, and the whole zombifying of the population made the city feel safe. She supposed there was a chance that not all the dead-head citizens were harmless, and she supposed now that they might still be holding a grudge over the Fortress thing and somehow figure out how to find them to exact revenge. But both felt unlikely, so the dark inside the dry cleaner didn't bother her. She and Hollis had raided a Wal-Mart (again; it's like their lives had a sponsorship) for camping lanterns in case they needed to spend the night, and they'd found out later that Theo and Carol, arriving while they were off finding the Fortress, had done the same thing at an REI. When they needed it, there'd be light.

But Mia used only the fading daylight now, watching dust motes stir in the air. The place wasn't small, and by the time she was finished they'd both called out. It was as empty as Hollis said.

"They're not here," she said.

"That's what I said."

"Don't get snippy with me. I wanted to check. Is that so crazy?"

Hollis patted the air. The gesture made Mia angry at first, but then she realized that her pop-up anger — like what she'd just said, which was snippier than Hollis had been — was out of place. She let it go, then. It'd been a long day, and burning the Fortress had, in some strange way, taken an emotional toll. She was glad it was gone, glad the problem was over. But still part of her wasn't sure. Part of her, she felt, would have stopped her from burning it if Hollis hadn't been as impulsive as he had.

That's not true.

Of course not. But she couldn't stop thinking about it, so maybe it was.

No.

Aaand ... now she was arguing with herself. Perfect. That's not what going crazy felt like or anything.

"Let's just think," Hollis said.

Mia bit back the first thing that came to her instead of spitting them out: *Good idea. Because I was planning to just stare at the wall.*

"Is there a note?" she asked instead.

They scoured the place, even breaking out the lanterns and a big, heavy 4-cell flashlight just in case the note in question had fallen off the counter and under a piece of equipment. There was nothing.

"They wouldn't just leave without a note," Mia said.

"Well, they did."

"Unless someone got to them."

"Who?"

"Beef. The Flesh Eaters. Maybe Brendan. We sure hauled ass out of town with a lot of enemies. It could have been Becky Bones, for all we know."

"Or your husband."

"What's that supposed to mean?"

"Nothing. Geez, girl. Settle. What's with you today?"

Mia made herself settle. Again. But looking at Hollis, she could tell that he was thinking the same as she was. They'd never confirmed that anyone had followed them from

Austin, but they'd both thought they'd seen people on their tail. In daylight, those supposed sightings felt like paranoia. But at night, she'd believed them just fine.

"Let's not jump to conclusions," Hollis went on. "They coulda just run out for something. Maybe they didn't think we'd be back already. They could be back in a half hour."

It was a sensible theory — the most sensible of all possible theories, perhaps — but Hollis was clearly working to believe it. He didn't sit down, and he had none of his casual swagger. This was uneasy Hollis, seldom glimpsed. But then again, maybe *he'd* felt something troubling at the Fortress of Refuse, too.

Finally Hollis did sit, and Mia reluctantly sat with him. Her body cried out. She'd been promised a rest, and now she had to wait for it.

They waited until the sun threatened to set, and dusk arrived. Then Hollis stood quite suddenly, left the building to make a lap as if maybe they'd been in the parking lot the whole time, and came back in agitated.

"If someone took them," he said, "it'd have to be someone from out of town, right? All the locals are zombies. So that means it'd have to be someone following us."

"We talked about this. How could anyone have followed us all that way across open roads without being seen?"

"Right. Especially since we made a point of looking back, taking side roads, stopping along the way ... all that. So it can't be that. It can't be them. And besides, *they'd* have left a note, right?"

"Why would they leave a note?" Mia asked.

"Who would want Theo or Carol?" Hollis said. "Brendan only wanted Carol because he wanted her help figuring out what was in the case, but he thinks the case was destroyed and doesn't know about the pictures I took of all the stuff that was inside. So Carol would be useless to him. Same with Theo, who I don't even think he knows. Nobody else we've pissed off cares about either of them — not enough to chase us down. Think about it, Green Eyes. There's a world of shit to do right now, so why chase us? What do we have that anyone wants? They'd only come after us out of spite. But ... chasing us all the way to San Antonio?" He paced. Either the Fortress or the coming dark had affected him, or he was just near breaking from the accumulated stress. "That means that *even if* anyone came all this way, and if their solution was to kidnap *them*, it'd only be so they could get to *us*. You or me, or maybe both. And to do that, wouldn't they need to leave a note?"

"Sure," Mia said. "Unless ..."

They both thought it at the same time.

Unless they're still here, waiting for us to come back so they could grab us, too.

They'd brought guns, but hadn't taken them to the Fortress. Neither had said why, but both knew: The Fortress's energy had been wrong, the way certain sounds can jangle the nerves. Who knew what might happen there ... and might it be worse if they had firearms, got confused or upset, and decided to use them on each other?

So they both went for the duffel bag they'd brought with them and left on a chrome table in the press room, not questioning whether or not it'd still be there until they'd grabbed pistols from it. Why wouldn't abductors have taken such an obvious bounty?

Pistols in hand, they rushed outside. Their movements were curiously coordinated. Mia wouldn't let herself think the thought that came next, though she knew it just the same: *Did that place do something to us? Are we connected* below the surface — growing into two parts of one whole, just like the aliens?

Mia was out the back, weapon up. Hollis took the front, but given the small building's configuration both doors were around corners, and the instant they were outside they could each see the other.

They locked eyes, then went the other way. She was keyed up. *Very* keyed up. She almost shot Hollis when she saw him again, despite knowing damn well he was coming.

But the building was clear.

The parking lot was clear.

There weren't many hiding places; they were in an exurban sprawl with low roofs and good sight lines. The same few abandoned cars dotted the area. No sign of anything at all unusual.

Still, they took to the streets, before the light failed. And found nothing.

"We need to relax," Hollis said. "I've been touchy all day."

"It was the place," Mia said. "That temple of junk."

"It's gone now."

It was. But the feelings remained.

Moving through the front door, Mia said, "They left, is all. They had to go, and for some reason they didn't leave a note. Or they just forgot. Or they meant to be quick, but got held up."

Or meant to be quick, Mia thought, and ended up dead.

"We'll just keep waiting," Hollis said. "We'll just hang out here and wait, that's all."

The front door, blessedly, wasn't glass. This must have been a questionable part of town, because the windows had bars. With all entrances locked, nothing could get in without artillery. The corollary, of course, was that if some-

thing did threaten during the night, they couldn't get out —
but along with so much else, Mia tried to forget that, too.

Mia fell into her nest of comforters. It wasn't as wonderful, now, as she'd hoped.

"I'll just close my eyes," she said.

But she slept until morning.

12

———

IN HOLLIS'S DREAM, he was being chased by a shapeless mass that dispersed and reformed like a swarm of bees. It was impossible to defend against; every time he struck out, its many parts just dodged and then cohered again. At first, he thought it *was* bees — some large and fumbling breed of insect. But after stumbling and falling, he saw it was actually the many pieces of the Fortress of Refuse: tossed-off miscellany thick with memory, after him for revenge.

He bolted upright, hand clutching his chest. A sunbeam flooded his face and chest, making him wince.

Mia came to him. She had a cup of coffee, and put it in his hands.

"Morning," she said.

Hollis looked at the coffee. "This is cold."

"No way to heat the water. And it's instant. It's absolutely terrible. But I did put a belt of whiskey in it."

"All that was in a dry cleaner's?"

Mia looked at him funny. "No. In your bag. Don't you remember?"

He did now. But he also remembered the leftover feeling

from his dream, still on him like morning fog. His tormentor's shape was already dissolving in that way dreams had, but the sense remained: that the reason it chased him was to purge him of memory. To make him forget.

"Yeah." He sipped the coffee. In the cold water, the instant granules hadn't fully dissolved and added a crunchiness that even Army coffee didn't have. It was hideous, but he drank it all before speaking again. The whiskey opened his eyes.

"Thanks."

"You looked like you needed it."

"What do you mean?"

"You were thrashing your sleep. If you hadn't gotten up on your own, I would have woken you."

"I was?" That was a little embarrassing. But last night, they'd both embarrassed themselves. He remembered *that* feeling, too.

Mia nodded.

"How long have you been up?" Hollis asked.

"Just long enough to sully the name of coffee."

"Did you sleep okay?"

"Like the dead. You?"

"Same."

"But not in peace," she said, referring to herself.

"Me either."

Hollis rose, forgetting that he was in his boxers. And of course he had morning wood, tenting his boxers. Oh well, nothing she hadn't seen before. Mia pretended not to see it while he pulled on his jeans.

After a quiet moment, Hollis looked out the window and said, "They didn't come back."

Mia shook her head.

"Part of me was sure they would."

"Me too."

"But not a big part," Hollis added.

"Me either."

Hollis sighed. He wanted to ask the predictable *"What now?"* but there would be time for that later whether they wanted to face it or not.

"How do you feel," she said. Then she sort of shrugged, sort of indicated her own head. "You know."

She meant the paranoia from last night. The surety he'd felt that he was losing his mind, that the brain-sucker the aliens had made from the Fortress of Refuse had infected them after all.

"Better," he said. Then he added, "Entirely." A weak smile tried to widen his lips. "Other than forgetting my own hooch, that is."

Mia nodded. "The feeling is gone for me, too. Maybe it lived for a while, after the fire. Maybe whatever the aliens did to that place had a half-life. But I don't feel it at all now."

Hollis had to agree. Last night he'd been sure something was after him. He'd felt connected to Mia in a way that wasn't entirely pleasant and didn't feel benevolent. He'd felt the place trying to call him back. But now the air — both literally and figuratively — was clear.

"So it's over," Hollis said.

"Theo said it would be, didn't he?"

Hollis wasn't sure. He remembered Theo's analysis, and his insistence that they get here and somehow put an end to whatever was feeding the database had, clearly, been the top order of the day. But now, without Theo or Carol to ask, he felt adrift. Mia knew no more about the tech parts of this than he did. They'd gone all mission-accomplished, but had no victory flag to fly. Strangely, even with their task finished, their future felt more uncertain than ever.

Hollis went to the door. Mia must have revisited this one after he'd seen it last, because there was a chair jammed under the doorknob.

She saw him see it, then rushed to remove it.

"Sorry. I guess I was a bit paranoid last night. It just felt safer."

Hollis wasn't going to argue with that.

He opened the door, and it was like stepping into the sun after a storm. The whole place felt different, even though it was the same.

He circled the building. Mia went with him.

"Nothing," Mia said.

"I wasn't looking for Carol and Theo," Hollis said. "I was wondering if the people would come back."

"The zombies, you mean? The people the Fortress of Refuse messed up?"

"Yeah."

"Do you think that's how it works? They'll just snap out of it?"

"I don't know. I hope so. But I don't know."

They stood there a while.

"Now what?" Mia asked. Voicing the obvious question after all, because it was time.

"Well," Hollis said, "I don't want to stay here. Certainly not at this dry cleaner's. So I guess we go back to Austin?"

"Why would we go back to Austin?"

"I don't know. It seemed as good a place as any."

"I can name five or six reasons it's not as good as any. Here's a hint: They're all people's names."

"Oh. Yeah. Maybe Dallas. Fewer people hate me in Dallas."

"Maybe not a major city," Mia said. "And while we're at it, maybe not in Texas. Texas was good to me, but it's still foreign soil. I don't think the governor and the president are going to get back together and decide to un-secede, given all the other things on all our minds lately."

She looked up, perhaps to point at the mothership, but San Antonio didn't have one. If not for the dead-husk feel of this place, maybe it wouldn't be a bad place. Or maybe, *because* it was dead, it would be good. But no ... Hollis didn't like its feel. After what they'd done, the city had an after-taste for him. The kind of thing an old-timer might post a hex sign to ward off.

"Oklahoma?"

"For a start. I guess it depends on how far the gas will take us."

Hollis nodded. "We'll leave them a note. We'll ... I don't know ... set up a drop point or something. A way they can get back in touch if they do come back."

"How would that work, exactly?" Mia asked.

"I'll have to think on it."

He did. They did. And the next day, they left the city.

13

North.

There was no other sensible way to go. Mia suggested Mexico, but Hollis made a valid argument that in the absence of real society these days, the cartel might be a significant problem. There was already a Murder Corridor south of the border, and it might easily creep north. Have gas, will travel — and there was so much good stuff in Texas that the cartel, if the thought occurred, might decide to come on up and get.

They'd talked about Oklahoma. That was north anyway. They'd have to go through Austin, or at least around it, but that was okay as long as they didn't park and make their presence known to any who might want to see them dead. Oklahoma didn't sound very exciting to Mia, but with aliens occupying the planet, anywhere was likely to be equally exciting or non-exciting.

Besides, heading north would, for now, delay the question of how to deal with Theo and Carol's absence. In theory they could have ended up anywhere. But after twelve hours at the dry cleaner's without word, it seemed safe to assume they either weren't in San Antonio or weren't *well* in San Antonio, which in practice amounted to the same thing. If they were being held without notice, what difference would it make? There were too many places to hide. They weren't going to go door to door, hoping to get lucky.

The truth was that if Theo and Carol weren't at the dry cleaner, there was nowhere left that seemed more likely than any other. They no longer had a safe base in Austin, meaning that even if that's where their friends had gone, finding them even in Austin would be like finding needle in a haystack. Hollis's idea of a drop-box was just a place-holder, meant to make them both feel better. Because how *would* that work? Any usable drop-box would have to be near San Antonio, and Mia, at least, didn't want to stay close enough to San Antonio to come back and check it.

As they left the city, Mia let herself accept that they'd probably never see Carol and Theo again. Easy come, easy go, she supposed. They'd met just days ago, but still it hurt. The world wanted for connection, now more than ever. Where they'd had a crew, now they only had a pair.

Still, when she was driving and Hollis slept, she cried a little.

Unwilling to go too far too fast — just in case, for reasons that were, in practice, absurd — they stopped in the little town of New Braunfels the first night. Hollis made a few jokes about making their new home there, riding the waterslides of an enormous three-section waterpark ... going back to the cleaner's, then, to leave a note for Theo and Carol to grab bathing suits and join them. Mia laughed, but the jokes weren't funny. New Braunfels was nearly as quiet as San Antonio, and the vibe was similar. Jokes no longer sounded funny to her anywhere.

The place wasn't abandoned, though; that much they

saw. People peeked out, as they hadn't down south. The faces Mia saw in windows and through the cracks of doors were intelligent, if paranoid. Faces of people not afflicted, at least. And that was good.

They broke into a motel. Spent a night. The next day, the mood was wrong for travel, so they stayed. They walked the town together, armed just in case, and tried to get the pulse. They did finally see a clot of people in the center of town, and made conversation. *Anything new with the aliens?* And the people said, *No, no news. All's well in the world of New Braunfels.*

The next morning they set out. They passed Austin, passed Rocky River, and took the freeway toward Dallas. They were north of Dallas when Hollis suddenly patted his pockets and said, "Shit."

"What?"

He reached into the back seat, rummaging in his bag. She could, of all things, smell gasoline on his breath as he searched harder and harder, almost in a panic. It'd been his turn to siphon at the last place — a parking lot full of cars with gas in their tanks, not a station. He'd reeked the car up ever since, and because of it they'd been driving with the windows down. They'd seen no alien ships. None at all. None, in fact, since they'd left for San Antonio. It'd been a few days. Had anything happened? The sense of not knowing — especially after growing up with the internet, knowing *everything* — was hard to get used to. It made things seem too quiet, as if a storm was brewing, or some deadly stranger was sneaking up behind her back.

"The phone," Hollis said. "It's not here."

"Is it charging?" She could see the cable in the car's socket, but not its end.

Hollis fished, then held up the cable. *Just* a cable.

"I think I left it back at the hotel. I was looking through the paperwork. There were photos in there — aerial views of the Austin datacenter. Home of the Astral app."

"The hotel in New Braunfels, you mean?"

"Yeah."

He punched the duffel. "I wish I could call the hotel. Dammit." He searched more, then asked Mia to stop the car so he could look under all the seats, in the console, in the glove compartment, in the trunk — everywhere and anywhere it might have gone. He looked through the bag again, every compartment in the bag, his pockets, Mia's pockets, then repeated all of it.

"It has to be at the hotel," he said.

Mia waited. He couldn't possibly be about to say what she thought he'd say.

Then he said it: "We have to go back."

"Hollis ... that's half a day away."

"I know. But it has all that information on it."

Mia breathed hard, once, then crossed her arms and looked into the distance, thinking. There was still no sign of aliens. No sign of conscious life. They might as well be on another planet.

"We can't use that information," she said.

"What do you mean? Don't you remember going through Hell to get it?"

"Yeah, but that was in order to find the trash monument in San Antonio. We found it. We destroyed it, Hollis."

"Mia, we can't just leave that phone behind. It's got everything on it. *Everything.*"

"We don't have Theo. We don't have Carol. What can we possibly do with that information? We agreed it was over. We stopped whatever the aliens are doing. You're not a network engineer and neither am I ... and let's face it, we're never going to meet up with the members of our party that were. So why can't we just let it go?"

"We can't. We just can't."

Mia had her arms crossed, taking heavy breaths that were more like sighing. She thought, and she stared into the distance, and she looked at Hollis and she looked at the road. The trip had been simple, without obstacles. She didn't like retracing that far on principle, but they'd gassed up twice by siphoning and although it was a disgusting task, it was easy enough to do. They *could* go back, if Hollis wanted. There was no reason, in Mia's opinion, but they could.

"I suppose we don't have anywhere we need to be," she said. "And if we go back and don't find it, I guess ... Well, what else were we going to do with the time?"

Hollis was nodding, seeming to think the same thing.

She looked at the sun. It was lowering again, and she was both hungry and tired. And even as event-free as their trip up had been, she still didn't like the dark. Not now. Anyone could hide in the dark. Any*thing*.

"We'll find a place to spend the night here," she said, "and head back in the morning."

Hollis nodded.

And so they found another hotel, so simple to break into that it was almost like someone wanted them to. They slept. *Over*slept. Mia, it turned out, was a lot more tired than she'd thought.

It was noon by the time they got back on the road. Back south, retracing their steps. Hollis drove. Mia, though she'd thought she was well-rested, napped on and off. Might as well. They didn't have a phone to play music over Bluetooth, and all of the AM/FM stations had gone to static. Unless they wanted to play road games, there was exactly nothing to do.

She awoke for the last time with Hollis shaking her.

"What? Where are we?"

She looked around. Blinking. Refusing to believe.

"New Braunfels," Hollis said.

But she barely heard him.

The streets were full of vacant-eyed people, all milling without a place to go — including some of the same people they'd talked to lucidly just two days ago.

They'd grown mindless, just like the citizens of San Antonio.

It wasn't over after all.

14

"No," Hollis said.

His voice didn't sound right even to himself. But he said the word anyway, then said it again: "No."

"They have to be from San Antonio," Mia said. "People who wandered up here after the Fortress burned."

"They ain't from San Antonio."

"They could get that far in two days!" She nodded. "They're just wandering, is all. Others went south. The same thing could be playing out in Mexico soon."

"For shit's sake, Mia. That's Debbie and Grandpa Joe right there. You talked to them for ten full minutes about the town newspaper." Hollis had forgotten their real names the second after he'd learned them, so he'd made up new ones. But it was true. That was them right there, eyes empty and drooling, yet when Hollis and Mia had left town, they'd been too normal to bother with.

She was shaking her head, trying not to see it. Trying not to believe this was happening, the way Hollis's first reaction had been to mumble the most basic imperative there is: *No.*

"We have to get out of here," she said. "Hollis? We have to go. Right now."

At first Hollis wanted to argue. The folks here were even less threatening than the crowd down south. At the Fortress, they'd at least had a focus for their crazy. That focus had given them an edge, and made Hollis wonder what might happen if the thing they loved so much was taken away. His feeling there had been right; the zombies had come after their car when the flames began. But here? They weren't even gathering around one thing in particular. They were empty-headed without a beacon to draw them together, not even remotely threatening.

But then the truth of what Mia had said hit him. They didn't need to leave because the people posed a danger. They needed to leave because whatever had made them dumb probably still posed a danger.

Hollis remembered the feeling from that night, when the Fortress had gone up and he'd felt both victory and loss. They'd gone to San Antonio to destroy the beacon, and doing it had felt right ... and yet at the same time, watching it go had felt like losing something precious — something old, deep inside him.

But even more, he remembered the way it'd gotten its hooks in him even while on the surface, he'd felt immune. That night, he'd felt like something was always right behind him. Like if he went to sleep, he might not wake up as himself in the morning. That sense of having forgotten something at all times, even when nothing went missing.

That's the way it felt here, too.

And what was worse: Even as Hollis felt something consuming him, that consumption had no direction. He didn't know why he felt the first tickles of desire — the kind that might slide into obsession. He only knew that he felt them. And he didn't know why he wanted to argue with Mia right now to stay where they were. He only knew that he wanted to.

There was no reason to leave.

No danger here.

In a way, it felt like home.

"Hollis?"

Mia, snapping her fingers in front of his eyes. Judging by the look on her face, she'd been doing it for a while. He seemed to remember that, plus Mia calling for his attention before that, using only her voice. He hadn't wanted to react. He just wanted to explore. Find out what the new New Braufels had to offer.

"I was just thinking we should see what's happening at Schlitterbahn."

"Schlit—?" She stopped. Then: "The waterpark? No, Hollis; we need to leave. *Now.*"

His focus snapped back. Yes, they *did* need to leave. It was so obvious. They needed to leave with extreme prejudice. With a vengeance, like a red-hot bastard. How had he missed it until now? It was just that the day was turning out to be so fine. The air smelled fresh. And someone had left on a radio station, and Hollis could've *sworn* it was Sun Radio out of Austin or maybe Dripping Springs, but how could that be? You couldn't get Sun out this far, could you? Unless you were listening online, or had one motherfucker of an antenna. But he was glad to hear it, hearing who he thought was Dale Watson now and knowing that any of his favorites could follow: The Killer Bees, Little Sister, Bob Schneider, David Garza and the Love Beads (pronounced *"Daveed"* to those in the know), or maybe Gary P. Nunn with the London Homesick Blues. Yeah ... this was the stuff. He could listen all day, or at least until—

"Hollis!"

Snapped back to Mia. She was practically dragging him now.

"Hollis, move your stupid ass!"

All at once, the trance was gone. He could see the people but didn't wonder what interested them so. He could still hear the music out someone's window or from a distant store's porch, but he wasn't curious what the station might play next. He'd noticed the smell of baking cookies, too — a real country smell that, if Hollis had to guess, either marked a late bloomer or a near miss. Whoever was baking the cookies had either gotten them out of the oven before losing their mind, or had left them in and were just getting started down the road to Crazytown while the house burned down around them.

He blinked and shook his head. Mia was staring at him.

"I'm fine. I'm back."

"You looked like—"

He moved back to the car without waiting for her. "I'm driving. I need to drive."

Mia didn't argue. He thought she might. You lose your shit while driving, you hit a tree, but Hollis really didn't think he was going to lose it now. What had happened in San Antonio, by all signs, had happened slowly. They found a wide range of activities abandoned over different time-frames, suggesting that there were at least 24 full hours between onset and full zombification.

The two of them had probably only gotten out because they knew what was happening, and had seen it all around them. But if you were in town and everyone was sort of going at once? They'd probably just gone with the flow.

Just like Hollis, without Mia, might have gone with the flow until there'd been no flow anymore.

As he got behind the wheel, Mia gave him one final look. "You're sure you can drive."

"I think I need to," Hollis said.

He gripped the wheel.

Now close the door. Then start the engine.

The simple checklist, so deeply ingrained, was stronger than whatever was outside. Hollis found his head clearing by degrees, shocked each time it happened that there'd been another layer of hypnosis to shed.

Now apply the brake. Now depress the clutch. Now move the car into first, and do the dance of gas and clutch. Gently, now ...

Mia said nothing until they passed the town limits. Then Hollis was the first to speak.

"I was going away," he said without taking his eyes off the road, "but I'm back now."

15

___

They were in a motel in San Marcos.

The people here were still normal, so far as they could see, but there was no way to guard against a slow decay here like there'd been in New Braunfels. It was true that unlike anyone else, Mia and Hollis knew what the disease (or whatever) looked like, and that might help them see it if things in San Marcos started to go bad. But the whole thing was a slippery slope. All that had pulled them out this last time was the way Mia hadn't gone down as fast as Hollis had. If they both fell apart together next time, chances are they'd be dead on their feet before they thought to start running.

There were two reasons Mia felt comfortable taking the risk, knowing how easily they could be pulled under. The first was that they had no choice. If the strange plague was spreading out from San Antonio in a wave, maybe they'd be safer if they drove farther. But who was to say that was how it was happening? The whole world could be going at once, fading like a time-lapse of bacteria covering an entire plate of agar.

The other reason was that, all things considered, quietly

losing your mind without a clue didn't strike Mia as a bad way to go. It sure beat a reptar attack, a bomb in your city, or even living in fear of roving gangs until you slowly died of starvation.

"You were just staring into the distance," she told Hollis, unsettled, feeling a flutter in her chest that once upon a time hadn't lived there. "It was like that scene in a movie where a beautiful woman walks by and the men can't hear their wives snapping their fingers and calling their names. You scared me, Hollis."

"You snapped me out of it." But he wasn't as cavalier as he put on. Mia had seen recognition enter his eyes when she'd started to pull. He'd been as scared as she'd been, just like anyone looked after a near miss. "But hell, lady ... If you hadn't been there?"

"It happened so *fast*," she said. "Nothing like San Antonio. You were there and then all of a sudden you were gone."

"*Me?*" He was just now noticing how she kept using the singular. "Didn't it happen to you?"

Mia shook her head.

"Not even a little?"

"It felt like being near the Fortress, before we set it on fire. Everything was just kind of interesting, but I knew not to stay."

"Why?"

"I don't know. But it's really, really hard to be serious right now, seeing as I've got all these great jabs about being stronger than you."

"Maybe you're not stronger. Maybe you're just more stubborn."

Mia fell back on the bed nearest the bathroom, feeling a little better. Talking to him was helping. They should have driven farther, assuming what Theo had said about "exponential nature" of the signal held true. The farther you moved from the signal's source, the faster the rate of decay. They'd driven for a half hour, but would have been four times safer at an hour. But Mia couldn't wait an hour. This was too hard. She needed to rest. Get it together. And only then decide how much to freak out.

"It *wasn't* like in San Antonio," he said. Then he described it for her — the way the simplicity of the day had drawn him in with its sights and smells and sounds. "It was just like I was a kid again, sitting on the porch and listenin' to Howlin' Wolf while my mama baked pie."

"Who's Howling Wolf?"

"Are you being serious with me right now?"

"I've never been that into music."

Hollis came over and laid beside her. Not on his bed, but squeezed onto hers.

"How the hell am I with you, if you don't like music?"

"Let's stay focused," she said.

But now he sat up on one hip, elbow on the bed with his head on his hand.

"No blues," he said. "No jazz? No funk. No good old rock n' roll? Don't tell me you like hip-hop. Not that I'm talking about the classics, mind. You like Sugar Hill Gang, I can respect that. I'm talking about the shit they play today."

Mia shrugged.

"Damn, woman. And you live in the live music capital of the world."

"We have a problem to solve, Hollis." But she was cracking a smile now, enjoying the distraction. That was one good thing about Hollis, to counterpoint his many annoying flaws: His tendency to deflect just about any mature topic made for a great vacation from her otherwise constant worries.

"Yeah. We do." He shifted again. "Like how you didn't even recognize the name Howlin' Wolf. How about B.B. King?"

"Didn't she sing that song, 'You've Got a Friend'?"

"That was *Carole* King. B.B. King is a blues legend. You know. *Lucille?*"

"Okay, who's she?"

"His guitar. Shit."

"Who names a guitar?"

"Who's got the nickname 'Titz'?"

He'd gotten very close. His smile was trademark-wide, just two inches away. She smiled back, and then it lasted too long and got strange, and Hollis retracted his grin and rolled away.

"Never have I ever," she said after the moment had passed, both looking up at the ceiling,, "heard a song with both ears."

He turned, looking at her profile. Then he reached for a bottle of water he'd set on the endtable, took a swig, and held it up. Mia shook her head.

"Ear infection when I was three," she said. She rolled to look at him, pointed at her dead side, and shrugged. "I guess it doesn't matter now."

He looked like he might crack wise again — surely about how big a deal that was, never hearing his Wolfman or Mr. King in stereo — but then out of the blue she started to cry. No idea where it came from. It just came.

She closed her eyes and sobbed as quietly as she could, willing it to stop. Willing for him not to be here to see her weakness. Willing him never to leave, sure all at once that the end had come, and that she was exactly one scoundrel away from dying alone.

In the darkness behind her eyelids, Mia felt the gentle

pressure of a hand laid across her stomach. Breath, subtle, was warm against the side of her neck.

I ain't going anywhere.

Her thought? It had to be, unless things were starting all over again. But the voice was deep. Soft, with a southern lilt. Nothing like her own.

His watch ticked.

There were no other sounds.

For a while, in the dark, everything went away and there were no dreams.

16

———

MIA, when she woke, gave Hollis a sheepish glance and went for the bathroom. At first she just seemed to splash water on her face, but then she stuck an arm out and grabbed the bag and he heard the shower start. San Marcos for some reason still had power, unlike just about every-where else they'd been lately. With the water heater still working, Hollis had been mulling a shower himself. About time to freshen up. Blow off the dirt of the road, which was building between his ears as much as beneath his fingernails.

By the time she came out, she looked better than she had just a moment ago with that damaged little glance she'd given him — better, by far, than she'd looked just two hours earlier. The sun was high and the day had grown better and brighter. In a way, it was a shame. They didn't even need to take advantage of the electric room lights. The phone was charging, though, and that was something. He wasn't sure why he'd wanted so badly to recover it. It was probably useless now, like Mia said, but at least he wouldn't have to wonder. It'd been right where he'd thought it'd be, on the nightstand in their last motel. If only that were *all* they'd brought back from New Braunfels.

They locked eyes just long enough for Mia to say *Don't ask me about last night and don't ask if I feel better* without words. She didn't like dropping her walls, so now they were supposed to pretend they'd never been breached. But it was fair. Over the past weeks, Hollis had asked the same courtesy from her.

"I've been thinking," she said. "We have to stop it."

"We already tried that in San Antonio, remember?"

"But it didn't stop, Hollis. We have to try again."

"How the hell are we gonna *try again*? Wanna build another garbage fort, then burn it down for good measure?"

"What else are we going to do. Run?"

"Yes," Hollis said. "Running sounds like a great idea."

"It's spreading. It'll continue to spread."

"You don't know that."

"It spread from San Antonio to New Braunfels."

"We ain't sure that's what happened," Hollis told her. "Coulda been there was already something there. Could be there are junk piles like that all over, and they just kick into gear at different times. For all we know, tryin' to burn 'em all down is a fool's errand, like a big game of Whack-a-Mole."

"If New Braunfels started on its own, where's the 'Fortress' for the town?" She answered her own question. "There isn't one. In San Antonio, they were all migrating somewhere. Bugs to a bug zapper, like you said. They weren't going anywhere in New Braunfels. It *had* to have spread there."

Hollis found himself getting irritated. Mia did this; she reached grand conclusions on the basis of *it-just-sounds-*

right-to-me and ignored the fact that her explanations were, in themselves, full of logical holes.

"Then how's it spread?" Hollis asked. "You got all sorts of explanations for why those folks in New Braunfels couldn't just be hypnotized by the wind, so how 'bout you explain the way it crept almost an hour up the road and attacked those good folks without the trash fort to make it happen?"

"Maybe they rebuilt it."

"Oh, the zombies? They couldn't rebuild a one-picket fence."

"Then how do you explain it, if you're so smart?" she demanded.

"I *don't* explain it! You know how I solve shit like this, Mia?"

"You walk away."

"Goddamn *right* I walk away! Look what confrontation got us. It got us downtown in a city that about imploded on its own, then took an alien bomb in the face. It got you caught by Brendan ... *twice*. It put us in the middle of an alien scrap-fight, more than once. I got stabbed and about got some guy wearing my jimmies as earrings. We got half the fuckin' city of Austin hating our guts and now two cities worth of walking freak shows in our dust. I 'bout got my eyebrows burned off trying to do things your way, then had my brain fisted like the main attraction at an S&M club. So, yeah: My pitch is to get the fuck out. Just *go*."

"To Vail?"

"It's as good a place as any!"

"And what if Vail's the same way?"

Hollis threw his arms in the air. "Then fuck it! I'm glad you pulled me away, Green Eyes, but to tell you the truth, goin' felt pretty good. Maybe it's not all bad, being outta your head. Better than what we been up to."

Mia stalked the room. "We're going back."

"Where?"

"San Antonio."

"The fuck we are!"

"We have to see if they rebuilt the Fortress. Maybe it's self-reorganizing. Like how when someone shot the T2 into a ton of little pieces, all that mercury just rolled right back together."

"What the hell are you talking about?"

"In the second *Terminator* movie, the bad guy—"

"I know what a T2 is, woman! I'm talking about your crazy fuckin' idea of goin' back where we almost got Swiss cheesed."

"How is my idea any harder to believe than the rest of what we've seen?"

"I don't care if it's true or not!" Hollis said. "I'm not goin' back!"

"We have to."

"Why? Because it's our *duty?* Who the hell died and made *us* king? I don't know about you, but I never signed up for this. I wanted to get the hell out of Dodge right from Day 1, and if you'd listened to me we'd be on some island right now, safe and sound. We wouldn't be MechaPope, charged to protect the kingdom!"

Mia stared him down, but then, unable to keep it together, spit a tiny laugh.

"*What?*" Hollis said.

"Really? You're going with 'MechaPope'?"

"You know what I mean."

"Was he built with a tall hat?"

"Yeah, I fucking suppose!"

Hollis could have laughed there, too, but he didn't.

He said, "You want to go back, be my guest."

"*We,*" Mia said.

"I'm goin' to Vail. You want to come along, come. But if you want to go back, you're on your own."

He crossed his arms.

No. No way.

17

———

EXCEPT THAT *YES WAY*, because when Mia began to pack her bags, Hollis broke first in the game of who'd call whose bluff. Who was he kidding? He'd always done well on his own, but Mia wouldn't. She'd get her stupid ass killed, and right about now the though of her dying wasn't something Hollis could stomach. So he caved, and he went with her. And maybe he also went because he'd grown accustomed to having her around, too. It was an outside possibility, though it remained an unofficial one.

Still, Hollis gave himself credit for the moral victory. It was clear, once he agreed, just how relieved she was. In that moment he decided that *he* could have been the one to successfully bluff, and that if he'd dug in his heels, she would have gone with him. It was enough, for now.

He felt differently, though, when they began to drive south again. His mind protested. Now that he'd gotten the idea of Vail in his head, it was stuck there like the worst of earworms. He could almost feel it calling him. Because it wasn't just Vail, now was it? In his mind's eye it was another place entirely. One where those who went were safe, and free.

And he thought, *Step behind Heaven's Vail* — almost a slogan, like some kind of subliminal advertising campaign. A thing that meant nothing once he began to feel the lure of the unknown all over again. At that point, there was just the tug of darkness.

"Are you okay?" Mia asked from behind the wheel.

"Not as well as I'd be if we were headed the other direction."

"So you're fine, then," she said. And he didn't bother to contradict her.

They went through New Braunfels, where the people stood fixed by nothing. Then to San Antonio. The air had the same sour tang it'd had before — nothing material; more a psychic ring a half-note out of tune. Hollis found himself wishing more than anything that they'd just stayed where they were. San Marcos was more alive than he'd imagined, once they'd spent the day he'd insisted before heading back out. The second day, they saw activity on the town lawn: people gathering, milling, not unlike a street fair. There'd been two separate ensembles playing in the open: one old-school blues, one a bit rockabilly. Why couldn't they just stick around? It beat this journey back into ...

Well, into nothing.

Because that's what they found when they returned to the Fortress of Refuse: *nothing*. It hadn't reassembled. No new monument had taken its place. All, he thought, was how they'd left it. But he felt differently as they began to explore — as they returned to the dry cleaner's, just in case, to see if Theo or Carol had returned or left a note. They'd done neither, but their old place of sanctuary was no longer sacrosanct. Just as there'd been dead-eyed people around the Fortress before, so were they across all the neighborhoods now. Only now, they were as they'd been in New Braunfels: dispersed, entranced on the spot, milling some but otherwise focused on no single object as before.

"It came back," Mia said, holding her hand up as if to feel the air. "Why is it different now?"

Hollis wanted to correct her. They'd felt the mood change in San Antonio after the fire, but it would be a leap to say "it came back." In truth, they had no proof it'd ever left. The Fortress — supposedly the antenna for all of this, according to Theo and Torchy in different ways — was gone, but the disease of the mind was not.

"Are you still okay?" Mia asked.

Hollis checked himself before answering. Then: "Yeah."

But they kept the windows rolled up anyway. It felt safer.

They didn't stay. Other than their quick tour of the old Fortress site (around which there were few zombies; music spilling from a house in the distance made Hollis think they'd all gone to a party), they didn't even get out of the car. Instead Mia drove them further south, through places called Pleasanton, Floresville, Karnes City. In a small town barely past Karnes City called Kenedy, they found a rollicking community that didn't even seem to understand the apocalypse had come. That town, like San Marcos, was having a festival in the town square. But Mia sensed something and Hollis sensed something, so they continued on to a bump in the road called Goliad, finding yet another motel, running up and back to Kenedy a few times until they saw it happen near dusk. It came all at once. On one trip, the festival was still rolling. The next time it was New Braunfels all over again. It was like whatever had spread from Karnes City had walked down 181 and taken them over. The band still sat on the lawn, instruments in hand, doing nothing at all.

So they went back to San Marcos — roundabout this time, lengthening the route to avoid San Antonio the way you'd skirt a chemical spill to avoid exposure — and found that it, too, had fallen.

"It's spreading, like I said," Mia told him.

"I know you said it. You don't have to keep reminding me."

"It'll reach Austin if we don't stop it."

"Doesn't change the fact that we have no clue how to stop it," Hollis told her. "Nor any desire."

Mia looked over at him, but let it go. Objectively, they'd both made their points over the past few weeks. Objectively, Mia had been right as often as Hollis and Hollis had been right as often as Mia. But Hollis didn't see it that way right now; didn't *want* to see it that way.

"You made us go back for that phone," Mia said. "What's it say?"

"Oh, right." He pulled the phone from the console and set it on his leg, then made a show of putting on invisible spectacles using just his free hand. "Let me just put my smart-guy glasses on and get right back to you."

"You don't have to be a wiseass," she said.

"Don't have to, but wanna."

"I'm just saying, there might be something in all those documents to help us."

Hollis had taken over the driving. Which was good, because it meant he could underline his next point by stepping dramatically on the brakes.

"What?" she said, looking at the now-paused side of the road.

He handed her the phone. "You look through it."

"You're the one who wanted it so bad."

"Yeah. Like a woobie. Sure; I'll admit it. I wanted to get this thing because we did so much to *get* it, whether or not it made any goddamn sense. I dunno, Mia — call me a sucker for sunk costs. But now that you're putting on the pressure to perform, I'll just say it. I can't get *shit* from what's on there. But hey. If you're saying we only had Carol and Theo for kicks and *you* were the one who understood all that code and schematics all along, then by all means. Flip through those thousands of pictures and tell me how exactly we're supposed to beat something we can't see, can't find, and don't remotely understand."

Mia didn't take the phone. She let him put it back in the console.

"Maybe we could go and talk to Torchy again."

"Good idea. I need to borrow a belt."

"What about Theo and Carol? They *might* have gone back to Austin, right?"

"We've been over this."

She splayed her fingertips across her forehead as if she had a headache. "I just need to think."

"Think about saving yourself. Think about not going out the way they all went out, trying to change what you can't change."

"Quiet."

"You ain't gonna solve it, Mia."

Then she perked up. "The datacenter. The one in Austin. The Astral app database. Of course! That's what all of the pictures are of, anyway, right? Before we even knew there *was* something outside of Austin, that's where they were focusing. That's what Carol was studying when we still had internet, back at the Spider House. That's what you showed to Theo when you went to Louisiana. *The datacenter,* Hollis! That's what we should be thinking about!"

"What about it?"

Mia seemed invigorated by this new/old idea. She was more animated than she'd been. Hollis, on the other hand, found all this enthusiasm obnoxious.

"Carol and Theo said the aliens were using all that data the app had gathered on its users to train an AI or something, right? And Theo said it was like a big-old brain. Meant to ... what? ... give them an average of human behavior? To predict our responses? To help them understand us?"

She seemed to be waiting for an answer, but Hollis shrugged in a way that suggested the minimum of given shits.

Mia lit up again, remembering faster now.

"They said was like a master decoder. Whatever the Fortress of Refuse was collecting, it was being sent back to the Astral center. It's analyzed there, somehow. Like, the Astral thing makes it make sense. Then whatever comes out is sent up to the mothership."

"They were just guessing, too," Hollis said.

"But Hollis! Don't you see? We *can't* get all of whatever's doing this to people. But we *can* cut it off at the source?"

"Wouldn't the 'source' be what we've already tried to destroy?"

"You know what I'm saying."

She was so animated, Hollis had to grab her by the arm to shut her up.

"No," he said. "I don't know what you're saying. Because what I'd *think* you were saying, if I didn't know better, was that you think you know better than the two Ph.D's who told us to destroy San Antonio's tower and leave Austin alone."

"Leave it alone *at first,*" Mia said. "But it might still—"

"Mia," he said, shaking her arm again. "You're full of shit. Listen to yourself. Burning that pile of shit down was one thing, but you must really think we *are* MechaPope if your plan is to blow up a building that's sure to be guarded if it's so damn important."

"I don't know that we need to *blow it up.* I'm just saying that somehow, some way, something else is doing the job the Fortress was doing. The Fortress made people feel and sucked those feelings and memories away, right? Out of nostalgia? Something else is doing that now, is all. If we can find it ..."

"Mia!" Hollis yelled. "You're not listening to me. I've played along so far, but this is some serious bullshit. Do you hear me? There's a problem here, yeah. But I'm just me and you're just you, and while your ass could launch a thousand ships, it ain't gonna save the world. I'll say this as clear as I can: *I've had it.* I've been asking around, when we've found a town with folks who can still talk, and I'm not the only one with Vail on the mind. It's out there, somehow, the way those lines of psychic rocks seem to put shit out there. I can feel it in my bones. *That's* where we should be going. And so if you insist on dancin' to the beat of a different band, you have at it. But — and I mean it this time — if you wanna dance there, you'll dance alone."

Mia's face looked shocked, then disappointed, then angry, and then finally something entirely different.

Her features fell slack. She looked like she'd gone the way of the zombies, brain finally slipping away out the back door.

"I don't dance," she said.

Hollis felt his brow scrunch. "Huh?"

She looked up at him, those big green eyes on wide display.

"I don't dance," she repeated.

Then: "Hollis. I think I know what's replaced the Fortress of Refuse."

18

MUSIC.

Hollis, Mia thought, still wasn't convinced. But for Mia at least, all the pieces fit. If the Fortress worked by evoking nostalgia for all the crap that it'd been built from, then whatever was still scooping out people's minds had to be something capable of doing the same. It had to be dispersed instead of focused on a single object or location, as had been the case in San Antonio before Hollis and Mia had come. Whatever this was, it had waited for their move, then adapted. They'd caused the aliens' plan to evolve, was all, like an infection growing antibiotic resistant from exposure, or going airborne so it could spread faster.

Same disease, even though it wasn't a disease. Different mechanism.

In New Braufels, where they'd first seen this new version, there'd been music in the air. Same for San Antonio, when they'd returned. In San Marcos, Floresville, Pleasanton, Kenedy, and Karnes City, Mia was pretty sure she'd heard notes on the air — even if only before the switch like had happened in San Marcos and Kenedy, as if music itself heralded the change. Sometimes, it had sounded like a recording — some ancient instinctual intelligence causing those in town to find a device that worked, to put in batteries, to insert media and have a listen.

"That doesn't even make sense," Hollis said.

Mia shook her head. They'd moved to a place just south of Austin, knowing the clock was ticking, their travel jury out while the committee debated. She'd been thinking this out for half a day now, while Hollis had sat in a chair on the abandoned deck of the lackluster pool, pretending none of this was happening. She wanted to be as bulletproof as possible when she talked to him. She wanted to preview all his objections, and have plausible answers ready.

"Sure it does. Music is a much better medium, if the aliens want to evoke nostalgia and memory from people. The only thing better might have been smell, but smell is so particular. You'll remember grandma's apple pie, but most smells evoke nothing at all. But music? It's everywhere. Even when we don't notice it, it's playing in the background. Haven't you ever heard a song, and remembered what you were doing the last time it played?"

"Not really," Hollis said. But she could see the shift of his eyes. He had. Almost everyone had.

"What about deaf people?" he asked.

"That's just the thing." She touched her ear. "Deaf in one ear, remember? I've never gotten into music. Maybe because I never heard much of it in stereo, or maybe some other reason. Still, I've heard lots of it in mono, and I can feel it tugging on me the same as you do. It's just less powerful for me, because I have less invested in it. I have fewer memories attached to it. I'll bet you have songs," she went on, "that make even tough old Hollis well up. I'll bet certain music reminds you of mom, or dad, or a best friend who's gone now. Or a girl, Hollis. Tell me you've never had 'our song' with someone you cared about."

"Dunno." But yeah, he had that, too.

"Maybe the deaf would be immune; I don't know. But you can still feel music, even if you can't hear it. It runs through you — not just the bass, but the treble. I'd think it'd evoke just the same, given time."

"I don't know ..."

But Mia had her ammunition ready. She'd planned this argument like an attorney with her closing argument.

"Why, with aliens in the sky and society going to shit, have people been gathering for public concerts?" Mia asked. "Think about it. A few times now, we've seen people gathering around music as the stage that comes before they go full zombie. Remember Kenedy? Maybe they're responding to some primitive calling. Like whatever drew people to the Fortress of Refuse, but now it's something new?"

"And the aliens just siphon off all that nostalgia. From everywhere at once?"

"Come on," Mia said. "Let's at least drive by the datacenter. Let's at least see what's going on."

Hollis didn't see the point, but Mia argued that it was up north anyway, on the way out of town. The city, so far as they'd seen from preliminary run-ups to check, was humming along better than they'd left it. Someone had cleared the roads. Someone had knocked out gang barricades. Someone, it seemed was out to clean up Austin.

That's what they found when they took I-35 through the city. Mia had never seen it not jammed. But now it wasn't jammed at all. Now it was as if a golden path had been paved.

Then they saw why.

Downtown, everyone was out in the streets.

"This is creeping me out," Hollis said.

But Mia had anticipated this. She'd thought they might see something similar. They kept moving. Passing neighborhood after neighborhood, seeing the city come to new life. Which was to say old life, entirely out of place.

"If your plan is to get me on board," Hollis said, "it's backfiring."

They passed the datacenter. Mia, driving, took the exit and circled the blocks around the facility as Hollis protested. But she could barely hear him anymore. They were inside the city, and if he wanted out, he could damn well get out. The idea was on her like a refrain. It felt right. It felt like an obsession.

"We need to do this," she told him.

"No, we don't."

"We can stop it."

"We really can't."

"If we don't at least try to make a difference," Mia said, "who will?"

"And if we do try to make a difference," Hollis replied, "we'll just become like the rest of them."

It was a shallow argument. Mia felt her brain on fire.

Go north.

So she drove them north. She got out, walked the streets for something to do. Austin was coming awake after its slumber. Live music capital of the world, and it seemed like everyone had a band. Hollis, between complaining, seemed to enjoy just a little of it. Only a tad, because the rest of him had his eyes on departure. But Mia, knowing it wasn't the greatest of ideas, let him fall under his favorite music's sway whenever they passed some that suited him. When she saw his eyes turn toward the past, she let him go. It felt dangerous, but she told herself,

He'll be fine,

and she was sure she was right, and so far reality agreed with her, because hour by hour Hollis became more pliable. Her intuition took her on a tour, and returned her to the Astral facility, which was guarded by enough alien ships to look like a modernist architectural wonder: all spheres, practically touching, forming a line that could never be crossed. Except that

You don't need to cross it. Not yet. You don't know enough yet,

and Mia agreed, because she hadn't yet sampled enough of the local flavor. And that felt more than necessary because Hollis had been right; you couldn't battle what you didn't understand. And Mia had never understood music, so how could she possibly comprehend what the aliens were doing and how to stop it unless she did her research?

Hollis and Mia, attending one of the outdoor concerts themselves. It was an all-girl band, too young to sing about the blues heartbreak the lyrics tried to reach. Then a jazz ensemble in the park, and a cool little bebop trio on the steps of the downtown Austin Java, a grunge band in the basement of a club.

Then out of the city. Into the city. Mia drove. Hollis stayed more and more quiet. And into that quiet, Mia wondered,

Is it getting to us?

But that was a crazy thought because she wanted to understand, and she didn't, but even with that one deaf ear she was starting to.

But after the second full day, she woke to find Hollis gone from his motel bed because he had—

19

—WOKEN UP EARLY, an alarm to vibrate on a pedometer device he'd found laying on the grass at one of the many impromptu concerts they'd attended. The band, that time, had been four boys singing in four-part harmony. Without excess post-production, they sounded horrible. It was the kind of band he'd always hated — manufactured, mass-market shit that had killed the indie game and was making true music obsolete. Making it an endangered species.

In that moment, Hollis had seen it all with perfect clarity. He remembered all of Mia's arguments about what had happened down south — how the aliens, deprived of the original beacon they'd converted from the Fortress of Refuse, had somehow bewitched local music instead. It seemed to be regional: just *listening to music* didn't doom you so much as *listening to music within a certain geographic sphere of alien influence*. How that might work, Hollis had no idea. He only knew that San Antonio seemed to be the epicenter, and that the ring was growing out from there. It had influenced Austin and made it come out to play — early signs, he now believed, of mind-sucking yet to come. And Hollis, as he'd been spellbound in New Braunfels, had been spell-bound the whole time that Mia had been dragging them around in loops like a crazy woman. He'd been half a zombie already, while she'd gone steadily manic. But hearing that shitty music popped him right out of it. Just as good music could get you in the mood, terrible music can throw you right out of it. And this music, with the four out-of-tune boys, had been truly horrific.

That was when his eyes had popped open for real and he'd seen the pedometer. He didn't know why he'd grabbed it at the time; some primitive part of him had told him to snag it just like he'd once snagged his Zippo. Later it'd occurred to him that you could set silent alarms on things like it, and he'd done so in order to rise without Mia seeing him.

He walked into the bathroom. Blinked into the mirror. He stuck out his tongue, widened his eyes, and generally peeked as much around his exterior as he could, to make sure the real and untouched Hollis was still inside. He seemed to be, for now. When Hollis had awoken at that bad concert, the rush-back of information had come to him. But by then, Mia had been too far gone. She was already talking about her new love of music, asking Hollis how long it took to learn to play an instrument. Or maybe she could sing. Hollis only heard some of her questions, though he took the rest from her body language. He could hear very little these days. At first, all he'd been able to shove in his ears were subtle wads of tissue, after he'd run to the bathroom. Later he'd managed to snag some bright orange earplugs that Mia, in her frenzy, hadn't noticed. He'd been able to duck into a pharmacy later and find some that were practically invisible, made out of tan-colored wax. With those in, he'd heard very little. And it'd been a waiting game since then.

The longer his ears stayed plugged, the more of his mind returned. Whatever the aliens had done to the air, *vis a vis* music, seemed to be reversible if you stoppered the sound in time. He couldn't pull Mia away, though. By the time his own head was clear, Mia's was half gone. She was no longer thinking logically, and wouldn't put in earplugs. How could she? She'd just learned so much appreciation for great local tunes!

After his ears were plugged — while he'd kept following Mia around, waiting for his chance to extricate them both — Hollis began to notice things. Things like the fact that the music scene wasn't as joyous and carefree as he remembered it, even though it sure had seemed that way when he'd been able to hear. The beats, which he felt through his bones, were just a little bit off. The clubs and public spaces where the bands played weren't as colorful and bright as they'd been.

It was all a sham. It was mind control, not true expression.

He also noticed the stones.

They were everywhere. Absolutely everywhere. The last time he'd seen so many of the monoliths, they'd been around Brendan's compound. Now they were embedded in the very streets downtown, along highway berms, on hills, through the lawns of the suburbs. There were ships, too — a *lot* of ships. Hollis couldn't help feeling scrutinized, like maybe he should be subtle if he meant to make waves.

And then he'd heard Mia talking to herself, and it'd become apparent that things, for Hollis and Mia, were a little different than they were for everyone else.

For Mia, anyway.

Before they'd gone to bed, Mia had gone into the bathroom, as he was now. She'd looked into the mirror, as he was doing now. And — still playing stupid, still pretending to be lost in the fugue of whatever the aliens were trying to do with their memory machine — he'd listened in.

We're coming, she'd told herself as if speaking to someone else — someone either not present or (and this was Hollis's bet) inside her head.

We can't make it, she told that unseen somebody. *Not yet.*

And the most troubling thing: *This was our deal.*

Deal? Hollis hadn't liked the sound of that. In the hours after that exhausting day at the Exchange, Mia had been more willing to talk about the ordeal they'd just come out of than she became in later days. She'd used the word "deal" then, too. Just like she'd used it when they'd still been inside, or when he'd merely sensed the word in the air.

Mia's hand on dark scales. Her lips pursing. *Shh.*

And her whisper: *Take him, and see what vengeance feels like.*

He hadn't remembered that at first. Not with all the injuries, fatigue, and built-up stress. But he'd remembered it later — the way Mia had spoken to the beast. The way she'd told it to take Dr. Greensward, lest he continue trying to take them.

This was our deal.

He sighed into the mirror. Then he went to the window. There were things to do, now, but he had to see what was out there first. He had to *feel* it. With one more night of silence and the clarity it brought (she'd even found the music on Ricky's phone, and with the thing cabled to an external battery had played it all night), things kept coming clearer and clearer. Maybe it'd been working on him for a while. For days. Since San Antonio, since he'd first gripped that chain-link fence and thought for the first time in years about his childhood.

There were stones outside. Dozens just within sight. They'd been slammed through concrete, buried in parked cars that were inconveniently in the way, planted in green areas, even dropped in the bottom of the leaf-filled hotel pool. But the stones, Hollis saw, hadn't been placed randomly. They were in rough concentric circles, spooling out from where they were right now — their room as dead center.

He looked at Mia as she slept, wondering how steadily it would work on her. She'd gotten infected after all, despite that bum ear and her apathy about music. Hollis had gone under fast, and chance had let him surface. Now he had to help Mia surface, if only she'd let him.

She mumbled in her sleep.

"We'll come when we can. Yes, I'm ready."

Ready. It felt final, as if preparations had been made.

"Of course," she said into her dream.

Who was she talking to? What was out there working on her specifically, going out of its way to circle her in memory stones as she slept?

He opened the door quietly, then moved to the room beside. She didn't watch as well as she thought, and over the past day he'd been able to stock up.

He looked out, past the rows of stones. Morning, on the external hallway fronting the motel, was chilly. There were ships there, now. And, he thought, aliens on the ground — or vague shapes moving between the stones that *looked* like aliens, anyway. Were they watching him? Did they know what he planned to do? Did they care? Why would they? Mia was just one person; Hollis was just one person.

Except that Mia, with someone, had made a deal.

If he tuned very closely into his thoughts and emotions, he could almost feel the bond. He could sense something intensely curious out there somewhere, reaching toward them. Toward her, in particular.

There was a bag beneath the bed. Hollis pulled it out, then sneaked back to his own room. He went into the bathroom and closed the door to prepare.

If he was going to do this, he'd need to be quick.

20

Hollis moved to the bed. Mia slept soundly, so he was able to get one end of the handcuffs around the posts without her stirring. He moved her right hand gently, flinching and holding perfectly still as she tried to turn over. Then the left hand was closer, so he clasped that one loosely with the cuff on that side — enough to slow her down, not enough for her to feel through her slumber. Then he got the other cuff on. He tightened both as she woke.

She wasn't dazed now. Now she seemed fully Mia, not at all dreamy, fully awake.

"Hollis." She looked at the handcuffs. "What the fuck is this?"

"You're sick."

"I'm not sick," she said. This was why he hadn't tried to talk to her first — why he'd gone right to such extreme measures. He knew a lost cause when he saw one. He knew that if he tried to convince her to do anything beyond that which clearly, now, felt like programming, that she'd tell him no. It'd put her guard up. If he argued or tried to persuade her to leave town, her guard would go up. Spellbound Hollis wasn't supposed to ask too many questions. Doing so might cost him his only chance.

It'd been the cuffs or nothing.

"Hollis."

"Just lie still."

"If this is some weird sex thing—"

"Shh. It's nothing like that."

She rattled the cuffs. Harder by the second.

"Let me go."

"I can't."

"Hollis? I said get these fucking things off me."

"I can't, Mia."

"Get them off or I'll yell 'rape.'"

"Nobody will hear you. Nobody will care." Then he said something he was quite sure of for no reason at all. "We're the only ones around."

The only ones inside the circle of stones. The only ones that someone was particularly interested in. They'd both heard about abductions the aliens had taken. They were returning some people, keeping others. To Hollis, who sometimes enjoyed sports, the abductions had the feel of a tournament. Those who were being returned had failed the first round. The winners were still on the alien ships, and it'd continue until only the ones they truly wanted remained.

Viceroys. The Nine.

Words without meaning to Hollis, coming maybe from within, maybe from Mia, maybe from something he couldn't see or feel or touch. All he knew was that if the aliens found some people special, they found Mia special, too.

"What the hell are you doing, Hollis?"

Man. She sure sounded rational right now. She sounded

like herself. She didn't sound like the spaced-out fruitcake she'd been for the past few days.

It's a defense mechanism. An allergic reaction: a fake personality cobbled to fool you into believing it's the real one, and the ditz she's been isn't a problem after all. What you see, at the top of her consciousness, isn't really her.

And yet it was, in a way.

"I need to fix you. Then we need to fix this together."

"How. Hollis?" Her eyes tried to follow him as he made a semicircle around the bed, being sure to stay away from her kicking legs. She was like a viper now, he knew. She'd play nice until she found her opening, then do whatever it took for the parasite in her mind to survive. "How are we going to fix it?"

"You'll see."

"Talk to me. *Hollis?* I'm scared. Please talk to me."

He kept his eyes averted: *Not her. Stick to the plan.*

"We're going to destroy the datacenter."

"You were the one who said that was impossible. You said we couldn't do it, and would be stupid to try."

"I said that when leaving was an option." He looked toward the window, unable through the blinds to see the rings of stones beyond. "Now, it's not."

"Why not?"

"Because of you."

Because I have to fix you first, or you'll bite my head off and run back the first chance you get. More thoughts informed by something else, in a chaotic sort of psychic stew.

"We can't destroy it. Hollis? Hollis, look at me."

He would not look at her.

"That was your analysis. Remember? They'll be guarding it. We've *seen* how they're guarding it. Dozens of ships. Maybe hundreds. That building is receiving tons of human emotion and memories, and they don't plan to lose it."

"Memories like yours. Feelings like yours."

"Others. Like New Braunfels. Like San Marcos."

"Like yours, Mia."

"*Hollis?* You're crazy." She rattled the handcuffs, now trying to yank through wrists that were too large for the steel. Determined to peel her skin off to get free, if that's what it took. "Hollis? Hollis? *LET ME GO!*"

And Hollis, reaching for the remaining item in his bag, said, "No."

"How is this going to work? What, you're just going to leave me here?"

He stood with the dangling white earbuds in his hands.

"Hollis? What are you going to do with those?"

Hollis, unnerved now and losing courage, wished he'd kept his earplugs in. He'd taken them out so he could try to make her understand. But now he saw: understanding wasn't just a luxury; it was also impossible. She was more out of her right mind than he'd realized.

He stuck to the script rather than fall into the trap of engaging.

"Brendan's compound was destroyed," Hollis said, "but he had bunkers underground. Of course he did. But the aliens? They don't understand paranoia like Brendan's. They didn't go deep. There's no way they destroyed all the vaults."

"You plan to get Brendan's artillery out of hock, then attack the Astral datacenter?"

"It's the only way to be sure. Cut it off at the source."

"Look," Mia said, voice softening, turning her head to try and meet his eye. "You don't have to do this. I'll go. Of course I'll go. Hollis? Listen. Uncuff me and I'll go with you without all of this. What do you say?"

Hollis reached for the floor. He'd already stripped one pillow of its case, and picked the case up now.

"Mia," he said.

He looked her in the eyes. She glanced up, waiting, hopeful.

"Do you love me?"

"*Yes!* Yes! Of course I—"

Not her. Not Mia in her right mind, thinking only her own thoughts.

He shoved the gag between her teeth, wrapping the pillowcase behind her head and tying it. That did not make her happy. She screamed against it, but at least now she couldn't keep trying to infect him.

He plugged the headphones into Ricky's phone. Then he put the earbuds into her ears.

"What are you doing?"

"Waking you up."

He found what he wanted. He pressed play. Then he took a second pillowcase and used it to circle her head at the midpoint, holding the buds in so she couldn't toss them away.

She thrashed. She fought. She kicked her legs like a body full of a demon reluctant to leave, raking marks from the metal handcuffs into her wrists.

Then Hollis took what he'd procured for himself: not earbuds, but big over-the-ear headphones. He put them on, then plugged the cord into the jack on an ancient iPod he'd scavenged when he'd scavenged the rest. He didn't want to take any chances, so he played white noise.

Then he sat in a chair in the corner with his arms crossed, watching Mia so she wouldn't somehow get away or hurt herself, white noise blasting to erase all sound.

He waited, then, for it to end.

21

Mia blinked, opening her eyes to find a popcorn ceiling filling her view. It was an ugly thing — the kind the home improvement shows always raked clean when they flipped houses. She tried to sit up, but her wrists were bound. There was something black in front of her face, and as she acclimated to whatever the hell this was, she noticed the subtle pressure of padding around her ears.

She raised her head to see Hollis watching her. And what was this? She was handcuffed to the bed. Seriously uncool.

But even that was just one thing of many. Hollis, for instance, was wearing what looked like a flight headset — the bulky kind of thing helicopter passengers wore so they could talk to each other over the roar of the rotors. And, she suspected based on the object near her mouth that she recognized as a boom mic, she seemed to be wearing one just like it.

"Welcome back," Hollis said. The voice was coming not from the man himself, but from the headphones. It was muted, somehow, though, as if the headphones weren't working right.

"You're wearing earplugs under those," he said, answering her unasked question. "I imagine the volume's loud enough that you can hear me fine, but I didn't want to take any chances."

"What's going on here?" She rattled her cuffs. Her wrists, she found, were both raw. She didn't remember getting into this and had no idea how long it'd been. Unless it'd been in a dream. Yes, she seemed to remember a nightmare that went something like this. She and Hollis had been trying to decide whether or not to enter Austin from the south, and then they must have slept on it. Her dream involved a lot of running around, a lot of music, a lot of fun, and a bit of trauma at the end. Or had that been real?

"You got an earworm," Hollis said.

She must have looked confused, because he went on.

"You know. One of those songs that sticks in your head, and you can't get it out no matter what you do."

"I don't even like music," she said. "Remember?"

"You learned. Over the last few days, you gave yourself a crash course."

She looked to the window. The drapes were pulled, but the light, versus her internal clock, was wrong. That's when she knew: It really happened. Somehow, what she'd seen spellbind Hollis had spellbound her. She'd lost days, out of her mind. What felt like a nightmare had actually happened.

"You can let me go now," she said through her microphone. "I'm better."

"Do you love me?" he asked.

"Of course not."

"Not even a little?"

"The best I can say, if you're going to dig for compliments, is 'I've somehow gotten used to you.'"

Hollis considered. Then he walked over and, using a tiny key, removed her right handcuff. Then the left. She rubbed her wrists. They were chafed, bruised underneath where she'd hung on their sharp edges.

"Better?" he asked.

She hit him in the testicles. Hard.

"Better."

Hollis was on the floor, gasping for air. He was also trying to climb back up, sure he'd made a mistake. He almost got one of her wrists again, but she got up and stepped over him. He was in a ball. She'd spared no mercy.

"I'm not sick again," she said. "I just wanted to show you that I'm in my right mind."

"Thanks," Hollis squeaked from the floor.

She went to the window.

"Don't look out," he wheezed from behind her.

"Why?"

"They might be watching us." Then a pause. "Watching *you*."

"Me? Why me?"

"I don't know. Maybe they got tuned into you when you got in that reptar's head. I'm hardly an expert." He got to one knee, pressing a hand into his abdomen just above the belt line. "But if you were to look out, you'd see we're surrounded by stones."

"I'm not special."

"They seem to think you are."

Mia considered this. Hollis still hadn't stood. She almost felt bad for him, but he'd cuffed her to the bed. The fact that he'd seemingly done it for her own good felt true but distant. Eventually, she supposed she'd need to thank him for doing what had to be done.

"Do I have to keep wearing this?" Mia asked, meaning the headphones.

He took his off, so she did as well. When he spoke again, he was much harder to hear and she had to work to listen.

"I've been wearing earplugs for days," he said, finally getting to his feet. "If they didn't work to block out the worst of whatever the music evokes for the aliens, I think I'd know by now. But it does make conversation hard. Hence: these."

"Where did you get them?"

"Brendan's."

"Brendan ... you mean Brendan Banks's compound?"

"It's not far from here," he said. Then he put his headphones back on and motioned for her to do the same, and then he went on with her much better able to hear. "And I was right about the vaults."

"What vaults?"

So Hollis told her everything. All they'd discussed, apparently, when she'd been chained to the bed at first, still out of her right mind. Plus all they'd gone through while she'd been in some kind of a trance, hopping from hotspot to hotspot until Hollis lucked into snapping awake, then laid his plans. And as it turned out, Brendan had some underground vaults still full of equipment — like working electronics, kept paranoid in yet another cage. He'd left her chained up, he'd said, after she'd fallen asleep during what he'd so far only called "deprogramming." He'd found the headphone set and some other goodies, extra guns, and a whole lot of potential. She was still weighing his plan to attack the Astral data center, but if Brendan really had the artillery Hollis claimed — including drone-aimed antitank missiles — then maybe it was possible after all. And if Hollis really meant to attack the place instead of running? Well, that was personal growth for you.

"Why not just run to Vail?" Mia asked. The answer didn't matter. She'd been off the deep end and he'd dragged her back, and now they were even. The nut-punch had settled her last remaining grudge, and now she didn't get to question his intentions. He didn't have to fix her, and he sure didn't have to stay in Austin to do it. There'd be some way to give anyone watching outside the slip, if Hollis had already run to Brendan's and back.

"I considered it," he said. "But then I realized: This is *my* town. And this is my *music*. I grew up watching bands play three nights a week, and now the aliens want to take that down? No way. *Nobody* fucks with my scene."

His response's words sounded satirical, but he didn't so much as smile.

"How did you ... *deprogram* me?"

"I played you a song called 'Mmm-Bop,' by a group called Hanson, on a loop for twelve hours."

"No, really."

But he still wasn't smiling. He said, "I'm not proud of it."

Mia seemed to remember, now. It'd been like holy water on an exorcism. She went to Ricky's phone, embarrassed for Ricky, and found the song to play it. It evoked nothing. Unless you counted hatred.

"So if we go out ..." Mia said.

"... we keep earplugs in. It's worked for me so far. I still feel something, but it's nowhere near as strong. Humming to yourself, if you can believe it, also helps. There's bands out there everywhere now. You thought you knew the Austin live music scene? You ain't seen *nothin'* yet. It's like the new alien plan was a flame and this city was dry grass soaked with gasoline. If they wanted to poke our emotions with melody, I can't think of a better place to do it. Except maybe for Nashville, but let's face it. They're nowhere near as cool as us."

Finally, Hollis's smile returned.

"So what do you think?" he asked. "Maybe a little hummer to celebrate?"

Mia shook her head. She took off her headphones, bringing them down to lay around her neck. Even saving her, he was an asshole.

"It's cool," he said, his amplified voice still audible, holding his crotch and wincing. "You probably broke it anyway."

22

Hollis had no idea how to use a rocket launcher, any of Brendan's big guns, or the mobile antiaircraft batteries he had a hunch would work just as well on ground-based targets if he just ... you know ... tipped them to lay on their sides. That, however, was a problem for another day.

They'd visited the vaults, finding them unguarded and honestly not all that hard to find if you thought like a human being. It hadn't been hard, either, to sneak out of the hotel. In Hollis's opinion, the whole alien *thing* — once you eliminated the obvious parts of arrival and destroying cities — felt ill-prepared. It was as if they'd had plans for humanity, then been surprised. He might be imagining things, but he got a distinct feeling of making it up as they went along.

They didn't take anything that first trip, though. Seeing what they had at their potential disposal, the question now was how to plan their attack. Brendan had acres of C4 explosive, but the idea of using it felt so crude. Had these aliens really come so far to be defeated the way Arnold Schwarzenegger defeated his foes? Maybe. Hollis, for once, figured a true plan was in order.

So: Recon. Gathering of resources. Maybe they could even find some allies, if they were lucky.

They moved mainly between Brendan's place and the Astral datacenter, which was now swarmed with ships like a hive at stasis. If they kicked the thing, Hollis thought, those ships might get plenty defensive. Maybe it had to be a suicide mission. Maybe it had to be the kind of attack they didn't come back from. Hollis didn't like that much, but it was hard to argue with the reason suicide attacks were so effective: If you didn't care about getting away clean, there weren't many limits on the damage a sufficiently motivated person could do.

They kept their earplugs in, to dull the effect of music and any other auditory attempts. They didn't go back to the motel after sneaking out the rear, down the fire stairs. After that, it was almost too simple — simple enough, they both thought, that maybe they were being let go, or still tracked but in a more subtle way.

Most of the time, when not trying to blend in, they kept their headsets on, too. And that all went fine until Hollis's crackled, and he found a voice intruding that wasn't at all like Mia's.

"Hey," it said.

Hollis looked around, expecting to see someone.

"Talking to you," the voice went on. "You on Frequency 6."

That, Hollis understood. The headsets, from what Hollis could tell, were next-generation: military surplus, perhaps, purchased well before they were obsolete enough to be surplus. They operated across a few different frequencies, supposedly coded, that the makers had numbered 1-9 on a dial at the rear of the right cup. Hollis had picked 6 for both of them, since any seemed as good as another.

"Who's this?" Hollis asked.

"I'm the guy who's headset this is," the voice said. "Who the fuck are you?"

Now Hollis caught Mia's eye. Her headset was on 6 as well, so they could communicate. She was hearing this, same as him.

She mouthed, *Brendan?*

Hollis stopped, then shook his head: *Nah.*

"You there, shitter?" the voice asked. *Clearly* Brendan. Because that was fair. All the people who died that day, and none of their foes had gone with them. They'd seen Vika and Beef after the dust-up at the Exchange, but some part of Hollis had been hoping Brendan had gone to his grave — especially since his property had been reduced to burnt twigs and nobody was guarding the ashes. It'd occurred to Hollis to check Brendan's underground vaults for leftovers, and he'd taken the fact that Brendan himself hadn't locked them down somehow as evidence that the man was dead, or out of town, or abducted. But no. He was still around, within whatever range these helmets had, and able to listen in on their conversations whenever he wanted, seeing as the headset he'd have to be wearing would easily decode the ones they wore.

Hollis scoured his recent memory. What had they said? Had they given away who they were — either Hollis or Mia? But no; for the past hour or so they'd been silent. The question was when Brendan had noticed someone else had one of his headsets and how — and if he'd eavesdropped for a while before finally piping in.

No. He's trying to figure out who were are now, Hollis thought. *If he knew, he'd call me by name.*

"That's not Hollis Palmer, is it?"

Well, so much for that theory.

"Come on, Hollis. You were never a coward before. Only a handful of people ever knew where my vaults were. Only people who bought from me — and crooks like you, who *pretended* to want to buy from me."

"Fine," Hollis said.

There was a light sound on the other end: Brendan clapping. "I knew it. I knew you were too slippery to get away."

"Where are you, Brendan?"

"Home. Above my comm vault. I just found two of my helmets missing. Who's with you? That fine piece of ass?"

"Nobody."

"Right. Well. You know where I am," Brendan said. "Why don't you come and say hello?"

"I think I'll pass."

"Found the carrier signal, did you?"

Hollis had been about to remove his headset — probably just toss it away for good. But that stopped him with a hand on each cup, pausing before the lift.

"What are you talking about?" Hollis asked.

"I've got smart people too, wiseass," Brendan said. "You didn't give me much, but it was enough for a start. I know there's something going on. And my people say that if you block all sound, you're more or less safe."

More or less. So he didn't know it all, and was covering all the bases.

"You really should come back, Hollis. We miss you."

"Right."

"It's the truth. You robbed me, I kidnapped and tried to kill you ... I figure it's all water under the bridge." There was a snap, as of fingers. "Mia. That was her name. Are you on the line, too, Mia?"

Mia looked at Hollis. He stabbed a finger in front of his lips.

"I'm sure she is," Brendan said. "Just trying to be quiet. It's okay. I might not trust me if I were you. But here's the thing, Hollis. You've known me for a long time, now. Have I not always struck you as a man of honor?"

Hollis didn't really want to answer that. At one point, yes, that's exactly how Brendan had struck him. But then he'd lost his mind a bit, and kidnapped Mia and Carol with intent to ravage and kill, and put Hollis in with the world's worst surgeon for a little bit of torture therapy. Maybe Brendan, as far as lowlives went, could once have earned a second chance. Not anymore.

"I'm going to go, Brendan."

"Really? But you must be so curious. I saw the way my explosives were moved, just enough for scuffs in the dust to give you away. What, you didn't want to just load up? Figured you'd think about it first, then come back and take more of my shit because I had to be gone, and my property was fair game?"

"Brendan ..."

Hollis could imagine the man waving a hand, waving it all away. "I don't care. It's fine. But to tell the truth, I've been looking at the datacenter, too."

Hollis and Mia traded a look. Superstitiously, they sat low. They were nowhere in particular, just about a half mile from the Astral building Brendan had referred to. But what if Brendan was there right now? It felt dangerous to risk being spotted.

"What?" Brendan asked. "You really think so little of me? And do you really think I wouldn't have a second home? I'm in the hills these days. *Under* the hills. But I come and go, because so many of my goodies are back at Old Home. Of course I was going to look into the shit you brought me, even with as little as I had. Clearly they're using it now. And clearly, as I'm sure you can see right here and right now, they don't want anyone else to have it."

That made them duck lower. The sky was alive with shuttles and from time to time they'd heard the low purr of reptars prowling the area. But what mattered most was the way Brendan had spoken about Hollis seeing it ... *right here and right now*. Could he track them, using the headsets? Were his people triangulating even now, and Hollis was only playing out line in continuing to listen, by which he'd later be snared?

"A lot of the locals know about it now, Hollis," Brendan said. "A lot of folks you'd know, walking around with earplugs or headsets. The general population wasn't so lucky. They're all having fun now, but I think it'll turn. What do you think, Hollis? Will things in town stay the same? Or will they get worse? My guys, they say the carrier signal is building. Growing. Or, to use their term: learning. I don't know what that means, but I don't really want to unplug my ears and find out."

Hollis pressed the mute button. To Mia, he said, "He doesn't know it all. He probably doesn't even know it's music."

And Mia said, "See if you can find out why he wants the datacenter."

Unmute.

"Why do you want the Astral center, Brendan? Maybe you're just pissing them off. Let it go. It can't help you now. What are you going to use it to predict: the outcome of a stock market that no longer exists?"

"Oh, hey, listen. That's a shortsighted game. There was a day, sure, that I wanted to see if I could hit their mothership. Maybe it'd have worked, and maybe it wouldn't have. But the writing is on the wall now, Hollis. Governor Garrett has all but disappeared — into a bunker, maybe; who knows. I haven't heard anything encouraging on any of the open networks. Do you know what that means, my friend? It means that the planet has spoken. Our authorities have given up. And in the end of days, the meek won't inherit shit. The new world belongs to the wolves."

"You want to join them," Hollis said.

"I want to see what a good collaboration is worth. And yeah, that means exploring all options. See what use they might have for an enterprising young Earthling like myself. Like *yourself*, if you want, Hollis. It's not a total shot in the dark. I got word just yesterday about a guy up north, named Nathan Andreus. They say he made a deal with the aliens, but deals like that, if they're real, have gotta be going fast. I know you; you know when to call done done, and you know a smart bet when you see it. The intelligent man, at this point, sees the writing on the wall. If you can't beat 'em, join 'em — and trust me, you're not gonna beat 'em. So if you're seriously planning to do something stupid, I strongly encourage you to reconsider. You won't get through their defenses. Trust me; we have good reason to know that's true. And if you try? Well, that might just be a really good chance for me and those in my camp to show our hosts just how dedicated to the cause we are."

"You'd attack me," Hollis said, "to help them."

"The question isn't where the chips will fall, Hollis. The question is where you'll choose to stand when they do."

"You're the coward," Hollis told him.

Brendan laughed.

"I've got my plan," Hollis said.

It wasn't true, and what he had would be severely handicapped by the fact that Brendan was now watching his vaults. There was no way to get the artillery he'd been hoping for, now. He should have taken it when he'd had the chance. He should have figured out how to hook the gun batteries to the Jeep Brendan already had at the bottom of the bunker's ramp, or how to drive and fly the self-contained equipment. He should have taken the time, then, because there wouldn't be another chance. If he meant to fight his way into the datacenter now, he'd have to do it with his fists.

"Well. I'll just say, 'last chance'. I'll give you my word that if you want to lay down the crap you've got in mind and join us, I'll give you a free pass. Bygones can be bygones, and I'll even protect you from some other people in town I happen to know want your head. Things have changed, and guys like us have to stick together. You have my word on all of it, Hollis." He paused, then added, "You too, Mia."

Hollis considered. Brendan sounded sincere. He even believed him — the offer of forgiveness, at least.

It might be nice. There was a lot of truth in what Brendan said, about the chips already falling where they meant to. It was the best offer he was going to get, and with far better odds. The aliens might not want collaborators, but maybe the Andreus guy Brendan had mentioned was real. Maybe his deal was real. And if it was, was Hollis stupid to keep fighting a futile battle?

"No thanks," said Mia.

Brendan almost made a little noise to recognize Mia's appearance, but instead just said, "And you, Hollis? Recent events excluded, we always got along well, didn't we? I always respected your ability to face facts head-on. We're the same, you and me."

It was a damn good deal. Better than any he was currently making for himself.

Mia, watching him, waited. She didn't like how long he

was taking to respond. She didn't like the thought he was giving Brendan's offer, free of judgment.

"They started this," Hollis said. "And we're going to finish it."

Brendan, sounding just a little bit disappointed but mostly just amused, said, "Yeah, you certainly are."

"I mean it."

"I know you do. And that's sad. Because you won't just be fighting them, Hollis. You'll be fighting us, too. You've got no allies, no weapons, and no chance at all. But I wish you luck. Honestly? I hope I'm wrong. I hope you somehow do what you mean to do, even if you kill us all. I'm serious. But I'm also not willing to bet everything on a dream."

"Goodbye, Brendan," Hollis said, reaching for the headset.

Brendan seemed somehow to nod in acknowledgement, even over audio. Then he said, "May the best man win."

He cleared his throat, then added a suffix:

"And woman, as it were."

23

———

MIA WISHED she hadn't heard. The picture Brendan painted was too bleak. Worse, she thought it might be true. She couldn't remember where or why or how, but she'd heard the name Andreus before. People talked about him like they probably once talked about Genghis Khan. To the ambitious go the spoils, same as always.

But she had heard. And she'd made her choice.

And she and Hollis, headsets driven far off-site for discard in case they contained tracking chips, had to face the fact that they had no support. No arms — certainly none big enough to punch a hole in the datacenter's defenses. He'd grabbed a single brick of C4 and a detonator he hoped (but was not sure) would be sufficient to blow it up, and that was it. Just having the thing in his backpack made him uneasy. Could they go off without the detonators? That's how little he knew, and he was almost literally going up against the world.

"Maybe you were right," Mia said. "Maybe we should just cut our losses and get out of town."

But Hollis got a curious look on his face and said,

"Maybe. But maybe we should do something stupid anyway."

She knew the look; it meant there was something beneath his surface, churning, waiting to find fruition. And so they recon'd all day, accomplishing nothing new, and through it all Mia waited to see what Hollis had up his sleeve. He *always* had something up his sleeve. Sometimes it was good and sometimes it was bad, but it was always there. Hollis seemed to fly by the seat of his pants, but you couldn't fly so reliably without a key to the back door. There was another way, in every situation. Maybe this was no exception.

But Hollis only stewed. Eventually she saw his mood for what it was: consternation, because as bad as he wanted a solution to come, it refused. There *was* no secret way. There *was* no back door. And that made the idea of "stupid" so far beyond stupid. Mia thought herself noble when it counted, but she also knew when to hold 'em, when to fold 'em, and when to run.

Then, while they were in the back of a Tacodeli harvesting what hadn't spoiled, Hollis sat at a table and sipped a glass of water and said out of the blue, "I know what to do."

"What?"

"We take out power."

"What power?"

"Power to the datacenter. We pull the plug."

"It can't be that simple, Hollis." She deflated. And to think: for a half-second, she'd been sure he had the answer after all.

"Sure it can. Think about it. All we need is to make them blink. You remember what Theo said, about how much data they're processing on the fly? The way he talked about it, the aliens don't even really know what they're getting. They don't understand our networks, for what those networks are still worth. They don't understand our distributed way of thinking — offloading so much of our interaction and thinking to what used to be the cloud. They don't even understand *us*, at all. You told me that yourself. When you were face-to-face with that reptar, I could feel its emotions, such that it had them. I know you felt them a lot stronger. You know as well as I do that it didn't want to rampage, so much as it wanted to *understand* what a rampage felt like."

Mia considered. It was true. How it related to his idea to "pull the plug," on the other hand, was yet to be seen.

"Theo made it sound like a delicate balance. Something they'd cobbled together. From where we're standing, it works ... but don't you think their goal is a little more lofty than 'to ruin people's minds'? We know it's *really good* at turning people into zombies, both in the Fortress of Refuse and musical versions. But what if it's only 'meh' at sucking what it wants out of us, and teaching what they want to know?"

Mia thought she saw where he might be going, but the connections he was making were tenuous at best.

"You think that somehow disrupting power will make their delicate system fall over? They're intelligent beings who've mastered interstellar travel, Hollis. Don't you think they built a mousetrap sturdy enough to withstand one guy with a single brick of explosive?"

Hollis was insistent. He shook his head, tapping a stainless steel table near a bowl of avocados that had seen better days.

"It doesn't matter. We're not trying to blow up the facility. That's what they're defending against, because it's not worth it to defend against everything. Destroying the building would be catastrophic, so they're watching it hard. But not just them; sounds like Brendan and whoever's with him are planning to do the same, just so they can lick some boot. But you saw the building. It's lit up like a Christmas tree, along with every block around it. They're keeping the lights on there because they need the lights on, and they know that if the power is ever interrupted, they can just re-route it. It's no big deal for them to fix the smaller things, but that's *exactly* why we should go after something like that. Because when I say, 'Cut the power,' it doesn't matter if the power stays cut. We just have to turn it off for a few seconds. We do that, their attention has to go to the problem, to fix it. When that happens, all that shit they're sucking out of people's minds will back up. It's already overwhelming them."

"This is a terrible idea," Mia said.

"Why?"

"Because you don't know what you're talking about! You don't know that a power outage will stop them at all — and if it does, you can't know that they'll care about the few minutes it takes to turn it back on. And in the meantime, it blows our cover. All those ships will come to find us."

"So we'll hide. We've done it before."

"*Hollis,*" she said, exasperated, dragging his name out as if saying it and doing nothing else would show him the stupidity of his ways. "*Even if* you're right. *Even if* it distracts them and causes some confusion. What then? If you had a squadron of fighters standing by, ready to swoop in and bomb the site once you'd caused a distraction, then fine. But you don't. You'll distract them, they'll fix the problem and maybe lose a bit of time and get a little confused, but then it's not like you're going to rush in there and end it all. You can't. Even with Brendan's arsenal, just the two of us couldn't have done that. And that's assuming they haven't somehow reinforced it with a shield or something, which they probably have, or rewired it all with alien technology that you can't just *'blow up,'* which they also probably have. So tell me. Tell me how this is a good idea."

Hollis shook his head.

"This is bullshit," he said.

"Bullshit or not, it's the truth."

But he was agitated. Tapping his fingers and tapping his feet, eyes wide, looking like a killer looking for something to do.

"We do it anyway," he said, "and take our chances."

"And die trying!"

"Come on, Mia. You're not this cowardly."

That did it. She wanted to scream at him, but instead she stared him down, eye to eye.

"Listen to me," she said. "Just put your goddamn ego aside and listen to me for half a second. Like Brendan said, it is what it is. The die is cast. The truth stands right where it stands, no matter what we do. They've got a stronghold, and that stronghold is sucking people's heads dry one by one. We aren't going to get in, no matter what you tell yourself! *Nobody's* going to get in. Real life isn't like the movies, Hollis. The good guys don't always win and you can't defeat a superior race just by flying your ship up into its primary weapon. I didn't like what Brendan said any more than you did, but all it really does is to put a cap on the whole thing, as far as I'm concerned. Before, I didn't see a way we were going to do what we both thought once upon a time that we could do. But now, after hearing what Brendan and the others are up to? What makes you think we're so smart? Why can the two of us succeed where nobody else can? Us against the world, is that right? Well I think we're pretty damn cool ... but if it's us against the world, I don't like the odds."

Hollis's face was ugly. Mia knew the look: He was hearing something he believed but didn't want to believe. It was a repugnant truth — one Hollis hoped to make untrue just by force of will. *I'll beat my head against it until it goes my way*; that's what he was thinking right now.

The right choice was to walk away. After all they'd gone through, Mia hated to admit it ... but they had to walk away.

"Sleep on it," Mia told him, "and you'll see I'm right."

Hollis stared into space for a long moment. Then he stood up and, in one fluid motion, raked a tall stack of serving trays across the room. Then he hit a refrigerator, kicked the base of the sink, and stormed into the office, where a chair and an ancient computer awaited.

Apparently they were staying here tonight, and furiously so.

"Stupid, stupid man," she said.

But noble, she thought. And even given how things were turning out, that had to count for something.

24

———

Hollis's eyes opened. It was still dark out. He had no idea what time it was. His watch was all the way across the room and he didn't feel like getting up to grab it.

He sat up. It wasn't his first time waking. Sleep, tonight, had been elusive.

He crossed the room, for once able to use illumination from outside to walk without tripping rather than feeling his way. Usually, things weren't so easy. Every night lately, they slept somewhere new. He was tired of motels. This time, they'd picked one within the power-up radius around the Astral datacenter, but they weren't the only ones with the idea and that created some trade-offs: the convenience of electricity versus their usual lull of solitude. This hotel, unlike most of the others, was as full as such places had been before the arrival. The people above must have kids because until 1am there'd been little running feet that the parents were too lazy to make stop. There was a guy in the next room with a cough so bad, it sounded like the plague was trying to make a comeback.

Hollis supposed he shouldn't complain. It hadn't been a

bad apocalypse so far, by apocalypse standards. They'd had plenty of problems with the city's criminal element, but criminals weren't pleasant during the best of times. They'd run afoul of a few aliens, a few citywide battles, many guns, and yeah, there'd been some brain-dead zombies. But you got that during rush hour around here anyway, so what was the harm?

Anonymous people, shockingly, weren't the problem. He remembered talking to Torchy Banner, and how the weirdo/psychic had predicted people getting worse. Maybe that would happen, but it hadn't happened yet. Much to the consternation of Hollis's old friend Dave, who was probably in a homemade bunker by now.

So the hotel wasn't all Mad Max. There weren't armed gangs going from room to room, offering rapey room service. The children, so far as Hollis had seen, hadn't yet gone feral. There weren't herds of orphans building their own cities, sacrificing adults to their new gods.

It was annoying, though. Hollis wasn't sure which option would be worse.

He went to the bathroom again. Looked in the mirror again. Studied his reflection again. He'd done a lot of reflection-studying. Maybe it had some sort of deep psychological meaning: Hollis confronting himself in some sort of internal battle, or some other happy bullshit. Normally, he thought such notions were stupid. What bothered him now was that they seemed to have traction. He'd noticed the change in his own eyes. He'd noticed his age, too. Had the wrinkles been there before? He still felt 25, and yet the guy staring back at him was clearly his real age: 36, and while nowhere near over the hill, also no spring chicken, either. A lot of guys had kids by this age. If he had kids, that'd be awesome. He could rent motel rooms above people who were trying to sleep and have them run back and forth. And also teach them to say funny things, like "Chicks dig scars."

He'd left the door open. Mia wouldn't mind the bathroom light. She was sleeping so hard, it sounded like there was a lumberjack under the sheets. She was sprawled in the least ladylike way she possibly could be, mouth open, beavers running chainsaws deep in her throat.

She was smart and she was clever and she was pretty, and that made her fun (he reluctantly admitted) to be around. But she wasn't right about this.

He had the backpack in his hand. Because he'd picked it up on the way in, even though he only sort of remembered doing so. More specifically, he had the detonators for the C4 in his hand. They were in a little box with instructions on the outside. Pushbutton army. Only an idiot wouldn't understand how to use them, now that he'd looked. Which he had. The last time he'd awoken, then never truly gotten back to sleep.

Or, he clarified, Mia might well *be* right about this. But being right didn't make her *right*. Technically, maybe it was stupid. But that didn't mean Hollis shouldn't do it anyway. Because even after all he'd thought and said about the virtues of cutting and running — of saving himself when things went bad — he didn't think he really believed it anymore. And *that*, ironically, he had to blame on Mia as well. She'd argued with him long enough and often enough that it was like his Lone Wolf muscle had broken. He wasn't capable of being quite as selfish. Some sort of pride — perhaps a kind of responsibility? — had grown where his Fuck-You used to be. Like a tumor.

Now she wanted them to cut and run. *Now*, really? Just a week ago, he would have jumped up and down to agree with her. He would have led the goddamn charge, middle fingers flying to the rear to greet all those who had something to say about it. Even a few days back, he'd been arguing for Vail first, with nothing in between. Now he still wanted to go to Vail (Austin was too hot — not in temperature, but in terms of those who wanted him dead), but only after settling this business. This grudge. This crew of dickheads — not just the aliens now, but Brendan and his turncoats as well — thought they could take over his city?

Not bloody fucking likely.

He looked again at Mia. Sleeping like a dude. She was still wearing her earplugs, impervious to stimuli.

"I'll be back," he said. And, because he didn't want to Theo-and-Carol her, he left a note.

But if all went well, she'd never see the note. She'd sleep through the explosion, and he'd be back before the dust settled.

This probably wouldn't work.

But really ... even if it failed, what was the harm in trying?

25

REBECCA ALICE LEGATTO, who'd been a semi-pro tennis player before the arrival had forced her to reconsider her sweet-girl appearance and doormat reputation, sat up in the truck trailer that Brendan Banks had provided to act as tech HQ. Brendan's stash of goods and weapons — even after the aliens had reduced his above-ground estate to dust — had made him kingpin, but Rebecca only planned to honor his rule as far as she had to. She and Vika of the Flesh Eaters (who used to be Joan Wylie, a cosmetologist) had talked about this. The men liked to swing their dicks, but deep down they seldom knew what to do. It was all bluster. And her new persona of Becky Bones, for one, didn't plan to go along with bullshit once it stopped serving her.

It was serving her now, though. Somehow, the aliens had turned on power around the building everyone seemed so interested in, plus a handful of blocks radiating out in all directions — and that, at least, had given power to the little mobile command she was sitting in right now. Night duty, but that was okay. She was nocturnal anyway. What's more, the electricity that powered Brendan's cameras and surveillance monitors also powered a Nintendo console that was a few generations old but still a lot better than twiddling thumbs. Most importantly, it powered a coffeemaker. There were worse ways to spend a night.

Except that nothing was supposed to happen. She was just supposed to sit here drinking coffee, playing Mario Kart 10, and keeping a sorta-eye on the monitors. The monitors showed the grounds of the Astral building, but those grounds were behind a few layers of fence. Nobody was going to get in. Nobody was going to cross those monitors. This was all a show; Becky understood that. Brendan and the other men (misogynistic lot that they were) wanted mainly to show the aliens whose side they were on. She'd laughed at that, but the longer they manned this post, the more she started to believe that the aliens actually understood. Just tonight, she'd entertained three alien patrol parties: two composed only of the big white ones, bulging with muscle and making her wonder secretly if they had penises that were as impressive, and one of the insect things.

That time, she'd been sure the bug patrol would cut her apart and eat her. She'd heard stories of how they killed from those who'd seen it: Thomas Davies and Raymond Fiest (who she refused on principle to call "Beef") among them. But they'd done no such thing. She'd almost have sworn they nodded at her, as if to say, *You're doing a bang-up job, Becky, and don't think your bosses on the mothership haven't noticed! You're a valued member of the team and we look forward to promoting you to middle management.*

Hey. Someone was going to curry favor with the new overlords. It might as well be them.

But then there was movement on the monitor. Someone who'd gotten through the fence, crossing the lawn alone. Stupid asshole wasn't even moving quickly. He was in a section where the spotlights were off, where only infrared showed him to be nowhere near as covert as he hoped to be.

She took out one of her earplugs and picked up the walkie.

"Carl."

It took a moment. He was probably masturbating.

"Yeah."

"It's Becky Bones."

"I know who it is."

"There's someone on the lawn." Then the someone stopped, and she moved the digital zoom in on his face, and although she'd expected just to give a general description ("Caucasian male, 30s, average height and weight"), she saw enough to bark laughter instead.

"What?" Carl asked.

"Jesus. I think it's Hollis Palmer."

"You're joking."

But she wasn't joking. She'd been pissed when a pair of assholes had stolen the car she'd bartered for fair and square, but after complaining to Vika back at Graffiti Park that night, she'd let it go. Only after Brendan had started recruiting and handing out protective earplugs had she taken new a new look at who he, too, had at the top of his Most Wanted list. And there'd been the same asshole, now with double the grudge.

"It's him. Tell me I can be the one to go get him."

"No, Becky. Don't leave your post."

"Who, then?"

"I don't know."

Carl didn't know a lot. He only knew his dick because it was usually in his hand.

"Wake up Foster."

"Foster rotated out."

"You, then."

"I'm busy," Carl said. And she imagined: *fap fap fap.*

"You're not helping, Carl. What good is watching the grounds if we're not going to go after someone if we see them?"

"Hang on."

There was a wait. She heard him talking to someone, then caught the word "Sonny." Then she wished she could hear their exchange, because Sonny had even less tolerance for Carl than Becky did. Sonny, if he wasn't half the city away laying demolition cones with Macy and Ahmed, would probably insist on going out himself. He'd come to town seeking Hollis, too — plus a former crony who'd left him to join Hollis's camp. A guy who, when Becky had heard his name and description, had reminded her for some reason of the movie *Die Hard.*

Carl's voice came back on the walkie. And now it sounded uneasy, as if someone had threatened to reach up his butt, grab his intestine, and turn him inside out. He'd be like an animal with a tail, digesting his food right out in the open.

"Becky? Go after him."

"After Hollis, you mean."

"But Carl," Becky said, playing dumb, "I thought you told me not to leave my post. I wouldn't want to violate an order. I'm trying to be a good little girl."

"Do it, Becky."

"Is *that* an order?"

"An order from Sonny."

"Sonny's not in charge. I'm not sure I should comply."

But now she was just fucking with Carl. Truth was, she'd been considering going on her own, no matter what Carl thought, the minute she'd seen their perp's face. There weren't a lot of rules these days, and she doubted she'd lose favor by beating Hollis Palmer until he peed red. The crew, it seemed, had been united by two things. First, they'd come together under Brendan's imperative to assist the alien invaders, indebted to him for handing out earplugs and keeping them all sane. But second, a surprising number of those in the crew had a problem with the guy on her screen right now. He certainly got around.

"Becky," Carl said, "please."

"Okay, Carl," she said. "But just for you."

She cut the transmission without waiting for a reply.

Then she put her earplug back in, grabbed the largest weapon she could find, and headed for the trailer's door.

26

HOLLIS STAYED LOW. Out of sight. There was no light on this section of lawn, and the fence, so far as he could tell, had no alarm on it. His bolt cutters (Wal-Mart again, formerly $18.72 but on sale for free) had made quick work of the chain link. There was true security further in, he saw. But as predicted, the power junction wasn't something anyone was thinking about.

Still, approaching the junction box, Hollis paused. He took in the lines of spheres around the building, packed close like pearls on a necklace. From here he could see patrols circling the spheres: some of the white things he'd heard called titans, lots of the bug types he'd gotten too close to inside Brendan's auxiliary barn. From a distance, it was obvious that they moved as a swarm. When one turned, the others turned. When they did separate and peel into two different directions (like Buckingham guard, doing their paces), they did so without apparent discussion. It happened at arbitrary moments, as if to keep potential burglars off-guard — but whenever it did happen, it worked like two arms of the same being, needless of coordination.

He didn't bother to open the junction box. The lock wasn't exposed, so his bolt cutters were worthless, but that didn't matter. He didn't have the knowledge to rewire the building's circuits in clever ways — perhaps crossing camera feeds to make his own passage invisible. No, what Hollis had in mind was a lot simpler than that. He wasn't going to finger this situation; he was going to double-fist it. He didn't need to be a rocket scientist to know that destroying what he was destroying would have *some* effect, even if it wasn't a long-lasting one.

Even if it works and the power goes out, he heard Mia ask in his head, *what do you plan to do after?*

He hadn't wanted to give her an answer when she'd asked it for real, but he definitely had one: *Nothing. He planned to do nothing.* In all likelihood, this errand would end up doing no good, making no difference. But he had a goddamn brick of C4, and that meant he goddamn well had to use it. This was about a statement, and it was about Hollis being able to look himself in the mirror the next time he had a sleepless night, as seemed to be a growing habit. One man can't make a difference. Not in the new world. But that didn't mean a man had to sit on his hands. It didn't mean he couldn't be obnoxious in whatever way he could, if for no other reason than to raise a middle finger and say — for just this one moment — that not all who lived in Austin planned to bend over and take it.

He scanned the directions on the detonators again, just to be sure. Then he stuck them into the C4, hooked up the timer with similarly straightforward instructions, and set the thing for five minutes. Plenty of time to get back through the fence and maybe even all the way back to the hotel, where he'd be close enough to hear it go off, then watch them scramble.

He pressed start, turned, and was perhaps twenty feet away when a woman's voice said, "Freeze."

Hollis's blood did exactly that.

"Hands up."

Hollis raised his hands, slowly. He wished he'd been holding a gun. Whatever was about to happen, he imagined, couldn't be pleasant. It didn't take a genius to make certain conclusions, and the first among them was that if any humans had been watching the place, they'd be Brendan's buddies. He'd soon be in front of Brendan again, and this time would be his third strike. He wouldn't escape again. He supposed, given his silver tongue, that he might be able to lie his way into the man's good graces — that if he played slippery enough, he could do to Brendan what he'd once done to Thomas Davies.

Yeah, sure, Brendan, that's why I came: to join your cause, just like you offered. Isn't rebellion for chumps? Not everyone is smart enough to hook their wagon to the winning side like us.

But the very idea raised bile in his throat. He'd lost his stomach for guys like Brendan. For that element in general. And that meant that if he wouldn't try to join them, he'd have to accept whatever they planned to mete out. Maybe they had more Dr. Greenswards in their midst to torture him for fun, or maybe they'd just keep things simple and shoot him. Either way, this was the end. If he'd had a gun, at least he could get the gal behind to shoot him now. End it fast, so it wouldn't have to drag.

"Nice and easy," the woman said. Her voice was muffled through his earplugs, but he could hear her just fine. "On your knees. Cross your legs at the ankle. Hand behind your head."

"I thought I was supposed to go right foot green?"

"Just do it."

"But you didn't say Simon says!"

She hit him with the butt of a rifle. It was sad, how easily Hollis could identify unseen objects that struck him lately.

"Let's try that again," she said, still behind him. He could hear the gun settling back into her hands, its plastic parts creaking minutely.

"Now I'm all lightheaded."

"Then concentrate."

Hollis did, but when he assumed the posture he wanted, he did it facing her. His days of being commanded from the rear were over. If she wanted to kill him for turning around, she could go for it.

It was a woman in a crop top with very short hair, dyed pink. And, most relevantly, pointing an automatic rifle at his chest.

"I know you," he said.

"Good for you."

"You're Bobbie Bones."

"*Becky* Bones."

"Is that a nickname, or was your granddaddy the Crypt Keeper?"

"You're hilarious."

"Thanks. I'm here all week."

She tossed him a pair of handcuffs. They were the same kind he'd used on Mia, probably because they'd both come from Brendan's stash.

"Put those on," she said.

"Okay, but next time I get to be the dom." He reached for the cuffs, picked them up. His eye spied the C4, which he'd planted on the far side of the box, opposite side from Becky Bones. Had she seen him plant it? He tried to guess the time on its face, but getting held at gunpoint always changed his perception of time. Slower or faster? Hollis could never remember.

"I know who you are, too," she said.

"Maybe you do and maybe you don't. I do really good impressions."

"You're Hollis Palmer. You stole my ride."

"To be fair," Hollis said, "it used to be my ride, and some asshole with a pink buzz cut stole it from me."

"I didn't steal your fucking car," Becky said. "I traded for it."

"With the person who stole my fucking car," Hollis added.

"Not my problem."

"No. Your problem is that haircut."

He thought she might hit him again, but she just smirked. He still hadn't put on the cuffs, but he was also still on his knees with his legs crossed behind him. Even if he moved fast, he was pretty sure her bullets were faster.

She ticked her head toward the building. Hollis looked again, seeing all those ships — in the ground, but also floating above — and a swarm of reptars moving past like pointy gazelles.

"We've got an understanding with them, you know," Becky said. "With the aliens."

"Yeah, Brendan told me how y'all sold out. Good on you."

"You're not terribly valuable to us. Really, holding you would just be a burden. So what I'm thinking is, maybe after you cuff your wrists, I hold you down and cuff your ankles, too."

"Kinky."

"And then I march your ass past the inner fence and

drop you right in the middle of all those bugs. See how funny you are then."

"That sounds like a plan. You're quite the go-getter, Billie Boner."

"Put on the cuffs," she said.

Hollis looked at the cuffs. He thought of all possible futures and of the timer ticking around the corner, now probably down to three minutes or less. This was your classic no-win situation. He was seriously considering going out with a bang, no pun intended.

"What if I don't want to?"

"Then I shoot you."

"You just told me you're going to feed me to the aliens if I *do* put the cuffs on. What's my motivation here, Bunny? Help me understand."

She was trying to stay cool, but her face kept wanting to twist. Few could irritate like Hollis Palmer. It was his super-power. It'd be written on his tombstone if he had one, which he sort of thought right now that he wouldn't.

"Maybe just shooting you now really is easier," she said. Then he saw her look at the weapon, sure that she was looking for the machine-gun equivalent of cocking it for intimidation. But Hollis didn't think he could be intimidated. Not anymore. He just had a few minutes left to filibuster, and then he'd be dead. All things considered, Hollis found himself surprisingly okay with it. He'd still get to make his statement, he wouldn't have to live out the rest of the End of Days, and the world would be rid of one more bad hairstyle. There was literally no downside.

"Oh, come on," Hollis said. "Don't you want to tell me your evil plan?"

"Put on the cuffs. Last warning."

Hollis searched for things to say, or ideally topics to discuss. How much more could really be left on that bomb? If it killed them both, cool. But if she shot him and dragged him off and only *then* did it explode? Well, that wouldn't do at all.

"Tell you what," Hollis said, holding the cuffs in front of him on straight arms, his fingers through both of the wrist circles. "'stead of cuffing up, how 'bout you and me play Cat's Cradle? Hard with cuffs, though. You got any yarn?"

She shook her head, rolled her eyes, and raised the weapon. Then her head slammed sideways as if of its own accord and she went down in a jumble of limbs. It took Hollis a half second to figure out that someone had hit her with something, coming unseen from the dark.

Someone with dark skin and black-frame Henry Kissinger glasses. Wearing a button-down shirt, tucked into his pants, and holding a baseball bat.

"Theo?"

Theo was looking at Becky Bones. "Did I kill her?"

"How the hell did you get here?"

"Do you think I killed her? Shit. I've never killed anyone before."

Hollis broke the stalemate first. As much as he'd wanted to filibuster when Becky had been in charge, he sure didn't want to do it now. He sprung up, grabbed Theo by the arm, and pulled him sufficient that he dropped the bat.

They rushed toward the hole Hollis had cut in the fence. Wouldn't be long now, and the aliens would see what minor inconvenience one man with a pop rocket could make. They'd be slowed down somewhat in their takeover of the planet, and wouldn't that show *them*?

"How did you find me?" Hollis asked as they ran — Hollis more fluidly than the geek on his arm.

"I saw you, and I saw her follow you. We tapped into

their cameras." He peered into the darkness. "We have to go. Someone may have taken over for her. They might be watching us right now."

Hollis looked around. Cameras? Now he felt stupid. "*We*?"

"Carol's with me."

"Why are you ... ? How are you ... ?" But he dropped both potential questions. There'd be time for that later. "Never mind."

Hollis pulled Theo faster, counting in his mind. Theo was still looking back at the slumped form of the woman he'd felled with the bat.

"I wish I knew if I killed her."

"It'll be moot soon," Hollis told her. "Come on. We have to haul ass before she ends up dead for sure."

Theo stopped. The sudden cessation of momentum caused Hollis to stumble. They were at the fence, but all at once Theo looked reluctant to go through.

"What do you mean?" he asked.

"I mean that in a minute at most, she's gonna be paste and you can stop wondering about her welfare."

"What? Why?"

"Because I planted a bunch of plastic explosive on that junction box. Come on!"

He pulled, but Theo now looked like Hollis had slapped his mother.

"You *what*?"

"You heard me, Poindexter. I'm glad to see you, but I'll still leave your ass."

Theo was looking at the junction box, now shrouded in darkness.

Then he took off running toward it.

Hollis, without thinking, followed. About halfway there

his senses kicked in and his mind showed him a brilliant fantasy in which his head was blown from his torso and continued to live a while, but he ran on anyway. If it blew now, he might just be maimed. In a curious way, it was better to be closer. Finish the job, so he didn't have to live as a thing in a bucket.

"Theo! Goddammit!"

But Theo didn't stop. Theo was Jesse Owens. He was Usain Bolt. Hollis couldn't catch him even if he had the last pound of fatty brisket that Smitty's ever made.

He made the junction box, almost face-planting into it. By the time Hollis got within ten feet, Theo was around the side, finding the C4, poking madly at it and breathing heavy.

Then all at once, he stopped. He exhaled, pulled the brick from the box's side, and handed it to Hollis. The timer said 0:07, just like in *Goldfinger*.

"There's something I need to tell you," Theo said between heaving breaths, "about what they're doing here."

27

MIA AWOKE TO A CALL OF, *"Honey, I'm home!"*

She roused, rolling over with every expectation of throwing the cheap hotel alarm clock at Hollis's face. The sky outside was still black and they had precisely no plans for the morning. She'd been beat — even more so after their argument, Hollis's pouting, and the silent trip here from the Tacodeli — and wanted more than anything to sleep in.

But instead of seeing just Hollis coming through the door, she saw Carol. And right behind her, Theo.

That changed her mood in a blink. She hadn't realized until that moment just how sad and hopeless she'd been feeling. It'd happened slowly: a gradual downward spiral of outlook and emotion. They'd been sliding since San Antonio: the Fortress burning, the zombies, the city-to-city drives with no brightness in sight, and the malaise they could only forestall with earplugs and nose-cancelling headphones — which, she'd noticed, only dulled her way of thinking about the world. Before San Antonio, at least they'd felt like they had a mission, and that if they pulled it off, tomorrow could be brighter than today. She and Hollis had lost that during their time alone, and their lost friends' return felt like a second wind.

Ebullient, she sprung from bed. She took Carol around the chest hard enough to break ribs. Then she hugged Theo, too, all three of them smiling like fools.

Hollis, who'd greeted them already, leaned against the corner. With a familiar smirk back on his face, he was sublimely cool in that moment. He waited for them to reunite, holding a baseball bat she hadn't seen before.

"Good news and bad news," Hollis said when they were finished. "The good news is that I found these two assholes."

"We actually found him," Theo told her.

"But the bad news is that I did something you wouldn't like."

"Tried to, anyway," Theo added, "but I stopped him."

Hollis gave Theo a look, either for stealing the spotlight or stealing the story. But then he got over himself and together they all caught her up on the night's events: Hollis's explosive errand and an implied willingness to die doing it (something that both angered and scared Mia), the arrival of Becky Bones (who, it turned out, wasn't dead, much to Theo's relief), and the way Theo had saved the day twice — once by dispatching Becky, then a second time by stopping the explosive. The *why* there was fuzzy, but Mia was sure there'd be plenty of discussion to follow.

When they were done speaking, Mia asked her most burning question: "Where did you guys go, back in San Antonio?"

Carol answered. "We were working on the new information Hollis's photos gave us. Remember, we'd only had it for a day or two then. My computer died in Austin, but we'd charged it on the drive. I assume we got to the dry cleaner while you guys were at the Fortress the first time, and the first thing I did was to find the phone where you'd left it for us, cable it to my laptop, and drag all the photos onto my hard drive so I could blow them up and look at them more closely."

"I remember seeing you looking through them between our trips to the Fortress," Mia said.

"Right. Because we'd seen a little before, when Hollis gave us that first bit of access while we'd been at the Spider House Ballroom, and we saw more when you first retrieved the phone. But seeing them on my laptop was our first chance to *really* look at them. And what we saw ... well, it surprised us."

"How so?"

"For one, there was no internet access in San Antonio. They had spotty cell service, but no internet. I had my phone, though — kept it charged to use as a camera. So I turned on the hotspot to see what happened. I tried to go to the old IP address, expecting nothing. But somehow, it connected."

"You said there was no internet."

"There wasn't," she said.

"They think the aliens did something to it," Hollis said from the corner, where he'd pulled up a chair, "so that they could get at the database, too."

Carol nodded, then returned her attention to Mia.

"Once we were in, we were both totally confused. The database was ... different than when we'd seen it last."

"Meaning it wasn't really a database anymore," Theo put in, eyes ticking toward the window, where the brightly lit Astral building — home to that strange database — was so heavily protected.

"It's more like ..." Her face became frustrated and she made looping hand gestures, unsure how to explain. "...

well, like no database I've ever seen. It was kind of like a program that *used* what was in the database, but not really."

"It doesn't matter," Mia said. "All the details are making my brain hurt anyway."

Carol, catching her drift, moved past the technobabble she'd been heading toward and skipped to the relevant part instead. "Point is, between our understanding of the original documents from the case and the new stuff we saw once we'd logged in, we began to see patterns."

"Without getting too technical," Theo said, nodding at Mia's cry of mercy, "we started to believe that whatever the aliens are doing with the datacenter and the Fortress of Refuse—"

"And then with music," Carol added.

"—it's not the only data source they have. They're looking for another cache of information, but haven't yet found it."

"What kind of cache?"

"We still don't know. Maybe something off-planet. But the way they seem to be searching, I have to think it's something already here on Earth, or they'd know where it was. So maybe it's something they buried. You've heard theories that aliens have visited us before? Like in the time of the pyramids?"

"Sure. Theories from crazy people."

"Maybe not so crazy," Theo said, "but that's a topic for another day."

Carol went on. "The second data source, if there is one, doesn't really matter. What matters is that the more we look at what they're doing with the datacenter, the more we think it's redundant. Strictly speaking, I doubt they need the information they're scooping out of people's heads. It's messy, for one. They *know* it's messy, too; there are things in the flow that make us think they don't like what it's doing to the humans."

"You mean they may not be happy that their meddling is turning people brain-dead," Hollis said.

Carol shrugged. "It's not a matter of 'happy.' I don't think they get happy, or sad, or mad. They're more analytical than that. It's probably more accurate to say they find it *inefficient.*"

"We have theories about why that is and what it means now," Theo said, "but when we were looking at it for the first time in San Antonio, we didn't have any ideas at all. It was strange, and alarming. Especially when we started to see that, if the Fortress of Refuse stopped working for any reason — say, if someone burned it down — they had other ways to 'scoop out' the same memories and emotions."

"Like with music," Carol said.

Theo nodded. "And if they *could* use music — not that we knew it'd be music, specifically, at the time — that meant it was something that spread through the air."

"Like a virus," Hollis said.

"Not exactly, but the same idea," Theo said. "So we went out with both of our phones, trying to triangulate a signal from opposite ends of the block. You can't triangulate very well with just two points, though, so we left Ricky's phone — your phone, Hollis — inside the dry cleaner and headed out a little farther. It was just supposed to be a quick thing. That's why we didn't leave a note for you — because we hadn't planned on leaving, and didn't think we'd be gone long."

"But you got sidetracked," Mia said.

"We ran into a caravan of aliens. They were on foot, holding devices of their own. What we think is, while we were trying to triangulate their signal, they turned right around and triangulated ours. They found me first. Even hiding, they walked right up to me as if they knew all along. I was terrified. I assumed they'd kill me. But they just put me in a sort of litter, which they carried, then went up the road and found Carol the same way."

"What about the third signal? From the phone you left in the dry cleaner?"

"Well, that's something we haven't figured out," Carol said. "There's no way they didn't detect it, but the phone was still there for you when you got back so they didn't take it. We do think they watched *you*, though, but didn't pick you up like they picked us up."

Mia swallowed. She had no way of knowing why the aliens might watch them but not abduct them, but an instinctual part of her couldn't help but pair it with her memory of the reptar — the way she'd seen into its head, and it into hers.

"Anyway," Theo said, "eventually they just let us go. But here's what's weird." He touched his ear, turning his head. "The first pair of earplugs each of us had? The aliens gave them to us."

"What? *Why?*"

"It sounds kind of funny," Carol said, "but our working theory is that they want our help to figure something out."

"They don't understand us, remember," Theo said. "They're curious. I've seen the way they approach our technology; it's like someone from an advanced civilization not quite getting our computers, so he assumes they're misshapen wheels and sticks them on his futuremobile. If you ask me, that second data repository we mentioned — the one we think they stashed somewhere on a previous visit to Earth but now can't find? I think that's Plan A and what they're doing with the Astral app stuff is Plan B. I think they ran across it, saw an opportunity to learn about us quickly, and are now trying to figure out if doing so was worthwhile, given all the collateral damage. Not because they mind zombiefying people, mind you. Because the sloppy nature of the thing corrupts whatever experiment they're conducting."

Mia's head was struggling to keep up. Her headphones were in and she should be safe from music-related mind control, but still her thoughts were a frenzy.

"So what did you do after they let you go?" Mia asked.

"Well, a few days had passed, so we assumed you'd've left San Antonio. There was no way to get in touch; we found out later that there only seemed to be a cellular signal that one day because there were aliens in the area, probably checking on whatever they'd done to the Fortress before you burned it. So since we couldn't tell you where we'd gone, we did all we could think to do, back in Austin where the aliens dropped us off. And that was to continue investigating. Trying to learn more about what was going on."

Carol picked him up. "I'd taken my laptop out that day, in case I needed any information from Hollis's documents while we were trying to triangulate. The aliens didn't take it away, so I still had it when we ended up back here. I studied, and Theo studied. The data — and the strange new systems the aliens kept building around it — started to look like boxes inside of boxes. The deeper we went, the stranger it got. Until we figured out, really, where the aliens stood on all of this. Not so much what their purpose is, though we think we know that, too; they're simply trying to amass as much information about human memory and emotion as possible, in an attempt to see what makes us tick. No ... I'm talking about their attitude toward their 'grand experiment' using the Astral data. I'm talking about their official position, as far as we understand it, right here and now."

Mia looked at Hollis, but this clearly wasn't something they'd all talked about before waking her.

She asked, "So what *is* their 'official position'?"

"That," Theo said, "is where Hollis's nearly-catastrophic errand this morning comes in."

28

———

THE LOUD PEOPLE upstairs had moved on. Mia saw them go. They weren't, as Hollis had griped from his bed, a family with small children. They were all hippies: four adults, all deeply in the trance that Hollis and Mia had narrowly dug themselves out of. They were more vacant-eyed than Mia liked to see — a significant step beyond the happy-go-lucky festival mentality they'd seen as a precursor to full zombification. In cities to the south, they'd seen people gather to play, dance, and sing, then seen them go blank as alien machinery sucked their memories dry. When they'd come back to Austin, it hadn't seemed much different than it had before the aliens even came. Austin was lively; live music in Austin was just part of the way things were.

Now, Mia suspected, the whole thing might be ruined for her. She'd never been into music, but she'd at least appreciated the culture around it. Now she saw it as something to fear. They protected themselves from it. Hid from it. Pitied those who fell victim to its literal siren song, like the quick-footed people upstairs — not nearly as quick-footed as they'd plodded down the steps and past their window, she'd noticed.

Now, Theo and Carol had taken the room above them. They were quiet already. The day that had begun with Hollis sneaking out to plant explosives, it seemed, had been stressful for everyone.

"You wanna watch something?" Hollis asked. "They got a decent Juke here. Figured we could take advantage while the power's on."

She said yes. Hollis started a movie she hadn't seen, but it was a dumb one they could both ignore, playing mainly to stir the quiet from the room. With its sound around them, they both felt comfortable taking out their earplugs to let their heads breathe. If, somehow, they both went bad overnight, it would be okay. They'd shared with Theo and Carol same as Theo and Carol had shared with them, including how to pull an entranced mind back from the brink. Mia had even shown them the bruises on her wrists to prove it.

After a while, Mia turned the TV down. She heard no music. It felt safe, for now.

Hollis, sensing meaning in the action, looked over.

"Why did you do it?" she asked.

"What?"

"We talked about trying to bomb the Astral building. I thought we agreed it was too risky."

"It's a good thing I did," Hollis said, "or we wouldn't have found our upstairs neighbors again. Theo told me that he'd heard from some of the goons that we were back in town, but didn't know where we were. He'd been watching their camera feeds just in case, figuring the more they learned about the datacenter and the people in place around it, the better."

"That was luck. It's a flimsy excuse."

He grew serious. Then he said, "I went alone because you didn't understand."

"You should have talked to me. I might have understood."

"I didn't say 'couldn't understand,' Mia. I said, 'didn't understand.' I tried. You said you didn't want any part of it."

"I assumed *you* wouldn't have any part of it, either."

"I'm not a little kid. You're not my mother."

She stood. Went to the window. Looked out. She remembered the rocks the aliens had dropped around their last motel — the one where he'd shackled her to free her. She remembered the mind of the strange, separated reptar. She remembered what Theo had said, about how the aliens were watching. There were no rocks now, but still she could feel their waiting presence. But now more than ever, she didn't want any part of this. Screw the datacenter. Screw saving anything more than they'd already saved. They'd done enough. It was time for them to go, and for the watchers to leave them alone. What made her so goddamn special?

Her hands made fists. She instructed them to open, to let the anger go.

"I'm pissed at you, Hollis."

"I figured."

She turned. He was still sitting on his bed.

"No. You don't understand. I hate you for what you did."

"Isn't that a bit extreme?"

"It was selfish. It was *you, you, you.* Fuck you for it, Hollis. Fuck you for even considering it."

Stress tears threatened. She forced them back, but still turned away.

Hollis stood.

"Hey."

He touched her. She hit him without looking at him.

"What the hell, Mia!"

"You heard Theo," she said, finding that logic granted the composure to face him. "If that bomb had gone off — if you'd managed to blow that power relay — it would have been the last straw."

"We don't know that."

"Carol agreed. The aliens have *had it* with this little experiment. I don't understand all that they said, but I trust their interpretation of it."

"It's a guess," Hollis said. Behind her now, but knowing better than to touch. "Just because Theo talks about the music thing like a virus doesn't mean it literally is one."

"He said they can't control it. He said it's out of hand."

"From a human perspective, looking at information they can't possibly know for sure."

"And you know better?" Mia turned, staring into his eyes. "You didn't think about any of it. Seven seconds, Hollis. Seven more seconds, and you'd have caused enough of a problem that they'd have erased it all."

"Look," Hollis said, "you can't possibly know that they—"

"I KNOW! I FUCKING KNOW, OKAY?"

Hollis stepped back. Mia wiped at her face, struggling to keep it together. He waited for her to speak next, looking like a man trying to disarm a bomb like the one he'd so recently used to almost end it all.

"I *know*," she said, quieter now. "It's that fucking ... *thing*." She rubbed at her forehead, as if that might make the intruder inside her mind go away. "Ever since I got close to it, I can feel it inside me. Not always. Not even most of the time. But ... it was cut off from the rest of them. The pain ...

the pain it has over that, Hollis. It's like losing a twin. It's all alone. So when I gave it something to sense, it's like it latched on. It might be half the globe away and I can still feel it now and then. And so when I say I know ... *I know.* I can see it from the inside. I'd never have been able to figure out what Theo and Carol figured out; that's not how it works. But when I hear the truth, I can feel it. It's like recognizing an old friend — or an old enemy."

Mia sniffed, wiping her face again. She hated this. This ... vulnerability.

"So believe me when I say this," she went on. "If you'd thrown that particular wrench in their plans, that would have been the end. You said you figured they'd just patch it up and move on, and nothing would change. Which in itself just shows how stupid you are: Why would you do it if it made no difference? For your ego? To prove you're a macho man? To prove you don't need anyone other than yourself — and if you can't win, you might as well go out telling the world to kiss your ass?"

Hollis stuttered. "I ..."

She cut him off. "But they wouldn't have patched it up and moved on. You heard Theo and Carol, and I agree: This is a broken machine for them already. It's a car firing on half its pistons. If you've got a car like that, maybe you keep right on driving it — because hey, it still runs, right? It'd be a waste to just throw it away. But when that car finally blows one more piston — or even gets something as simple as a flat tire — that's all the excuse you need to finally say fuck it. You'll keep on rolling as long as it rolls, but it's not worth so much as taking the time to get the jack from the trunk, to fix it. That was what you almost did this morning. You almost popped a tire on this mind-control thing the aliens are doing. And if you'd succeeded, the 'virus' would have been out of the box. Maybe they'd have left the planet, then, or maybe they'd have stayed to watch what happened. But I'll *tell* you what would have happened, Hollis." She tapped her head, because this, too, was something she'd seen through the reptar's mind — or felt. "The problem would have spread, and other than the few people who figured out to wear earplugs in time, it would eventually have gotten everyone. Soon the whole world would have been like San Antonio. All of humanity, everywhere, walking around dead, with no mind at all."

Hollis didn't argue. He had that much sense. But he did pause, and keep his distance, and then say, "I couldn't have known any of that, Mia."

"But you didn't think. And you had no good reason to do it."

Motherfucker. She wasn't keeping it together anymore, no matter how hard she tried. She turned again, but this time he took her shoulders and turned her back.

In a voice nothing like his cocky own, he looked into her eyes and said, "You want the truth? All right. Fine. I've been thinking about it. Because you're right. There *was* no way to win. But it wasn't just a way for me to say fuck the world. Honestly? I think I wanted to die. Because it's not just the aliens, now. It's also Brendan Banks, your husband, and even Sonny from Lafayette. The fat black guy with all the gold. The Flesh Eaters, and that girl that came at me with a gun. Somehow, all the people who hate me got together on the other side, and you know what? *They're gonna win.* That's the worst part: Their side is gonna win, and they're gonna be the new leaders of the new world, and they even asked me to join them. And I said no, out of some stupid sense of duty, or honor, or some other thing I never used to give a shit about. And because of that, things for me — for everyone — are only gonna get a whole lot worse." He shook his head. "I guess I just wanted to end things in a way that was still under my control, doing something other than kneeling to kiss some asshole's ring."

Mia watched him as he spoke, feeling the walls crumble. She wanted to be angry.

"Not fair," she said.

"What's not fair?"

And then the crux of it: "You left me behind."

"Mia—"

"Don't," she said, a bit of anger returning — now mixed with something else. "You left me. We were a team. We were *partners*. You came for me at the Exchange and then I came for you. I pulled you out of New Braunfels and then you tied me down and pulled me out of my trance in Austin. After all that, you can't just leave me. You can't." Her head shook, slowly, tears re-forming. "It's not fair."

"I was going to die."

"Then you should have taken me."

"You didn't want to go. You wanted to live."

"Not alone. The world is so *empty* now, Hollis."

Tears fell. A wall broke. Because now she saw that all along, this had been at the heart of it. Through thick and thin and adventure and misadventure, she'd been able to count on nothing other than his infuriating presence. There was the two of them and then there was everyone else — especially this morning, before they'd re-found the others. Even in the worst of times, she'd known he was there. Somewhere. She'd hated him through so much of it, but the alternative was emptiness. Desolation. The bleak downward plummet of nothing at all.

"Hey," he said, wicking a tear from her cheek.

"You're a bastard."

He kissed her. He pulled away with eyes wide.

"Say it again," he said.

"Bastard."

"Bitch."

He pulled her close and kissed her again, harder this time. He pushed her until her back was to the window. Then Mia shoved him in the other direction, into an end table, mashing her mouth into his while their four hands explored.

Onto the bed, their limbs a frenzy.

What came next, for both of them, was the opposite of lonely and dark.

29

New plan: Get the fuck out of town.

"I like it," Hollis told Carol, who proposed it. She even said "fuck." Hollis was definitely a bad influence.

"But," she added.

"I like it less," Mia said. Carol looked over at this, but mainly because Mia's hand had been atop Hollis's. She pulled it back. Hollis, feeling it happen, realized only then that the hand had been there. He looked at her, then looked away when she turned her head. He wasn't sure how he felt about last night, except that he secretly was sure, and it was pretty awesome. They'd woken in the same bed, Hollis naked and Mia in panties. That was new. But it hadn't been weird, especially when they'd started insulting each other again.

"But," Carol tried again, "before we do that, we need to settle some bad juju with your enemies, Hollis."

"Not interested," Hollis said.

"You *should* be interested," Theo said. "I'm not sure whether we're fooling the aliens or if this is something they're feeding us for reasons unknown, but the connection they've made to the Astral databank is just one node in a wider network. I'd have to do a whole lot more poking to be sure, but I think it's something the aliens are laying over top of our internet. Whether they have any clue what we built or not doesn't matter. They're able to follow fiber optic lines the way you'd follow a rope tied to a tree to find your way out of a maze, and that's what I think they're doing. Our network doesn't mean much to them, but it's still a network like our brains are networks. *That*, they understand. They know it's a thinking machine, for whatever that's worth. So they're building their own, better thinking machine on top of it. It's like a new internet, alien style."

"Why would they build a new internet if they think as a hive mind?" Mia asked. "Why would they need it if their natural process is telepathic and ..." She made inarticulate gestures, trying to articulate. "... *wireless,*" she finished.

"The working theory is that the new network they're building isn't for them," Carol said. "It's for us. For humanity."

"They destroyed our internet," Hollis said, "then built a new one?"

"One they understand, yes. One that works, but that also works with us, insofar as they understand us and our 'singular, disconnected' minds. I've previewed it. It's admirable. Our internet grew like a fungus, spreading opportunistically. This is deliberate, the way we'd've planned the internet if we'd created it all at once, from the start. It's the difference between a small city growing outward into urban sprawl, versus a city that's planned to succeed from the start, right down to well-thought-out public transportation and sensibly located facilities."

"And to be fair," Theo added, "the aliens didn't destroy our internet. The facilities that stopped working — power, water, network — stopped working because the people who ran them abandoned their posts. Luckily, places like nuclear plants are designed to shut down safely if the staff behind them take their hands off the wheel. With the exception of the cities they've destroyed, the aliens haven't done much to damage our planet."

"Yes," Hollis said. "Except for the destruction of cities, the mass abductions, and all the murder."

"The alien network is remarkably quick-spreading," Carol said. "I looked into the fatality statistics, so far as they've been centralized and compiled. And from what I'm seeing, most deaths and damage have come from humans fighting humans, not aliens."

"Now you sound like *you're* on their side, just like Brendan," Hollis said. He'd heard this before. *Humans destroy the planet, yada yada.* Just more hippie bullshit. Didn't change the fact that this whole invasion thing was a major pain in the ass.

"Funny you should mention it," Theo said, "because that brings us to the question of Brendan and the others."

Carol picked him up. It was clear they'd talked about this last night, rehearsing this little performance while Mia and Hollis had been getting better acquainted. This was Theo and Carol's plan, and Hollis and Mia were just hearing it for the first time. Hollis, having gotten laid for the first time in a long time, was feeling particularly cool with the idea of going with the flow. He liked the idea of heading off to Vail without giving the city his final middle finger now that Mia had explained her position in a very sexy way, twice, but he was unsure whether this plan amounted to that or something else. It was all very confusing, but it didn't matter. Not a lot really mattered right now.

"The reason I mentioned the new alien 'internet,' for

lack of a better term," Carol said, "was because it looks right now like it's centered preferentially on a few cities. Not the ones you'd expect, either, like New York or Beijing. Vail, coincidentally or not coincidentally at all, looks to be one of those cities. A hub, basically. So is Teotihuacan. I'd have to see a full geosurvey to be sure of the other clusters, but I think there's another cluster in Cairo and another somewhere around Uluru. The reason any of this matters," she said, holding up a finger just as Hollis was about to ask what this had to do with the "enemies" she'd mentioned to start the discussion, "is because it all points not to a random post-apocalyptic world in our future, but one that's being crafted in a very deliberate way."

"You're saying the aliens are planning to ... *what?* Remake Earth in their image?"

"All I know is what I see," Carol said. "Which, again, might be deliberately being shown to us."

"Why would they be deliberately showing you what their plans are?" Mia asked.

"Maybe they want help."

"Fuck their help," Hollis said, again thinking of Brendan.

"Now, hang on a sec," Theo said. "There's a difference between collaboration and working to make a bad situation better. The people we know who are 'helping' them are, for the most part, trying to secure positions of power for themselves, and don't mind throwing the rest of humanity under the bus to get there. What we're talking about is working within a system that we probably can't change. It's not assistance. It's more like understanding cloud patterns so you can go to where the weather is best."

"But if you do that, it still helps the aliens," Hollis said. "They still benefit."

"In that they know we'll trumpet our plans and that

because of it, more people will head to protected zones and fewer people will die, yes," Theo told him. "As far as we can tell, they'd rather we live, so they can study us."

"Or enslave us."

Theo shrugged. "I'm just telling you how it seems. Could they be fooling us? Of course, but I don't see why. They've proven they can just *take* whatever they want, so why bother with subterfuge? In my mind, if they want to give us tips, I'm not too proud to take them."

Hollis considered. It was a convoluted argument, but he was still willing to trust. Theo and Carol, not the aliens.

"If they really are building a network for the future of the planet," Carol said, "they probably mean for the prominent cities on their 'internet' to be prominent cities, period. Now, there's no way to know if we'll be able to use whatever they set up, to let one city talk to another, or even if that's the point of it all. But if they are, a whole new economy will develop. This is just the beginning of the beginning of the beginning. But ask yourself this: If there are to be big cities on the new Earth, what will be between those cities? Will it be sprawl, like there is now? Because so far, there are no nodes throughout most of the planet. There are large clusters on the network and smaller ones between, but absolutely nothing between *those*. Have you heard about Nathan Andreus?"

"I think Brendan mentioned him," Hollis said. "Who is he?"

"Someone with admin access to the new network, that's who. According to the permissions I've seen, he's got satellite surveillance, voice access to other connected parties, the works. Since we've been tapped into Brendan's systems for a while now — which is how Theo located you to begin with, Hollis — we've heard all that's being said over their scrambled walkies, too, and if I had to guess, I'd say two things. First, Nathan Andreus stands to be a major power in the southwest in coming years if things keep going the way they're going and second, that Brendan's already put out feelers to him. The aliens are facilitating that connection, too."

"Wait," Mia said. "Are you telling me that the aliens are helping Brendan Banks get in touch with this warlord Andreus guy?"

Theo answered. "That's exactly what she's saying. Now, Hollis — you know Brendan better than we do. Do you think that if Brendan *does* start talking to Andreus, they'll get along?"

Hollis's lips pressed. He answered, but only with a nod. The truth was, Brendan was just as slippery as Hollis. He was just as good with people as Hollis, but he had bigger balls, a more violent temper, and usually a lot more guns and money to offer as part of the deal. Oh, yes ... if Andreus was a player anointed by the aliens, chances were excellent that Brendan and his buddies would be, too.

"So Brendan wins?" Mia asked. "He's decided that the way to get ahead is to be a traitor to his own kind, and he's going to actually be rewarded for it?"

"Looks that way," Carol said, more frankly than Hollis was comfortable with. "So Theo and I got to talking, and knowing this group and its goals over the life of its time together, we have a proposal for you."

"Getting the fuck out of town," Hollis said.

"But stopping to 'settle bad juju' with our enemies first," Mia said. "I assume you were talking about Brendan and Company?"

"Yes."

"This is a terrible plan," Hollis told Carol. I don't think

you understand this group and its goals as well as you think you do."

"Hang on, now," Theo said. "We've got access to the new alien network, too. It's clumsy as hell, but the way I figure, only two kinds of people will be on it right now. Either privileged citizens like Andreus, or nerds like us."

"I prefer 'hackers,'" Carol said.

"And so, knowing that, I snooped around," Theo said. "And I found a guy working out of a lab in Moab, Utah, who's uncovered a lot of the same stuff we have. He doesn't know about the Astral app database; that's unique to us thanks to the information in Thomas Davies's attache case. But he knows about the over-air signals, the piggybacking over the old internet ... all that. Anyway, by doing some technical things you'd be bored by, he and I set up private communication. Or at least, it's private as far as we can tell. It uses some of the technologies that the aliens seem most confused by, anyway."

"And?" Hollis asked. He was already bored, Theo's disclaimer aside.

"We think it's worth stopping by to 'make amends' with Brendan," Carol said, "for two reasons. The first is because if the world goes the way we think it will, Brendan will be a worse enemy to have then than he is to have now. If you got to Vail, he'll know every move you make. He'll make your life miserable, or just have you shot on arrival."

To Hollis, Brendan having him shot wasn't exactly a new threat. But he went with it anyway. He shrugged and said, "Kiss Brendan's ass to avoid a beating later. Fine. Check." He didn't like it, especially since the original plan involved disturbing Brendan's credibility with the aliens by blowing something up instead of buttering him up. But whatever.

"The second reason we think you should talk to Brendan

before going north," Carol said, "I think you'll like a lot better."

"Lemme guess," Hollis said. "I get to give him a rim job?"

"Actually," Theo said, "we want you to give him something else. Something I got from this guy Terrence."

"What?" Hollis asked.

"A virus," Theo answered, "called Canned Heat."

30

———

SO THIS WAS THE PLAN: Not to set off a bomb at the datacenter (which they all agreed would be stupid and pointless), but to leave town and serve Brendan's crew a poison apple along the way.

It wasn't the same victory as they'd been hoping for at first, but the only thing that could destroy the alien presence at the Astral center now, Theo told them, were the aliens themselves. This was the best workaround he and Carol had been able to come up with — and, once Mia understood it, it really *did* feel like it fit their group and its goals. It gave Brendan a better middle finger than blowing up the switching box would have, seeing as it'd probably ruin his chances to become a warlord like Andreus later on.

"So if we do this," Hollis said to Mia as they got behind the wheel and began to drive toward the Astral building, "it's going to ... what? Somehow mess up Brendan's access to the alien network?"

"I think so," Mia said.

"I didn't follow half of what they said back there," Hollis admitted.

"Me either."

"So if Brendan lets us inside, I'm just going to plug this thing into one of his machines and see what happens." He indicated the thumb drive Theo had given him, supposedly containing Terrence-in-Moab's Canned Heat virus.

"Sounds like a plan."

"Even though I don't get it."

"Plug it in," Mia said. "And it screws things up. That's the limit of my knowledge."

"Will Brendan know we did it?"

"I don't know. Carol seemed to think it was important to kiss Brendan's ass, just in case the virus doesn't work and he ends up king anyway. I think that'd be hard to do if he knows we farted on his plans."

"Farted. Really."

"It's better than 'MechaPope.'"

"Definitely isn't," Hollis said. She looked over. He couldn't stop smiling. It was cute, but also weird. Things were different between them now, but Mia wasn't sure *how* different she liked it. Their old way had worked, what with her punching him a lot and all.

His hand was over hers, her hand atop her thigh. He was driving with one hand and looked uncomfortable. The hand moved away, letting hers breathe. Thank God. Her hand had been getting sweaty, but she wasn't sure if she could just ask him to knock it off.

"I don't think I'm a hand-holding guy," he said.

"It's okay. Me either."

"You're a guy?"

"Fuck you."

"This is better," Hollis said. "With me not touching you."

"Much."

"I mean, unless I touch you in a way that's really inappropriate. Maybe even illegal."

"Try it," Mia said, "and I'll break your fingers."

"Asshole," he said.

"Asshole," she replied.

They drove in silence, a tiny smile kissing the corner of her lips.

"Do you think he'll shoot us out of hand?" Hollis asked.

"Who cares? Be a man."

"He invited me to join their camp. You too, actually. Just because Bobby Bones got coldcocked while trying to sneak up on me, that shouldn't change anything."

"It will probably change things for Bobby Bones."

"I think her name is actually Bonnie Bones."

"I don't think her name is actually either of those things," Mia said.

"But she's not in charge. And Theo didn't kill her. He checked. Abundantly. It was sort of embarrassing."

"Well, Theo's a warrior," Mia said.

"So the way I figure, the offer should still be good. We didn't move against them."

"Except that you tried."

"Yes, but they don't know that," Hollis said. "Becky Bones—"

"Bobby," Mia corrected.

"She didn't know I'd planted the bomb. And she was unconscious when we went back for it. So nobody knows I tried to ram C4 up their asses. Therefore, I should still be at neutral, as far as Brendan's opinion of me goes."

"What do you think Thomas will have to say about you," Mia asked, "now that you had sex with his wife?"

"Thomas is with Brendan, too?"

"You knew that."

"True. I just wanted to hear you talk about me having sex with his wife."

"You made his wife come like four times," she said.

"His wife really isn't big on discretion," Hollis said.

"Maybe she's been hard-up for a while."

Hollis watched the road. It wasn't far to the datacenter from the motel, and even less far to the spot where Brendan had parked his Mobile Command Unit. Hollis could see it now: a big, boxy tractor trailer with a bunch of equipment in the back. It struck Hollis that Brendan, with his stupid truck thing, was basically a classroom kissass. You know that kid who got his reports professionally bound so the teacher would praise him? That was basically Brendan right now.

Aliens! Aliens! His stupid-ass hand waving in the air. *I know the answer! Let me help you clean the whiteboards after class!*

Oh, fuck you, Brendan.

Hollis looked at Mia's hand. She stowed it between her legs, lest he get the feeling he was supposed to hold it again. Not that "between her legs" was a place Hollis was unwilling to go.

"Did you like me all along?" Hollis asked.

"No."

"I mean, over the past few weeks. Did you find me charming, like what we ended up doing was bound to happen?"

"No."

"But you thought I was sexy."

"I'll meet you in the middle," Mia said. "I'll grant that you thought *I* was sexy."

"That's not really meeting me in the middle."

"What do you want, a love letter?"

"Throw me a bone, at least," Hollis said.

"Tell you what. Later, when all this is over, I'll let *you* throw *me* a bone."

"Again," Hollis clarified.

"Again," Mia agreed.

They drove.

"I'll take it," Hollis said.

They pulled up to the tractor trailer. A man was waiting outside with a machine gun. He was wearing a shirt that read, in giant letters, CARL.

"Excuse me," Hollis said. "We're here to see Carl."

"I'm Carl."

"Prove it," Hollis said.

Carl's face twisted. "I know who you are. You're that Hollis guy."

"And that Mia guy," Hollis said, indicating Mia. Mia raised her hand.

"I should shoot you, for what you did to Becky."

"You like Becky, do you?"

"No. But she's a comrade of mine."

"Way to dispel the rumors that you're a communist, Carl," said Hollis.

"I would shoot you," he said, "if Mr. Banks hadn't told us to bring you to him if you showed up."

"And a bang-up job you're doing at it," Hollis said. "What was your name again?"

"Wait here," Carl said, turning.

"Is Thomas Davies inside?" Mia called after him.

Carl looked back. "He's around. Not here."

"Can you get him a message?"

"Maybe."

"Tell him there's a guy here who fucked his wife."

"Who?" Carl looked at Hollis. "Oh. Very funny." Then he went inside.

"You're going to get us killed," Hollis told her once they were alone.

"Nah."

"What if you're overestimating our value, in Brendan's eyes? Our primary goal here isn't to be obnoxious, though that's always *something* of a goal. This is about Canned Heat."

Mia, now grinding her heel in the dust, said, "Do you remember that old song, by that guy with the funny name, called 'Canned Heat'?"

"No."

"It was pretty hot."

"Come on, Mia. Stay focused."

"Did you know that your orgasms sound like porpoises mating?"

"Do not," Hollis said. Though he'd heard that exact thing before, in those exact words. It was uncanny.

Carl was back. His shirt still said CARL.

"Brendan is on his way. He told me to offer you coffee."

There was a long pause.

"Are you going to?" Hollis asked.

"I just did."

"That didn't really sound like an offer."

So Carl said, "Would you like coffee." More like recitation than a question.

"Nah," said Hollis. Mia shook her head.

They all stared at each other for five minutes, and then Brendan drove up in a camouflage Jeep. Mia, looking at Hollis, could see him holding back jokes about how none of them could see Brendan, in that Jeep with all its blending-in.

Carl went inside. Mia found she missed him.

"So," Brendan said, smiling. "You came. He walked up to

them and, shocking Mia, hugged them one at a time. "Wonderful, wonderful," he said. "Come in. Mi trailer est su trailer."

Hollis followed Brendan, and Mia followed Hollis. And Mia could see Hollis, as he watched, fidgeting with the thumb drive in his pocket, both of them feeling shared nerves.

31

BRENDAN WAS CRAZY, Hollis reminded himself.

It'd be easy to forget that. Right here and now, he was charming, magnetic, and had a lightness to his conversation that even Hollis would have had a hard time faking. But he needed to remember at all times that Brendan could turn on a dime. He'd been homicidal before and could easily be homicidal again. And in fact, his whole stupid forecast was kind of homicidal, if you read between the lines. "Clearing areas" had to involve killings, right? Hitler was probably great at a cocktail party, too.

So Hollis didn't let himself relax. He kept his guard, and kept flashing warnings to Mia, too.

This is the guy who kidnapped you and meant to sell you as a sex slave. This is the guy who tied me to a chair, then sent an insane surgeon in to cut me apart piece by piece.

Mia, however, didn't need the reminder. Judging by appearances, she never fully relaxed into Brendan's charm. She faked it whenever Brendan looked her way, but it was all a facade. Her eyes said, *Let's do what we came to do and get the hell out.* But of course Brendan didn't make that part easy.

The Command Center looked large from the outside, but was even larger inside. It'd been partitioned like a mobile home, into a few distinct rooms. Up front was a kitchenette, behind it (in the truck's middle) were all the computers arranged in dual utilitarian banks that flanked each of the side walls, and to the rear was something like living quarters. The last is where Brendan took them upon entry. They passed through the computer area, through a drape, and into a surprisingly plush sitting area. It was nice on the human end, bad on the mission end. Even as Hollis settled, he realized it'd be hard to plant his virus in a recliner or a coffee table.

So at first, all they could do was talk. It wasn't easy. Hollis hadn't come prepared to bluff his way through a discussion of trading sides, or of allegiance to what he was now already envisioning might one day be called the Banks Army, ruling the barren wastelands between cities. His eyes kept wandering back up front, where he'd seen all sorts of slots into which he could plug his drive. Back here, there were no slots and no end in sight. Worst of all, somehow Hollis had lost the best of his smooth-smiling guile. He used to be so good at bullshitting, but it seemed his mind no longer had a taste for it.

Instead of nodding and smiling along with the grand plans Brendan was laying out for the group's future, Hollis kept wanting to rise and punch him in the throat. Instead of agreeing with Brendan and making up some good-sounding shit of his own to go with it, he found himself wanting to argue. For every point Brendan made, Hollis kept coming up with counterpoints that he couldn't voice — that he had to bite back like a good little soldier. It was the absolute worst.

Finally Hollis got up in the middle of one of Brendan's insane speechifications and said, "I have to go to the bathroom."

Brendan, surprised at first by the whiplash change of topic, quickly recovered. He gave his host's smile again, pointed to the trailer's rear and said, "Of course. It's back there. My engineers even got the plumbing hooked up: water *and* waste disposal."

Something about the way Brendan said, "... and waste disposal" struck Hollis as both a boast and a promise. Didn't RVs have a tank for waste? They didn't hook right into a sewer, did they? The way Brendan was smiling looked proud, though, as if he was bragging on the way his team had given even this temporary command structure the comforts of something permanent. *Join me and I'll make sure you have all the plumbing you want,* that look seemed to say. *And water, and food, and the comforts of home. I'm the one with the resources. Versus the suckers out there, I'm the one with the means to survive in style.*

Hollis looked toward the bathroom, realizing he should have seen this coming. Of course the bathroom was to the rear, inside the living quarters. But he didn't want the rear; he wanted forward. Where all the computers and their tantalizing slots were.

"Actually," he said, "I really just want a glass of water."

"There are glasses in there," Brendan told him.

"A really *big* glass. I'm really thirsty."

You sound like an idiot, Hollis thought. *He's going to see right through you.*

But instead of raising an eyebrow, Brendan shrugged good-naturedly. "We have bottles in the kitchenette. And cans of pop. Whatever you want." Then he stood. "Come on. Let's all head up there. I could use something to drink, too."

Brendan tried on a smile. This was all so much harder than it had seemed when Theo had described it.

Just put the drive in a slot, Theo had said. *The program will do the rest.*

Only now did Hollis think to ask whether he was supposed to leave the thumb drive in the slot (which didn't seem right; that left evidence behind) or take it with him. And if he was supposed to take it back, how long did it need to stay in?

Hollis went to the counter, just inside the forward quarter of the truck. If he leaned back from here, he could almost touch one of the console-mounted computers, built in rather than freestanding for stability while moving. Nobody was sitting in front of it. It showed a camera feed of the facility, either mounted close or zoomed in.

"Coke?" Brendan asked.

Hollis, turning, almost jumped.

"Uh, sure."

Brendan gave it to him. "Cold, right?"

Hollis nodded. The can was almost cold enough to give his palm frostbite.

"How long's it been since you had a cold can of pop?"

This morning, actually, seeing as power was on at the motel and they'd said fuck it and raided the minibar. But instead he played to Brendan's boast: "Long-ass time."

"They tell me we'll always have power, if we want it."

"The aliens?" Mia said. "You ... *talk* to them?"

"No, not them," Brendan said, his manner approximately a hundred times more relaxed than Hollis felt. "I meant my engineers. See, we're plugged into a plain old outlet here, but do you know what the outlet is plugged into?"

"A bigger outlet?" Hollis said.

"Not the power grid," Brendan said. "If you go out a few blocks, you'll see that power's on in a big circle. It's like the Austin Power plant's working again, but only for this little circle. That's not actually the case. Austin Power is down, from end to end. What the entire grid is actually plugged into is ... " He smiled in a secretive way, stepped around them to re-enter the computer section, and ducked beneath a console to retrieve something. "Check this out." Then he held up something that looked like a triple-size Rubik's cube covered in glowing blue lines.

"What is that?"

"Alien technology. My guys have been studying it and have no idea how it works. It's like a battery, but it's extremely powerful. Here."

He handed the thing to Mia, who hefted it and handed it to Hollis. It was much lighter than it looked, and seemed to vibrate just above his ability to detect.

"The whole area is plugged into one of these?" Hollis asked.

"In a manner of speaking. There's no actual plug. See?"

Hollis turned it over in his hands. There were no holes. Just smooth surfaces.

"The creepiest part is, it knows what you want it to do. The aliens hooked up the one powering all of this, but we took that one out of the powered zone and would just set it somewhere, and then whatever we'd been thinking we wanted on would come on and that thing there would start to pulse. Somehow it was powering whatever it was just by grabbing our thoughts."

Hollis handed the thing back. It had an oily feel, even

though no oil came off on his fingers. He didn't like to touch it.

"As long as we have one of these puppies with us," Brendan said as he set the cube on the countertop, "we'll always be able to power anything we want. And it gets better. Right now, I've got teams out there fixing up cars — electronic ones that were fried during that EMP a while back. We're all pretty confident that if that cube will run a toaster, it'll run a car. Or *many* cars. They pack a punch. Remember, something like fifty city blocks are being run by a cube just like that right now."

Hollis found himself staring at the thing. Brendan, if he wasn't such a shitbag, would actually be making a compelling case. Access to a cube like that was almost worth joining a bad cause. With neverending power (and hence fuel, for electric cars), Brendan's people would be able to manufacture all sorts of advantages. Water could be purified with enough power, food could be grown, and more. Hollis got the feeling that was only the tip of the iceberg.

He looked around, wondering what it'd take to steal the thing. But he nixed the idea immediately, because if you used the cubes by thinking at them, chances struck him as excellent that it wouldn't work for thieves. Taking that cube and trying to use it might be like drawing a target on his back. Hell, it might even self-destruct, if it got bothered enough.

Hollis, now that he was closer to the computers and had an excuse, bent low to look at the monitor he'd noticed from the other side of the counter. It showed a close-up view of the alien line of ships around the Astral building — and, if Hollis still had illusions about trying to get inside to destroy the place, dispelled them immediately. There were hundreds of aliens on the ground, moving in waves. Most of them were the black reptar type, blue sparks inside their many-toothed mouths.

Still Hollis considered. If he'd blown up the power relay, the database would have remained to perpetuate, corrupt, and eventually ruin the minds of everyone it could reach. But if the database itself were nuked? Well, that would solve the whole shebang.

And that gave Hollis an idea. Maybe, if he could somehow re-attach the truck part to the trailer they were in right now and drive the whole thing toward the line of alien spheres, they might be fooled into thinking Brendan was behind the wheel, and they'd part to let him in like a Trojan horse, and ...

"What's going on over there, Hollis?" asked Brendan's voice, from deeper in the kitchen.

Just thinking some idiot ideas again to get us all killed, Hollis's brain said. *Stupid, stupid man.*

Hollis blinked up from his moronic fantasy and said, "I was watching your camera feeds."

Brendan came around and looked at the one Hollis meant.

"That's east side. Light patrols today."

Hollis looked at the screen *Light* patrols? What did the heavy ones look like?

He pulled Mia closer. She shuffled, surprised, but came willingly. She was acting the way she had when he'd held her hand in the car, but then he caught her eye and she understood.

When Brendan started talking again about the alien patrols, hunched to focus on the screen, Hollis pointedly looked at Mia, then at a spot just beneath the console's countertop. Then at her, then at the spot.

Mia looked. There was a line of controls there ... and ports.

Her eyes widened. Hollis returned his attention to Brendan, but at the same time he pulled the drive from his pocket and slipped it into Mia's hand.

"How many ships are there?" Hollis asked, shifting his body to shield Mia from Brendan. His heart was pounding now.

"It changes. Usually at least a hundred, if you count the ones parked on the ground and the ones in the air."

Mia, moving behind him. Bending her knees enough that she could reach the ports without actually bending. A few seconds later Hollis could hear her trying to find the port by feel: a small sound of thin metal against plastic, like a cat scratching at the door. After a bit the sound was so *obvious*. How could Brendan not hear it?

"Huh," Hollis said, his attention now more on Mia's sounds than Brendan's words.

Fortunately, Brendan picked up his non-response. "They've always got patrols walking the perimeter. They ..."

Hollis lost track of what Brendan was saying. Mia was still scratching, still not getting the drive in the slot. Damn things were impossible to get right the first time. You always put them in backwards — or more likely, put them in the right way but not quite, then switched to putting them in backwards and wondering why you got nowhere. Hollis could barely put the things in right when he was using his eyes, let alone by feel.

Brendan stopped. He looked at Hollis. "What?"

"Nothing."

"You feeling okay?"

In the quiet between words, Hollis heard Mia finally

slide the little drive home. Somehow, Brendan heard nothing.

No. Not feeling okay. But he said, "Yeah. Absolutely." He pointed at the screen again and said, without antecedent, "What's that?"

Brendan studied the screen and Hollis sneaked a look at the drive. Its little light flashed for a while, then stopped.

He looked at Mia, who'd also been watching the light cease blinking.

Does that mean it's done? she seemed to ask. *Should I pull it out now?*

But she didn't have to decide and Hollis didn't have to guess at the answer. The cube, farther down the corner, began to strobe as every monitor in the place went blank. Brendan looked around, then saw the non-subtle looks that must have taken up residence on Mia and Hollis's faces, then looked where Mia couldn't help glancing and spotted the drive. After that, he made a face himself. And this one, unlike the host's face he'd been wearing for a half-hour now, was decidedly less friendly.

"*What the fuck,*" he asked, "did you just do?"

Hollis didn't feel like answering, and the drive was already beyond grabbing. So he rushed at the door, which Mia beat him to, praying there was no one with a gun behind it.

"Run," he said, quite unnecessarily. "*RUN!*"

32

CARL WAS OUTSIDE, but he was sniffing daisies or something, his attention away from where it should have been. Mia, in the lead, took him down using the most aggressive block she could muster. He got the gun a quarter of the way raised before Mia was throwing her shoulder into his chest, her forehead colliding half-intentionally with his nose. The impact rattled her brains; there was no other way to describe it. Post-strike, she would have fallen if Hollis hadn't caught her, dragged her, practically thrown her into the car. Thank God they were still driving the Shit Bomber; thank God the roof was down.

Mia had her face in the footwell by the time she heard Brendan emerge. She couldn't see him from way down low, but he must have had a gun because Hollis, not yet in the car himself, was ducking behind the door for cover.

"It's okay!" he said. "Give me the gun from the glove compartment and I'll stay low and—"

But Hollywood got that wrong, too, because when Brendan started firing, his bullets ripped through the car door like tinfoil. She could see daylight through the steel.

One shot, two shots, and Hollis was in the car too, half-ducking but now protected only by the windshield, which wasn't bulletproof and may not (being a vintage car) even have had laminate between the layers to make it shatterproof. Brendan popped off two more shots, shouting now, so Hollis laid so far down, his neck was where seat and back met. He'd started the engine; he'd somehow gotten it into first gear. The only problem was his total lack of visibility. He floored it anyway, heading toward the shots rather than away from them, and after two more slugs (one in the headrest and another gone astray), the car struck something heavy. Their forward progress stopped and after a quick beat Hollis peeked out, sat up, and said, "Got him in the jimmies."

Mia didn't understand that at first, but by now she'd extricated herself from the footwell and was sitting upright, staying low, too. No more shots came, though, and after a quick inspection she saw why: Carl was on the ground to one side, holding a broken nose and groaning. Brendan was to the other side; clearly he was what they'd hit. But he wasn't dead and didn't look like anything had broken. Instead, he was clasping his testicles in pain and then Mia remembered: There was a life-size He-Man head mounted to the grill, right at crotch level.

Mia had managed to fish the gun from the glove compartment. She flicked off the safety and aimed it, but found she couldn't shoot a man — even Brendan, who'd threatened her, sold her, and just tried to kill them both — in cold blood.

"It's okay," Hollis said, seeing her. "He got Canned Heat, and we were outta here anyway."

He slammed the car into reverse, made a three-point turn, and peeled back onto the road.

"Vail," she said.

"Vail," Hollis agreed.

They just had to make one stop first because someone, like Lucy, had some 'splainin' to do.

33

Mia kept looking back. What she saw was both fascinating and horrifying. The Astral building never left her sight, and as Hollis topped-out the Shit Bomber the wind whipped her hair into a cyclone. She watched as the alien ships first began to wobble like BBs on an unstable platform, then began to take to the air. It was harder to see the reptars and titans on the ground from here, but they moved in large enough numbers now that she got the drift. They, like the ships, stirred without obvious direction. It was like a hornet's nest that'd been struck by a rock, thousands of stinging soldiers rising in search of a culprit to blame.

"Jesus," she said.

Hollis wouldn't take his eyes off the road. At this speed, it would have been suicide. "Is Brendan's crew chasing us?" he asked.

"Yes, but that's not what I was talking about. It's the aliens around the building."

"What about them?"

"They're ..." But she wasn't sure how to finish that sentence, and after the few more seconds it'd taken to have this exchange with Hollis, the alien threat had begun to strike her less as an immediate threat and more as nonspecifically ominous. Part of her had been sure their cloud would become a line of ships with purpose, shooting toward them at lightning speed to blow them from the road. But that hadn't happened. They'd been jostled, and they'd risen like a fog, but after that they'd gone no further.

"They're what?"

"I think whatever that Canned Heat thing did, it somehow affected them," she said.

"How? We were with Brendan, not them."

"Theo said Brendan was connected to the new alien internet. Maybe they saw it come through."

"Are they coming after us?"

She'd been watching. She shook her head. "No. Doesn't look like it." In fact, they were settling again, also like hornets after the antagonist was gone.

"What about Brendan?"

"I think we lost them. Or will lose them. They were pretty far back, and you're ..."

"Yeah," Hollis said when her sentence dangled. "I'm just glad Sonny gave me a Chevelle, not a Kia."

Mia watched for another second, then turned back to front. Hollis hadn't slowed. She had a very distinct thought: *After all we've been through and all we've risked, this is what's going to kill us.*

"I think you can slow down now," she said.

"Are you sure?"

She looked back again. "Yeah. I think we're okay."

Hollis let off the gas. The car slowed, but only to seventy.

"I thought it was supposed to be subtle," Mia said. "The virus was supposed to go onto Brendan's system, then leak out onto the alien net. It was supposed to corrupt his end and ruin his connection to the aliens."

And yeah, that *was* how it was supposed to work. At least according to Theo — who, now that Mia thought about it, hadn't always looked them in the eye. She'd had the feeling that neither Theo nor Carol were telling them the whole truth and half-wanted to ask, but at the time she'd chalked it up to lack of understanding. Every time she or Hollis had asked a question, the other two had given them answers — which made things worse, given how overloaded with information they'd already felt.

They hadn't planned to rendezvous at the motel. Somehow, that had seemed like a bad idea. There was a fruit stand on Old Jollyville that they'd passed earlier — one they'd all noticed because the sign said "FRESH" STRAW-BERRIES rather than FRESH STRAWBERRIES, the quotes seeming to indicate that the strawberries were fresh only by some abstract definition — that would do just fine. There was a row of trees behind it, perfect for hiding until a joining party arrived.

Carol and Theo were walking toward the car before Hollis had fully stopped. They climbed over the top to get in so the front-seat occupants wouldn't need to stand or lean forward.

"So?" Theo asked.

Mia told them what had happened. While she did, Carol set up a miniature workstation on the bench seat between her and Theo. She had her faithful laptop and her cell phone, and from the arrangement, Mia assumed she'd managed more magic: getting a connection, on a dead network, over the air without need for a hardline. A month ago, doing what Carol was doing to find the internet would have been easy. Now, it deserved a Nobel prize.

Theo made a face when Mia was done speaking. The car was moving fast again, heading out of the city.

"I thought that might happen," he said.

"You *what?*" Hollis said.

"They're sharing space with alien technology. Naturally it's smarter than ours."

"Wait. You *knew* it might set off alarms? You knew we might be caught with our pants down? When were you planning to tell us?"

"You're good on your feet," Theo said, now turning to Carol's screen, rotating it for a better view. They exchanged a glance and Carol nodded.

"What the hell, guys," Mia said.

"Water under the bridge," Theo said, apparently deciding for all of them. "This actually isn't a bad thing. We just move to Plan A."

"You mean Plan B."

"I mean Plan A," Theo corrected. "Plan B was setting a Trojan to spread out and corrupt the connection later. But I don't think that's what any of us really wanted."

"Except," Hollis said, "that's *specifically* what we went to Brendan's to do."

Carol spoke up. She had to shout, over the wind and through the earplugs they were all wearing. "We explained all this. Weren't you listening?"

Mia looked at Hollis, now just a little sheepish. *Technically listening? Yes. Understanding every detail?* Not in the least. She distinctly remembered letting her attention wander in the name of sparing brain cells, figuring Theo and Carol had done the thinking for them.

"Pull over," Carol said.

Hollis looked at the others, but then pulled to the side of the road. She then told him to raise the convertible's roof, which he did, too. After that, with the wind noise dampened and the sealed atmosphere safe to remove earplugs, it was much easier to have their conversation.

"I have the network up right now," Carol said. She turned the laptop to show them the screen, but to Mia it looked as much like a vascular diagram as a computer thing. "Now, the bad news is that Canned Heat didn't really do anything. We told you Terrence was still working on it? Well, it seems he'd better keep on keeping on." She tapped the map. "See? They've got antivirus that's a whole lot better than ours, and it appears Terrence didn't really understand their system."

"So we did nothing," Hollis said. "Brendan still wins."

"Looks that way. His connection is unaffected, and from what I'm seeing the network has already purged Canned Heat entirely. So that's Plan B, gone."

"What's the good news?"

"I'm actually not done with the bad news," Carol said.

"Oh." This wasn't any fun. Mia wondered why they'd invited these killjoys along. Why they'd bothered trying to make a last stand at all. Vail awaited. She wondered if there'd still be skiing this winter. Probably, she decided. Mountains were still mountains and snow would still come. And if the lifts weren't running, they could hike to the top of the hill.

"The cube thing you described," Carol went on. "You said it reacted when you plugged in the drive?"

Mia nodded.

"Sort of figured. That part, I'm sure you remember."

Mia nodded again — but no, she didn't remember that. Not specifically. Both Theo and Carol had a way of using overly complex terms to describe simple things. They'd probably mentioned the cube, but if so they hadn't called it a cube. They'd probably said "inverted spectral quantum power relay" or something.

"Theo told you that we're tapped into their surveillance, and that we've pulled a few tricks so we can surveil them right back. Thanks to that — because we've been spying on all of their discussions for a week now — we're pretty sure that ..." Her eyes flicked up, then down at her screen. "Hollis. Pull off again. Slowly. There. Park behind that big bush."

Hollis did, but his eyes didn't understand. Then, after they were stopped, Mia began to see movement between the tight-knit branches of the bush. It was indistinct, impossible to catch beyond a distant sense of motion. She got curious when it was past, and over Carol's protests opened her door with the softest of touches. She went around the bush while Theo hissed for her to stay down and come back, and then saw what they'd barely avoided.

It was a party of reptars, all in a line, heads swinging side to side. Despite a few big psychic rocks nearby, Mia felt nothing from them as she'd felt from the one at the Exchange. These weren't separated as that one had been. They were moving as one mind, driven by the basest purpose. If they saw her, they'd come for her — and what came after wouldn't be pretty.

Still Mia stood, mostly concealed, and watched until they were out of sight. Only then did she return to the car.

"You knew they were coming," Mia said.

"Sort of," Carol told her. "Their network isn't like the internet. It's both intelligent and intuitive. It's not really that I knew they were there so much as I was able to see a peak in their level of interest. Their interest in finding the two of you, I think."

That gave Mia a chill.

"Now, I don't really know what I'm doing here," Carol said. "You get that, right? These are all guesses."

Mia nodded, but Carol's guesses had been scarily accurate so far, as had Theo's.

"But based on the network activity I saw when you planted the Canned Heat, and ..." Carol actually picked the laptop up, scrutinizing the screen. She zoomed in on a section of a rolling graph that showed a double spike, the second peak much higher than the first. "Wait. The cube you mentioned. Did you touch it?"

"Was I not supposed to?" Hollis asked.

Theo and Carol shared a knowing look that, given the situation, only served to piss Mia off. She was getting a little tired of their superior, *how-can-you-not-know-this?* attitude, especially since she and Hollis, from the start, had gone on all the errands and taken a hundred percent of the risks.

She said, "How about you just tell us what you think is going on instead of acting like you're smarter than us all the damn time?"

Theo answered. He avoided the barb in Mia's question, and was courteous enough to not point out the fact that everyone knew — that he and Carol were, objectively, smarter.

"From listening in as they studied the cube," he said, "we're pretty sure it imprints on its users. That can be mental, or it can be physical."

"You're not saying that—" Hollis began.

"It might have 'sampled' you when you touched it, Hollis," Carol said. "That explains this first peak. And it explains why they're zeroing in on us so well. It'll get better as they chew on what you gave them. If that same patrol came by in a few hours, I don't think they'd have passed us by."

Hollis went quiet. Mia went quiet, too.

After a minute, after Mia was again facing forward, Theo's voice came from the back seat. He was speaking to Carol.

"You know," he said, "this could work to our advantage."

"How?"

Mia turned in time to see Theo shrug. "Brendan's people have all the same information we have. They have to, if they're on the network."

"But they don't know what they're seeing," Carol said. "That's the only reason we're staying ahead of them. If they could interpret the data the same way we are, it wouldn't just be reptars and titans and big round ships chasing us. It'd be Brendan and Sonny and all the humans, too."

"So we should haul ass toward Vail," Hollis said.

"Except that it's a network," Theo said, now with a strange look in his eye. "That network is *stronger* in Vail, not weaker."

"Somewhere else, then."

Theo was looking knowingly at Carol. Then Carol had the same look, too.

"Somewhere else," she agreed.

"Somewhere familiar," Theo said.

"Like staying right here, in Austin?"

"Now hold on a second," Hollis said.

"That's what I was thinking," Carol told Theo.

"Excuse me," Mia said. "Care to let the rest of us in on what you're talking about?"

"Plan A," Theo answered.

"Plan A," Carol told them.

Then, as they sat in the parked car, Theo and Carol told them everything else.

34

"THIS IS NEVER GOING TO WORK," Hollis said.

"It'll work," Mia said.

"He's not that stupid."

"I'm willing to bet he's that stupid."

Hollis put his hand back into the bag Mia was holding. He came out with a handful of spun sugar, its color somewhere between radioactive yellow and radioactive orange. His next words came out garbled and with a great volume of crumbs.

"Bet me," he said: *Beff meef.*

"What do you want to bet?"

"Five bucks says he doesn't fall for it," Hollis said.

"I don't have five bucks."

"Then how about a handjob?"

"How about fuck you, pig?"

"You just know you're going to lose."

"I'm not going to lose," Mia told him.

Hollis took another handful. Then Mia did too, to see what all the fuss was about.

Theo, while he'd been spying on Brendan's crew, had

heard where Beef kept his stash of Beaver Nuggets. It was hidden but not guarded, so at some point while they'd all been separated, Theo had raided the stash and taken something like twenty bags. Hollis had been offended, just a bit ago, when Theo told him this. Specifically, Hollis was bothered that Theo hadn't told them earlier.

Mia didn't get it. The Nuggets tasted like something between the bottom of a cotton candy machine and a honeycomb made by very distracted bees.

"Win or lose," Hollis said, "I think we can appreciate the real victory here."

"That we're not the ones on the other side of that fence," Mia said, nodding.

Meaning the electrified fence surrounding Brendan's tactical unit, which Beef seemed hilariously to be in charge of. Theo had some hack for not getting electrocuted or setting off any alarms, but cutting through the links had still taken forever. Carol and Theo had gone and for once, Mia and Hollis were the ones outside making judgments like armchair quarterbacks. It hadn't been hard to turn the tables and get the others on a mission for a change. All it'd taken was bullying.

"These are terrible," Mia said, spitting out what remained of her Nuggets.

"I know, right?" said Hollis, reaching for another handful. Apparently he'd taken it as a compliment.

Theo came around the corner of the building ahead, moving fast. Carol was with him. Theo held a garbage bag, almost empty now, and Carol was in charge of reaching into the bag, grabbing bags of Beaver Nuggets, and dropping them on the ground.

"You have to move faster," Mia called out. "Don't you know that?"

"Yeah, guys," Hollis said around more Beaver Nuggets. "We've talked about how neither of you ever pay attention or are smart enough."

Both Theo and Carol looked harried. They were rushing, Carol more throwing the bags frenetically behind her than dropping them as discussed. Neither seemed to appreciate the jokes, which was tragic.

"He's coming," Theo said.

"No way," Hollis said.

"Five bucks," Mia said, holding out her hand.

They rushed through, the garbage bag snagging on the cut fence's tines. Theo pulled it free and they all looked toward the building.

"Do we have time to close up the fence?" Mia asked. "That'd make this less suspicious."

"Less suspicious than a trail of snack foods showing up on the ground for no apparent reason?" Carol asked.

"I hear him," Hollis said. Listening close, Mia could hear grunting and heaving and panting. It was like a dog trying to do calisthenics.

"He didn't see us drop the first one," Carol said. "But I don't think he's moving fast."

They waited, expecting Beef to round the corner any second and bring his vaguely sexual sounds of exertion into the open. But the sounds continued and nobody came.

"I think we have time to close the fence," Hollis said. So he went forward and, taking his time, did.

Still they waited, listening as the huffing and puffing grew more insistent.

"If he has a heart attack trying to pick up all those bags," Carol said, "then nobody wins."

"Oh, I'm sure *someone* wins," Mia replied.

Three minutes later, Beef's blinged-out form came

around the corner, his arms overflowing with bags of Beaver Nuggets. Mia, Hollis, Theo, and Carol were hiding deep in the weeds, watching.

They waited.

Thirty feet away, Beef looked at the now-closed hole in the fence. It wasn't like they could hide the thing; it was a circle cut in chain-link that, by all accounts, was supposed to be electrified. He was wearing a Kangol hat and had so many gold rings on his fingers that Mia found it hard to believe he could bend them. He was wearing twenty pounds of gold chain, just like Mr. T used to.

He went to poke the cut in the fence, and Mia considered betting Hollis that this — not exertion — would be the thing that'd stop his heart. But mostly she wondered why they'd closed the fence anyway. With the ruse they were playing, it actually made sense that, as far as Beef was concerned, someone would have cut out and run away.

There was a piece of paper stuck to the fence. They'd planted it there before Theo and Carol had run in to lay their trail. It read,

* * *

MIA -
MEET ME AT 5PM WHERE THE PATH TO THE ASTRAL
BUILDING HITS THE MAIN ROAD.
- HOLLIS

* * *

"HE'S NOT dumb enough to fall for *that*," Hollis whispered.

But Beef snatched the note, scanned it, then crumpled it up and threw it outside of the fence. Mia, though she hadn't thought to brag, had anticipated him doing that, too. Because if Beef was going to bring some piece of insider news to the boss, he wouldn't want to give anyone else credit. He'd want to pretend — big, important man that he was — that he'd figured it out himself through means he'd later refuse to share.

Then he ran off, still with Nuggets overflowing his arms. A few dropped, but he waddled off without stopping.

"I can't believe that worked," Hollis muttered.

"Now you have to give me a handjob," Mia told him.

35

Carol and Hollis sat in the car. Hollis was driving and Carol was in the backseat with her laptop open and an earpiece in her unplugged ear. The engine was idling. Ideally, they wanted a critical mass, but that would only work if anyone watching the car was content to wait for Mia to show up for the supposed rendezvous. Hollis wasn't sure that would happen; it was his DNA (or whatever) that had imprinted on the alien cube, meaning it was him they'd be able to track. What's more, Hollis was the one who'd pissed everyone off. Mia had mostly just been along for the ride.

"I see something to my left," Hollis said.

"Don't look over," Carol told him. "Don't let them know you know they're there."

"Who is it?"

"Hard to say." She pressed the single earpiece, listening closely. She consulted her computer, which showed a whole lot of alien network crap of which Hollis could make neither hide nor hair. "It might be Beef. He blabbed to Brendan over the walkie, meaning everyone would know — but given what we've seen of the guy, he'd probably want to give himself a head start before telling anyone else."

Hollis agreed but didn't nod. He was hyper-aware that right now, someone — and maybe several someones — was watching him through binoculars, waiting until Mia showed up to grab them both. Carol was low. She needed to be in the car to guide Hollis and answer his questions, but it was important that she not be seen.

"Did Brendan respond?"

"Yes."

"And you're sure everyone could hear when he did? About me and Mia meeting here?"

"Everyone with a walkie-talkie," Carol said. "They both used the general channel. They think it's secure, but not from the likes of me."

She tapped her keyboard. Hollis didn't like how completely he had to trust Carol, given all that had gone wrong the last time he'd trusted her plan. But she was in the car with him, and that meant that again, she was taking the risk. He tried to breathe, but it was hard even to stay still when every fiber of him wanted to run.

Because, he thought now, it was entirely possible that some of those who were watching him weren't doing so through binoculars. They could just as easily be doing it through the scopes of high-powered rifles.

"What does your little computer map show you?" Hollis asked.

"Well ..." Carol tapped her screen, hit a few keys. "That might be a problem."

"Don't say that, Carol."

"Just try to breathe."

But Hollis was finding it harder and harder to breathe. If you try to corner a fox, he'll usually rise to the occasion, call on his instincts, and calmly slip away. But if you tie that same fox down while the bigger animals came, he'd lose his cool. He'd panic. And that's how the fox that called itself Hollis Palmer felt right now.

He wanted to bolt.

Every sense within him was *screaming* for him to bolt — anything but sit here and wait for the trap to close around him.

"I see more movement," Hollis said.

"Yeah. I was going to say that. You've attracted a few more fans who I think are arriving now."

"Who?"

"Sonny Malone. And Thomas Davies."

"Not Brendan?"

"He just told the others he's coming." She bobbed her head in the tipped-down rearview, then corrected herself. "Actually, he *warned* them that he's coming. He told the others that you belong to him, and that anyone who goes after you early will have to answer to him."

Yes, that sounded like Brendan. Just because he'd somehow ended up holding the alien cube, he fancied himself the leader. But in reality, Brendan was just one more alpha trying in vain to lead a pack of other alphas. They wouldn't listen. Every one of them had a reason to be excited by Beef's news: that Hollis Palmer, who they'd just rather coincidentally realized they'd been able to track using the alien network all along, was about to walk in front of them with his neck exposed.

"How did Sonny and Thomas respond to that?" Hollis asked.

"Sonny said he's got a score to settle with you, but that's not really an answer. But Thomas ..."

"What about Thomas?"

"Well, turns out your buddy Carl delivered Mia's message."

Hollis remembered that one: *Tell him there's a guy here who fucked his wife.*

Dammit, Mia. And Dammit, Carl. You were supposed to know that was a joke.

"He's not happy," Carol added from the backseat.

"Who else?"

"The ladies, of course. Though to be fair, Becky Bones sounds like she has a bigger problem with 'the asshole who hit her' than you." Carol shrugged. "Probably thinks it's Mia. Let's *hope* she thinks it's Mia, so she hangs back until Mia arrives."

Hollis wanted to tell Carol to tell Mia not to arrive at all, but that was cowardice talking. If they were really out there waiting, then what would stop the waiting and start the clock would be Mia showing up. And that, Hollis knew, could be soon. If the bigger threat could just hold off until ...

"Shit," Carol said.

"What?"

"Reptars. Heading this way."

"Maybe they'll eat our buddies."

"Sort of doubt it. They're on the same side these days."

"How long?"

"Hard to say. But not long." Now Carol's voice, which had remained calm, was starting to falter. Hearing it made Hollis's composure drop a notch. As long as she'd been cool and acted like he was the cheese in the trap — which he was — then he could manage. It was like watching the flight attendants on a bumpy flight: If they stayed calm, there was no reason to worry. But Carol's cracking voice and shallowing breath was like wild eyes on a stewardess. Shit was about to go down, and it was too late to run.

"They'll ruin everything," Hollis said.

"Just stay calm. Just ..."

Something crashed through the brush to the side of the road. Hollis barely saw it. It sprung before he could get eyes on it, looking in that brief flash like an oversized panther. A moment later it was on the roof, ripping through the steel above. Hollis flinched down, forgetting the wheel in a second of panic, thinking only: *Thank God Sonny got a hardtop.* If the Chevelle had a cloth roof, he'd be dead already.

Hollis was breathing hard and fast, feet stabbing at the ground, hand moving to the gearshift.

"Wait," Carol said.

But another reptar came. And another, and another. Now there were two on the hood and one on the trunk, staring in at him with their alien yellow eyes. More were arriving by the second, circling the car like gunslingers. Their mouths opened wide, showing concentric rows of teeth and that hideous blue glow they held deep inside. But worst of all was the purring sounds they made, like bones rattling inside a crypt.

"Not yet, Hollis." Carol, barely keeping it together. Her lifeline was the computer. He could see her, now unafraid to turn, hugging the thing like a child. She kept staring at the screen — better, surely, than staring at the monsters outside.

Claws pierced the roof. The windshield shattered. They were only playing with him.

And then humans, from the weeds, beginning to shoot.

"Hollis? *YOU HAVE TO WAIT!*"

But fuck that.

Hollis's foot mashed clutch, gas, clutch. He went from first to second gear automatically. But now he could hear shouting and knew it wasn't aliens, knew it wasn't their pursuers, knew it was shit hitting a very particular spinning fan.

"That's them," Hollis said, hitting the brake. He'd dropped three of the reptars to the ground but the one on the hood remained, others climbing back in a swarm as the car came to a stop ahead of the closed gate. "That's Mia and Theo."

"It's too late. They surrounded us." She was looking at her screen, tapping madly. "They know we're on the network. They know we can watch them watching you."

Hollis shot the car forward again, then broke again, then reversed and blind-dashed backward with the pedal to the ground. He knocked a few of the attacking reptars aside but seemed to harm none. Those on the car had spilled again, but again came forward.

They were playing with him, like a cat with prey. They weren't killing him outright, just as he could tell from the screams that the monsters from the other flank hadn't killed Theo and Mia outright, either.

That, more than anything, snapped Hollis out of fear and into high-octane flight. Because if they were really toying with them? Well, that *seriously* pissed him off.

Stopped again, he rammed forward. It was like swatting flies; if he stayed still for more than a few seconds, they regrouped and swarmed him again. The only way to keep the reptars at bay was to keep the car moving — and that wasn't going to last long.

He could see the humans now, their opportunity for ambush usurped by the reptars — and, now that Hollis looked to his rear, a trio of approaching spherical ships. He spied Brendan, arrived after all, standing tall from the roof of his Jeep. The reptars were leaving him alone.

"There's turbulence on the network, Hollis," Carol said, barely calm. "Turbulence!"

Hollis barely remembered why that mattered, though they'd talked about it in detail. Right now? Fuck the network. Fuck whatever Carol was bothering to check on, over the air, in the middle of an attack. Why would he care about something so mundane? Once upon a time he'd cared about the Fortress of Refuse, and music as a weapon, and mind control, and cuffing people to beds for their own good. Right now, that felt years in the past.

Mia.

He could still hear her. Just as he could hear Theo.

Hollis sat tall, stretching to look around as best he could through all the insect-like bodies suffusing them. As he stretched, someone (Sonny? Vika, who he'd now seen as well?) nearly blew his head off. He heard rat-a-tat and the passenger side window shattered, falling onto the seat in safety cubes. In its place; the limb of a reptar and then its face, black jaws opening, breath like rotten meat.

He stomped the pedal, swerved, running over something with a satisfying crack. He heard a new scream now — one of the reptars under the wheels, its limb broken.

"Oh, hell," Carol said from her position now deep in the footwells. "The hive mind did *not* like that."

He couldn't believe she was still back there, all attention on the computer, monitoring turbulence and alien mood and a bunch of shit he'd long ago stopped considering. In some distant way, he understood its importance. *The right amount of turbulence ...* But why did it matter when the world was ending?

It'd probably only been thirty seconds since the attack began, but to Hollis, it felt like a lifetime. How was Mia still screaming? And where the hell was she?

Another volley of fire. Slugs hit the velour of the dashboard, the cloth of the seat. There was a tremendous screeching sound — reptars screaming, it seemed — and one whole side of the vehicle cleared as they rushed away. He could see Mia now, crouched with Theo to one side of the road, surrounded by reptars who wouldn't strike, would only taunt. And the anger returned.

He shifted into first, jockeyed the wheel. Released the clutch, punched the gas like he had a grudge. Which, he supposed, he had.

The reptars that had fled the car's side, he saw now, had surrounded a two-woman open-top vehicle: pink-hair and Vika, ridiculously with their hands up. Vika still held a weapon, but was making a show of keeping her hands off it.

That's why the reptars had left. They'd gone over to the people shooting, to make it clear that they'd better not do it again.

This fight is theirs, Hollis thought. *They won't hurt Brendan's people if they don't have to, but they won't have them shooting where aliens might be hit, either.*

Hollis centered on Mia. Hit the gas, swerving right, knocking one side of the reptar circle aside like bowling pins.

"*Critical disturbance!*" Carol shouted of her laptop's screen. "The network activity has gone from—!"

Reverse. Forward again. Carol rocked and spilled in the back seat as Hollis worked the stick and wheel, thrashing the car like a living thing. It had worked so well last time, using Sonny's jacked-up Chevelle to bash away the creatures holding Mia and Theo. The idea that they'd thought this would be orderly — that they could fool the people without having to fool the aliens and that Mia might have approached the car calmly — felt like a distant memory.

"They're agitated, Hollis! Give them a focus!"

But Hollis could barely hear Carol. He slammed the car beside the huddle one last time and then leaned over and kicked the passenger door open almost hard enough to break Mia's face.

Mia was up. It was farther than he'd thought. Too far to go. She rose anyway — clothes ripped and hair a mess, but seemingly whole. Whatever she'd done with that first reptar wouldn't be repeated. These, once they were done playing, were aiming to kill.

She wobbled, in shock. Another reptar came from the right, seeing her, now starting to trot.

"RUN!"

But the beast was faster, faster, almost on her. The others were shifting, watching, almost pausing to see what was about to happen. Mia stumbled, saw it, tried to move. But she was too slow, and it was coming, and the entire melee had frozen with Mia at the center and the villain coming from stage right on articulated legs of keratin or some alien analogue, Mia stumbling, almost falling, and she wasn't going to make it and Hollis's outstretched arm wasn't going to reach her until—

She flew suddenly forward, against the car's side and barely missing a smack on the frame. As she climbed in, Hollis saw what had happened. Behind her was Theo, off-balance with his arms out. He'd rushed, he'd shoved, and Hollis could see on his face that he knew exactly what it was about to cost him.

He was gone in a blink. First there was Theo, and then there was a blur of alien, and then there was nothing. Hollis didn't see where he went and didn't want to look. He saw the blood, and that was enough.

Mia, jolted from her shock, closed the door just as the

wave of departed reptars returned, the lead creature shoving its head immediately inside, teeth out, turning, ready to finish what the one that'd missed Mia hadn't been able to.

"DRIVE! NOW!"

Carol from the backseat footwell with glass shattering all around her, not remotely necessary.

Hollis hit the gas, first to second without a hitch, to third gear just as the front of the Chevelle rammed the gate, into the Astral building's grounds, headed directly at the hundreds of ships and on-ground aliens, into Hell.

36

———

THEO WAS GONE, but Mia couldn't think about that right now.

Her hands, moving ahead of her brain, moved into triage: patted her chest and stomach, *whole*, fingers to her head and hair, *also whole*. Somehow she was intact. Things wouldn't have stayed that way, though. Theo was proof of that. One of them had been coming for her, and she'd barely seen it before Theo had pushed her out of the way and taken the brunt himself.

The blood, on her shirt, was his. Her hands made their lap again: *confirmed, no holes or slashes in Mia.* Just bits of her friend. Just bits of the man who saved her life, at the cost of his own.

You can't think about that now, the voice of instinct — of survival — said from deep within her.

And that was fine, really, because the path from the main road to the building, was mostly a road but half a path — rutted, and no good at all at whatever speed Hollis was driving right now.

"Head down," he said.

"What?"

Mia's own voice, too loud, compensating for the wind whipping by where that great black thing's head had so recently been. But Hollis didn't answer. The collision answered for him. He struck the gate, slapping it open like a pinball defeating the paddles at the bottom of a machine. Something broke off from gate or fence, shot toward the cab, and turned the windshield white with the instant spiderweb of its impact. Hollis compensated gamely, the Chevelle swerving only a little. His eyes went to the rearview, but in Mia's opinion the real problem was ahead. She saw it now, even through the smashed windshield, even while her bones and teeth rattled in time with their thrumming wheels. She saw it even as Hollis hauled ass toward it with both ships and reptars behind — driving them into the throat of the alien beast, like hounds to the hunters.

Carol was behind them, impossibly still minding her computer's screen. In her hysteria, Mia wanted to shout at her: *Didn't you see what happened to Theo? Don't you understand that we're about to die, smashed between two halves of an inescapable pincer?*

The rules of Carol's plan were laughable now, yet she was still watching the network chart, still checking stats and usages, still shouting out values that neither Mia nor Hollis could possibly give a shit about.

"Let them catch you," she said.

Mia couldn't possibly have heard right. Not only was Carol not panicked and not screaming; she'd just said the most idiotic sentence in the history of the world.

"Don't you dare!" Mia shouted at Hollis, as his eyes ticked back and forth.

"HOLLIS!" Carol barked. He looked back again, face lost,

eyes wide. There was no way out, and this was the face of a man who knew it.

Why did we come here? Why didn't we run?

And a voice said: *Plan A, Mia. Slow your roll. Settle. Cool your jets. Take a chill pill. Put your feet up, and sit a spell.*

Carol, meeting Hollis's eyes as Hollis's eyes ignored the road ahead and all its troubles, went on calmly: *"Let them catch you."*

She didn't mean the reptars chasing them.

She meant the humans chasing them.

Recognition came to Hollis's eyes. And then Mia remembered what they'd said — Carol, but especially Theo: *The humans and the aliens made a deal. If anything is a ticket to the grand ball, it's those assholes who'll come for you.*

Because that had been the plan, right? They were supposed to wait, let Brendan and all the others who'd come gather in full, and then drop Mia into the car and do ... well ... exactly what they were doing now — the surprise shit-ton of aliens ready to bite them in half not withstanding.

Hollis slowed. The reptars were in the lead, but predictably the humans were behind them, following the chase into the Astral compound. So instead of just slowing — which would cover their car with alien assailants all over again — Hollis made a slow loop. He came behind Brendan's Jeep before Brendan saw it coming. Then all of a sudden they were surrounded: Brendan to the front, Beef and Sonny sharing a car to the left, Becky and Vika in a car to the right. There were other cars in the high-speed caravan as well, one of which probably contained Mia's ex-husband (or actually *current* husband) Thomas. *Thomas,* who had the most personal grudge of all.

The herd of alien insects made the same loop and came in just behind. Now there were just two groups storming the compound: the humans with Hollis, Mia, and Carol in the middle and their enemies confused all around them, and the horde of reptars rushing behind with three spherical ships in tow.

"Critical," Carol said. "We're at critical."

Still calm. Still focused. Mia knew this, but still struggled to make sense of what she might be talking about.

"*Where do I go? Where do I go?*" Hollis asked, frantic. Through the windshield, an impassable line of shuttles loomed. There were alien troops there as well — both types, this time.

There was only one place he could go, and that's what Carol told him now. He could only drive straight ahead, into the line of spheres. He couldn't dodge and he couldn't evade — not as long as the beings who ran those ships cared to stop him. The trick, Carol had said, was to make them stop caring.

They don't hate us, Theo had said. *They're too logical for that. They don't hate us because they can't hate us, and that's how we're going to win.*

Whatever best served the aliens, Theo had said, was what they'd do. They didn't hold grudges. They didn't harbor hate, or consider revenge. They were efficient above all else. The job, then, was to create a problem worth correcting — and to become a problem worth letting go.

It was all academic to Mia, who was scared out of her mind.

But in the end it didn't matter. The opportunity to run — to truly *run* — had passed. And that, Mia remembered, was why they'd agreed to this suicide run in the first place — why they'd baited Beef, waited for him to spread the word, then lined up and let them all amass like sitting ducks. There'd been no question of evasion after Hollis had touched the cube inside Brendan's trailer; that's when the die had been cast. They couldn't go to Vail or anywhere else and just escape. The aliens could now track Hollis better than Brendan had once tracked Mia ... and because the aliens could do it, so could the humans who were privy to the alien network. Hollis was forever on the grid now, whether he liked it or not. He was a blinking dot, like a beacon.

"Remember," Carol said from the back seat, "it's the humans we have to worry about."

Mia knew that, too — or had at least once believed it — but could no longer remember why.

Just as it seemed they'd run into the shuttles and waiting alien soldiers, the line of spheres split and let them storm past. Their human partners had an all-access pass. The aliens didn't understand humans — hadn't quite gotten the message that they didn't think as a collective whole. So the ships had behaved exactly the way Carol and Theo had predicted: If they were with Brendan's party, the gates would open.

And they did, and seconds later they were in.

"Carol! Now wh—?"

But their victory was short-lived. A car T-boned theirs, shoving it violently sideways. They were inside a courtyard outside the utilitarian-looking building and the newcomer had circled to come from starboard. The Chevelle stopped suddenly, engine smoking, the shaft of the T-bone now locked tightly to the upright. He'd hit the front, near the engine. Good thing, or Mia's door would have been crushed and she'd surely be dead.

But she wasn't dead. She was still thinking, still moving, now climbing out the passenger side door with her wrist wrapped tightly with Hollis's hand. The man inside the new car exited too, and for a long second, with the alien horde now blending into the already existing horde around the building and encircling them like spectators to a grudge match, both drivers stared at each other across the smoking hoods of the two destroyed cars.

Thomas.

And Hollis.

37

"HEY, HOLLIS," Thomas said. He was holding a semiautomatic handgun. His eyes flicked to Mia, then to the point where they conjoined — where Hollis had her by the wrist. It was a dragging posture, but it was also contact: skin-to-skin, with a woman who'd been his wife. Or was still, as the case may be.

"Thomas," Hollis replied.

"It's been a long time."

The reptars weren't attacking. The ships, from around the building and beyond the fence, weren't attacking. Maybe the aliens didn't understand. Carol and Theo had both agreed: Based on all they'd seen, the deal between Brendan's group and the aliens was already underway. The aliens were openly sharing access to their network and the humans were ... well ... still alive to use it. Between the parties in the deal, the aliens had a clear upper hand. But both were honoring it, for better or for worse.

Right now, the human players were getting out of their cars, forming the inside of the open circle around Thomas, Hollis, Mia, and Carol. Mia couldn't see Carol right now, but she'd seen her stir and knew she was unhurt. Then Mia turned her head and *did* see her, without her computer but still holding that uber-jailbroken phone of hers. She was looking at the screen and watching the territorial display unfolding in front of them. They were now only fifty feet from the building — big, boring-looking structure that it was.

Carol looked like she might say something to Mia, but she didn't dare. Everyone was watching. In the encircling crowd, Mia spied Brendan, Sonny Malone, Becky Bones, Beef, Vika of the Flesh Eaters, plus a few additional Flesh Eaters and other miscellaneous crew. Everyone had turned out. That was a talent Hollis had, and Mia supposed that even now she had to admire its power. The whole world might be ending, and yet this troupe had formed, in part, over their common hatred of Hollis Palmer — their desire to right some petty wrong he'd committed, and watch him pay.

Thomas and Hollis were still standing-off.

"So what now?" Hollis asked. "You gonna kill me?"

"I'm not sure," Thomas told him, shrugging with the gun in his hand, keeping this light. "You know me, Hollis. Normally I'd make a speech. I'd set you down around my big table, with all my knuckle-breakers and face-beaters, and you'd have the place of honor across from me. A lot of times I could get the guy in that seat to piss his pants before we even got to work. It was an art. But right here I got nothin.'"

Hollis looked around the circle. This had started with Thomas, and it looked like it was going to end with Thomas. The other humans all wanted their piece of Hollis, but they were standing back, all with weapons at the ready should Hollis or Mia decide to try their trademark vanishing act.

Hollis pulled Mia closer. Pointedly, he put an arm around her waist.

"You *do* got nothin,'" Hollis said.

Thomas pretended to ignore this, but a cloud passed his face before he spoke again.

"What did you even do with my case, Hollis?" he asked. "There's no way you sold it."

"He tried," said Brendan from the edge of the circle.

Then Sonny: "But then he stabbed the buyer in the back and destroyed it."

Thomas clearly didn't care. He put on a face anyway and said, "That wasn't very nice of you."

Hollis raised his free arm. The other stayed around Mia.

"Just do it, Thomas. Just shoot us. Everyone's watching. If you don't do it, they will. So go ahead. I don't need a big exit. You draw this out, you lose your turn. You make that big speech you'd normally make, Becky Balls over there is gonna get impatient and come in to do it herself."

"Becky *Bones*," Becky Bones said through gritted teeth.

"Yeah, I'm sure she does."

They stood. Watched. Waited. Mia realized that nobody knew what came next.

One second. Two seconds. Three.

She stopped trying to be subtle. She stopped just peeking at their surroundings with her eyes and turned her whole head instead. Nobody, it was clear, had any idea what was about to happen — or, more accurately, what was *supposed* to happen. All the hoodlums dotting the circle's inside perimeter had put on brave faces, but on closer inspection Mia could see fear — *deep* fear — in every single one of them. There might be two hundred aliens in a ring outside of the human ring, most of them the insect-like reptars, and not one human in the group trusted their fragile alliance enough to have faith they'd remain at bay. The line of car-sized shuttles had shifted: many still hovering a foot above the ground, many others swarming the sky. Mia could see unrest in their movements. The way unrestful thoughts would buzz in a disturbed mind, that's how the shuttles were buzzing now. Their very lack of unison spoke volumes. This was a hive mind in the midst of a decision it found hard to make.

What that decision was, Mia couldn't guess. Although Carol had. And Theo had.

Carol had come up behind them. Mia whispered, "Why aren't they attacking?"

And Carol said, "I think it's because they want to see what happens."

Alien curiosity. It was the one common denominator in everything they'd seen.

A shadow fell over the gathering on the lawn. Most human heads looked up. The aliens stayed focused. They already knew what they'd see.

It was the downtown mothership high above, moved in to rest above the complex.

Without the sun, the temperature dropped. But that wasn't the only reason Mia started shivering.

Thomas's gun came up. But it was shaking on the end of his hand.

"Do it, Thomas," Hollis said. "I ain't got all day."

Thomas's arm moved like a hinge. Now he was pointing the gun at Mia.

"Maybe I'll shoot my whore wife first," he said.

Mia's heart hammered in her chest. She watched the gun's muzzle, on the end of that fearful arm. His attempt to hide the fear made him dangerous. She saw Thomas swallow. She saw him regrip the weapon, as if his hands were growing slick.

Go on, Mia thought now, but it was more of a mental goad than a wish. *Go on and do it, you coward.* But then her lips made the tiniest, tiniest of smiles. She realized he couldn't do it. He wouldn't. He'd want to save face in front of his human audience, but it was the alien one that bothered him. They were going to let him shoot whoever he wished, but there had to be a catch. The moment felt surreal, in the shadow of the mothership. The city itself was holding its breath.

"What the fuck are you smiling about?" Thomas demanded.

What came next was the most curious of sensations. Mia had never experienced anything remotely like it. It was as if the entire world had erupted in whispers, only no mouths opened. She heard snippets of rumor and supposition, as if a great crowd was weighing in on this, giving its opinions — yet nobody spoke. She could pull out no true words but could feel all the emotions. And yet, the emotions themselves felt fake. They were facsimiles of feelings, not feelings for real. They were things copied but uncomprehended. They were words mouthed in a tongue the speaker didn't know, hoping the right meaning was being conveyed.

She was hearing them all. Inside her mind.

All the other humans were looking from one to the other, unsettled. They weren't hearing any of what she was; that much was clear from their faces. But they were sensing it, the way you'd sense a cold spot in a room. It was ghost phenomenon, like the surety that you're being followed even when you're technically not.

The alien mass began to shift. A non-auditory murmur percolated through them.

"What?" Thomas asked.

But of course nothing, objectively, was going on at all. He was responding to nothing concrete, doubly unsettled because he was self-conscious. Spooked like a kid entering a basement, irrationally scared of the dark.

His eyes moved side to side. It seemed, at any moment, that he might start shooting without focus. Shooting his allies dead, just for looking in his direction.

Across from Mia and Hollis, behind Thomas, the clot of reptars began to part. There was one — only one — reptar in a newly formed corridor.

And she heard the minds again. The mind. It was singular, yet disjointed. Because about this one being, the collective had an opinion. Questions. Uncertainties.

And she knew without question that this was the reptar she'd faced at the Exchange. The one who'd been cut from the collective, seemingly plucked from the Exchange and partially reabsorbed.

But only partially. Because the others, who'd never left the hive mind, couldn't quite understand its singular experiences. Its soft-formed habits of thinking alone.

She felt the group defer to it. Ask it questions.

Thomas turned. Looked behind him.

"What's going on?" Hollis whispered to Mia and Carol — whoever might be able to answer the question.

Carol shook her head. Mia watched the reptar. All she could get from it were senses of the indistinct. All she knew was a wave of thought, diluted but heavy with intention.

Thomas remained perfectly still while the beast approached him. When it was a foot away, his lack of movement turned into outright paralysis. The gun hand had fallen. The sawtoothed thing sighed near enough to riffle Thomas's hair.

Then it reached up with its front legs. The legs moved to his head. Thomas shivered as the point-ended things ran along his cheeks and pressed into his ears.

But just when Mia thought it meant to skewer his brain, it made a flicking motion and something hit the dust at Thomas's feet. It was his earplugs.

More reptars approached the others around the circle. With the same flicks, they removed all the humans' earplugs. Then Mia felt a chill behind her, and she heard Hollis and Carol's breath quicken. Something entered her own ears, and when it was gone, she could hear so much better. The world was both loud and quiet. Loud because all the little noises were back. Quiet because into the stillness, nobody dared to speak.

Something descended from the mothership on a beam of light.

And then the sounds — nothing like music, this time — began.

38

HOLLIS KNEW it wasn't music, coming out of the thing the mothership dropped. But still he heard the strains of Beto y Los Fairlanes, playing live at Liberty Lunch. And from the same venue, the early days of The Toadies and Sonic Youth. He heard Trish Hinojosa — unknown to most, collected once upon a time by Hollis. Guy Clarke, Jr. and Dale Watson. He heard blues. He heard rock n' roll. Inside his memory, he felt the birth of something new.

It's not real.

But did that matter? It was so comfortable here.

Some part of Hollis knew exactly where he was. He knew Thomas was right in front of him, still holding his gun. He knew there was a veritable who's who of Hollis haters ringing him and the two women, and he was very aware that the lawn was filled with creatures and their ships. He remembered the mothership arriving; he'd watched the object descend to settle on the grass. But as clear as all of that was to Hollis, he found he didn't really care.

A gravel-voiced singer. A soulful saxophone. A six-string guitar in a dimly-lit basement, the ceiling low and made of unpainted concrete. The wet scent of draft beer wafted from the tap. He could feel the seat beneath him — padded but worn — and found himself back in time, younger then, not carefree but caring differently, the whole world ahead of him both wonderful and terrible at the same time.

And a woman — a girl, really, about the age he was now — was sitting to his left. She had wavy dark brown hair, a spray of freckles, and a little upturned nose. She wore a summery dress, the kind that worked only on the young. On her feet were thin, brown-leather sandals. Her toenails were painted pink, to match both fingernails and lipstick.

When he turned, and she turned, Hollis saw that the girl had deep green eyes — the kind a guy could fall right into.

He gave his devil's smile. He had all night to talk to this girl, to go wherever their whims took them. He'd been sitting at this bar for ... oh, he had no clue how long. Somewhere in the back of his mind, he knew when he'd arrived — or did he? This was one of those moments that existed out of time. When you were in it, you were *in it*. When you left it, the spell was broken forever.

When I was younger, the girl said, *I used to come here all the time.*

Hollis turned fully to her. He said, *With your parents? Were they into music?*

She smiled. It was an expression neither patronizing nor confused, yet he knew clearly that she understood why he'd asked the question even though it wasn't relevant — or even sensible — at all.

With my friends, she said.

He was watching her lips when in a blink, the entire bar behind her became somewhere else. It was a restaurant with vinyl-upholstered booths and bright, cheery lighting. He saw half a dozen girls flanking the one he'd been talking to (how'd he missed them before?), all sipping from straws. A waitress passed, holding a pot of coffee.

Then it was the same old bar again.

Hollis shook his head. Seeing things.

There was this little bell over the door, the girl said, *like an old-fashioned diner. To this day, whenever I hear a bell ring, I think of this place. It takes me all the way back, just like that. Just one little ring of a bell, and I'm back here in this booth with these same girls, talking about school and parents and boys.*

Hollis looked at her barstool. There was no booth. There were no other girls and no bell. There was just the music, reeling Hollis back in time.

The girl stood—

(Mia. Mia is her name.)

—and took his hand. It was forward of her, but for some reason it didn't arouse him so much as intrigue him. She felt as right as this place. She felt as right as this time.

Do you want to get out of here? she asked him.

And go where?

Anywhere, she said, *that they aren't.*

At first Hollis didn't understand. But then he followed her pointing finger and saw that there was a ring of people lining the outer walls of the bar. They covered every inch of the perimeter, two or three deep. How had he not noticed them before? They weren't dressed for the mood at all. Most were in all black, without a speck of color on them. A few were in all white. All wore helmets — not the kind motorcyclists wore, but something closer to a welding helmet, with an opaque face shield. Or perhaps they weren't helmets at all. Perhaps the oval things atop their necks were simply their heads, smooth and featureless.

Who are they? Hollis asked.

Judge, the girl said.

Jury.

And executioner.

The bodies around the perimeter stood with their arms in front, hands clasped at the waist. As if watching. As if waiting.

The room seemed to grow colder. The soft lights darkened. The music faded, becoming something different. Something worse. The whole world seemed to swim. And through the haze, Hollis felt some long-forgotten thing begin to emerge. Or *re*-emerge, because it'd been there all along.

Mia held his hand. But Mia, too, was different now.

Why are they here? Hollis asked as the illusion began to dissolve — as he began again to hear the sounds from the alien device for what it'd been all along.

She met his eyes and said, *Because they think they understand, but want to know more. Because they know got to know me a little, or think they did. Because they're interested in me and want to be interested in you, too. In all of us. All of them. Because they want to know.*

Want to know what? Hollis asked her as the room vanished and became grass and open air again.

Before the mental bubble popped the rest of the way, this younger version of Mia gave him an answer.

Who chooses to stay, she said, *and who chooses to go.*

39

MIA HELD HER FOCUS. Held her center.

She had an unfair advantage. She'd done this before. She'd looked a reptar in the eye and shared its mind. She'd felt the press of all those thoughts from outside herself, and made space for them inside. She and Hollis had both fallen into trances, then been extricated. They knew. *She* knew.

With Hollis's hand in hers, she pulled. The illusion was strong, but she made herself push it away. Reality, right here and now, kind of sucked. The days of sitting in the booths at Mackie's with her friends, as evoked by the alien machine, had been so much better. Back then, she'd had all the freedom of adulthood but none of its responsibility. Her parents had still paid all the bills. Life had been fun — the very definition of carefree. The girl she'd been back then would never have plotted to marry a mobster and con him blind. But this was the world she lived in, and those days had been whispers on the wind. They'd lived only for a time, and there was no way to go back now.

She pulled Hollis. Pulled and pulled, until his eyes cleared.

Across from them, down the hollow the others had made for it, was the reptar. *Her* reptar.

She met its yellow eyes.

We are not saving you. We are not sparing you.

Mia understood. What the aliens were doing, with their memory machine, was not a trap. It was not a reward or a punishment. It was neutral. It just *was*. They would all respond as they would — Hollis and Mia and Carol for sure, but also Thomas and Beef and all the rest. She looked, now, at Beef. Dreaming of a hot tub full of ho's and drinking Cristal from a blinged-out chalice, maybe? Judging by the smile on his face, it could be anything.

Stay in peace, the reptar's mind said to her, *or go in death.*

To Mia, the dichotomy was a false one. *Staying* was death. Going was ... well, it sure wouldn't be peace, but it wasn't dying, either. Yet she saw the alien's point. She could imagine how this must seem, watching individual human dreams from their hive-mind perspective. Living, for all of them, was its own breed of unrelenting torment. Buddha himself had said that existence was suffering, and the aliens, ironically, would probably agree.

Vika was smiling in her false vision.

Stay in peace.

As was Sonny. As was Becky.

Or go in death.

The machine in their middle was a bomb. Now that she'd made her choice — hard reality over easy fantasy — she could see that plainly.

"Carol," she said.

But Carol, who'd never experienced the trance before, showed no signs of budging.

Mia shook her. *"Carol!"*

The alien mind — mostly shared, but with one sharp

edge where the re-integrated individual reptar hadn't quite come all the way back to center — whispered in Mia's ear.

Let her stay.

"Carol. Come on. We've got to go."

Tugging. And tugging.

The frontmost reptars stepped forward. Again the voice said, *Let that one stay, if that is her choice.*

"It's not a choice," Mia said.

Hollis looked at her, confused. But before he could ask, he saw the bomb, too. It was the same as what they'd dropped in Ukraine. The same bomb they'd dropped in downtown Austin, when the armies had begun their fighting. It had the same mechanical face, its parts chugging and clanking, counting down.

"Do you hear me?" Mia shouted at the reptars, still advancing. *"It's not a choice!"*

She wishes the illusion.

But Mia knew the aliens didn't understand. They didn't know the human mind. They expected it to be like their own.

"Then show her," Mia said. *"Show her* that it's an illusion."

Hollis was looking between Mia and the reptars, surely wondering why she was holding up what appeared to be only half of a conversation. But in the end it didn't matter. Now fully awake — and immune to re-immersion even without earplugs now, it seemed — Hollis simply ducked low and lifted Carol over his shoulders in a fireman's carry. He stepped forward, found himself faced by a mixed line of buglike and humanlike aliens, and waited. If they were going to kill him, his body said, then so be it. But if they weren't going to end him, they'd better let him through.

The reptars parted. As viciously as they'd come after

them all before, they seemed uninterested in harming them now. Hollis stepped through.

"They're letting us go," Hollis said as they reached the back of the line and began to run. Carol was heavy on Hollis's back, but his legs found their own motivation to push on anyway, as the giant device clanked behind them.

Mia didn't reply to that. She didn't know the answer. She'd probably never know the answer.

They reached the gate. It was easy to pass, after all the damage the car had done. And when they were past — when they'd reached the road beyond — they finally turned back to look.

What they saw chilled Mia's blood. The reptars were parting in a unified wave, heading for the spherical ships, boarding them, taking off. More ships came and more aliens came from the building. Then those ships left the ground as well, and rose to the underbelly of the mothership, and together all of the ships began to float away.

The lawn was once again drenched in sun, now with only the ring of glassy-eyed humans and the big alien machine.

"Rats from a sinking ship," Hollis said of the exodus.

Inside Mia's mind, she heard Theo's voice — poor, departed Theo, who'd kept her alive. Kept all three of them alive, as things turned out.

This isn't going well for them. The Fortress? The database? It's barely worth their effort.

Then: *We can't destroy the Astral building. The only thing that could possibly destroy it is—*

Hollis's words: *Rats from a sinking ship.*

—is themselves.

40

BRENDAN WAS, he was pretty sure, in a loud little punk rock club with a thriving, thrashing mosh pit. That was strange, because a moment earlier he could have sworn he'd been part of a group of people managing a very tense, Mexican stand-off type of situation.

He knew there was someone he was very mad at

(Hollis)

and someone he was rooting for, yet wished he'd let someone else have some of the glory,

(Thomas)

but most of all he remembered a feeling of peril. He was sure, in fact, that he'd been convinced he might die, no matter what deal he'd struck.

But, whatever. Now all that really mattered was the club. And the sound. And the band onstage, which was one of his favorites. The speakers were so loud, he had to shout to be heard, and even then it was hard to hear anyone who spoke back. He'd had a dream, once, that he'd gone all survivalist, moved to the woods, and started amassing both weapons and an army. It'd been very quiet, then. But this was no dream. This was real life. And right now, Brendan (who thought he was maybe 17 years old, but was for some reason unsure) wanted nothing to do with the woods, guns, or armies. Life, right now, was just a series of concerts. The mosh pit kicked you around; you left exhausted with sweat soaked through all your layers of clothes; you got three hours of sleep after driving all the way home and then maybe went to school the next day or maybe didn't. Depended whether Mom was still drunk or not.

But here? In the club? This was Brendan's jam.

"You can go, if you want!" someone was shouting.

Brendan looked over. It was a tall women, mid-30s. Attractive in a MILF sort of way.

"What?" Brendan shouted back.

"I said, you can go!"

She'd leaned very close to his ear to say that. But what she'd said still didn't really make any sense.

He turned away. The lady was nuts, but so what? This was one of his favorite songs. The pit was hopping. Brendan, who couldn't quite remember how he'd gotten here, was feeling good.

The woman tapped his shoulder. What was worse, somehow she'd turned down the music. The club, so vivid and sharp a moment ago, was now a little cloudy, as if filled with smoke. Punk shows were supposed to be dark, but the walls had grown thin and now he could see inches of sun between the boards of his vision.

Brendan turned.

"What?" He didn't have to shout to be heard. The music was quieter, and the band was harder to name. Brendan didn't like that. The whole thing had felt good, and now this bitch was taking it away. He was ... He was ... Well, he was *some* young age, knee-deep in what people that age did.

Was he eighteen?

Twenty-five?

Or was he, as he was starting to suspect, well past thirty with his head stuck in a dream?

The woman was no longer speaking to Brendan. She was speaking to someone else — a dark shadow that it hurt Brendan to look at too closely.

"Then show her," the woman said. "*Show her* that it's an illusion."

So, clearly, not talking about Brendan because Brendan wasn't a "her." But she *had* spoken to him earlier (or had she?) and she *had* tapped him on the shoulder a few seconds ago (or had he just imagined it?), so the same words could probably apply to him. They should, really.

Show him. Show him that it's an illusion.

That what was an illusion? Brendan knew of no illusion. He was just hanging out, listening to some of his favorite tunes way back in time.

Except that he wasn't, and never had been. He was, in fact, standing on the lawn outside the Astral building — not wearing his favorite teenage band's T-shirt, but instead wearing camouflage pants and a sidearm he planned to use to shoot several holes in Hollis Palmer's head.

He blinked. The club was gone because he'd never actually been in a club. The music was gone because he'd never actually heard any music. That had been some alien mind trick, the illusion finally obvious.

Disoriented and a little lost, Brendan looked around. He saw a handful of people on the lawn with him — Thomas Davies, that pink-haired warrior chick, and all the others that Beef's revelation over the walkie-talkies had drawn together.

Hollis Palmer is meeting someone at 5pm outside the Astral facility? The same Hollis Palmer we've been chasing for God knows how long, finally pinned down to one spot? Count us right the fuck in!

A whole club coming together, united in hatred of a man against which they had a score to settle.

But something was missing.

Before his mind had taken its little trip down memory lane, they'd all been standing in more or less the same spots. But at that point, there'd been a whole lot of others. Hollis, Mia, and that other woman for one; right now there was nobody in the middle of the circle to hate. But also all the aliens. They were gone now. Not a single bug in the distance, not a single ship in the sky.

There was a sound, though. It was coming from the big boxy thing his eyes had seen but his mind still hadn't bothered to register. It now formed the circle's center, as if they'd all come to this empty lawn outside what now looked like an empty building just to pay it homage.

The sounds it made were enormous and mechanical, like the operation of a hydraulic press.

The others were blinking now. Coming out of their own memory-scented delusions, perhaps. They were all looking around, noticing the absence of both prey and predators, mumbling various versions of, *What the hell were we doing and where did everyone go?*

But Vika was the first to name the noisy object in their center — something Brendan had previously seen first-hand in another time and place.

"Shit," she said. "It's one of those bombs."

Its face chugging through permutations: senseless glyphs in an alien language, counting down to zero.

"It's okay, yo," Beef said with his mouth full of marbles, looking down at a watch the size and brilliance of a bar of gold. "They count down for sixty-six minutes. We still got—"

That was all Beef said in the moment.

It was all Beef ever said again.

41

———

THE EXPLOSION KNOCKED Hollis onto his face. They'd probably gotten a half-mile away from the Astral building and the bomb on its doorstep, yet the shockwave was still like six giants punching him in the back. He didn't, in any way, see it coming. One minute he was rushing on as best he could with Carol over his shoulders, the road ahead. The next he was eating grass and gravel. There'd been no transition. No sense of falling. It was as if the world itself had blinked, and there'd been pain and a whole new point of view.

Something crushed his head, making the impact worse. It was Carol, falling from high, hitting the ground like a sack of bricks. Luckily her head had been on Hollis's right side; if she'd been slung the other way she'd probably have struck the concrete of the road's surface rather than the berm. As limp as she was, her head would probably have whip-cracked against the stone and that'd have been it. When Hollis was a kid, they used to call any scalp wound "cracking your head open." But for Carol, with that degree of impact, the expression might have been literal. Like a walnut crushed beneath a boot, hair parting to show pink brain.

But instead, she was merely as dazed as Hollis. Merely as bruised as Hollis — and Mia, who'd been thrown into a roadside ditch full of fetid moss-water.

Hollis looked back. It took airburst to create a mushroom cloud, but the explosion of the alien bomb had created something like an enormous white bush. Like fog in a very contained spot, wider than three Astral buildings set end-to-end.

"Shit," Hollis said. He'd inhaled gravel. That's how it felt, anyway. He was bleeding. But whatever; he'd bled so much lately, it'd lost its novelty.

Mia was up, also looking back. She met Hollis's eye.

"You okay?"

"I doubt it."

"Carol okay?"

Carol groaned, then rolled over.

"I thought we had 66 minutes," Mia said.

"I guess they were feeling more decisive. No need for suspense." But, Hollis realized, the quick-fire of the bomb meant something else, as well. When they'd left the circle, all their human buddies had still been staring into space — probably trapped inside of mindfucks like the bar fantasy he'd been in himself, before Mia had yanked him out of it ... *again*, he realized. The bomb's radius wasn't as large as it'd been in Serpukhov (if it had, they'd be dead right now), but it'd been enough to level the Astral building and any assholes still left on its grounds. So Plan A had worked after all. He hadn't believed it would — or that if it did, it wouldn't be kind enough to take Brendan and all his buddies with it.

Carol sat up, blinking with confusion. She looked at the

explosion cloud, which was sticking around like a show-off, then at Hollis and Mia.

"I was with my husband," she said. "We were dancing."

"Maybe go back," Hollis said. "It sucks out here."

"I thought about it," Carol said, though Hollis hadn't expected a response. "But then I got this very clear impression that I was in a dream, and I could choose to stay or go."

"So you took the red pill," Hollis said.

She clearly didn't get it. People these days. "I decided to wake up," she said.

That made Hollis look back at the Astral grounds. Had *they* woken up? Probably didn't matter much now.

Carol shook her head. Then she stood up, even though Hollis and Mia remained sitting. She started to walk in circles, pacing herself back to reality.

She looked at the explosion again.

"The whole building?"

"Plan A," Hollis confirmed.

"I wasn't sure it'd work," Carol said.

"Thanks for letting us know," Hollis said. But he knew why she hadn't, and why Theo hadn't. Hollis had had a hard enough time steeling his balls for the waiting game outside the gates. All that'd kept him from turning yellow was his belief that Carol could read the alien network as well as she claimed to be able, and was sure that if the balance tipped the wrong way, the aliens would decide to end their failed experiment. Ideally without killing all of them at the same time, though the probability of dying for the greater good had always been Plan A's biggest downside.

Carol tossed Hollis a look, conveying what he already knew. Then she slipped her phone from her pocket. Its screen had been cracked, but from where Hollis was sitting, it looked otherwise whole.

"I can't get on the network," she said.

"Shit."

"No, no," Carol said, holding up a hand. "I was getting in through the connection they gave to Brendan. If I can't get on, it means that connection was either cut off or destroyed."

"Along with the Astral building?"

"Separate, but related." She tapped a bit, but without a way to see the network, there was little to check. She re-pocketed it.

Mia stood. Hollis stood as well. He watched Mia's face before she spoke, seeing her concern.

"Theo said that if Hollis had blown up the power station that first morning, the aliens probably would have abandoned their project as not worth fixing ... but because the database was still intact and running, the 'zombie' thing would have continued to spread out of control."

Carol nodded. "The ultimate catchy song. Yes, that's what I think would have happened, too."

"But if the database itself was destroyed ..." She trailed off.

Carol shrugged. "I don't know. Maybe it's still spreading, or maybe it's over like we thought it might be. What do you think?"

"Me?" Mia asked.

"Well," Carol said meaningfully. "What do you *feel.*"

Mia blinked more, seeming to try and focus inward. But the Zen-like calm she'd shown about the alien mind before was gone, and in its place Hollis saw only raw edges.

"I don't know. I can't feel anything at all."

"You were talking to that thing before we left," Hollis said. "To the reptar."

Mia nodded. "I think it was the one I connected with at

the Exchange. They must have let it back into their collective. Maybe that's why they all stopped: they recognized me because it had once recognized me." She shook her head. "No. I was feeling it before the bomb went off. I understood some things, like I understood some things before. But it's all gone now. I can't feel anything. After the Exchange, I still felt *something*."

Hollis watched her. It was a question for another day. But if ending the Astral database experiment had cut Mia's connection to the alien hive, that was just fine with him.

"What about me?" Hollis asked.

"What *about* you?" Carol countered.

"Am *I* still on their radar? You said the aliens could track me."

"I imagine they still can. But in your shoes, I wouldn't worry. If they wanted you dead, they would have killed you already."

His mind turned, then, to the most pressing of questions.

"Why do you think they let us go?"

On this, though, Mia did still have an opinion — and it came with a sense of informed authority. "I feel like we passed a test," she said.

"Because we chose the real world over the Matrix?"

Mia shrugged.

"I don't know," Hollis said. "I don't really think they flew millions of miles just to hover over us like a nosy mother-in-law, judging us."

"Actually," Mia said, "I think that's *exactly* what they came to do."

Hollis looked at the explosion, which was finally starting to dissipate. "Well," he said, "I guess they can't do it now."

And Carol said, "We'll see."

42

THREE LONG DAYS LATER, walking luckless through wild lands northwest of the city, they finally found a car that still had gas in it. Gas, already, was getting harder and harder to find. Mia, though she tried not to think about it, understood why. The world often felt empty now, but in reality it was as full as ever — something they were reminded of when they passed the rare outside gathering of people. All those people still had to live, and there were no central resources anymore. Within a year, all the gas would have gone bad. After that, only diesel would remain, an increasing percentage of it home-brewed biofuel — something you could make from used cooking oil. Humanity would adapt, in time, but only after enough of the population died off and nature found its new equilibrium.

The car's contents were sparse, but when added to the few items still in Hollis and Mia's backpacks, it was enough for a road trip. They took things carefully, always with an eye out for cars from which to siphon fuel. At yet another Wal-Mart (this one intentional; Hollis was making a game of it), they took big red plastic gas cans and, at the next mall parking lot, filled those, too.

In Colorado Springs, an hour south of Denver, Mia found herself unable to take it anymore. They'd taken over a small mansion just to use the indoor pool, so while Hollis and Carol swam in clothes they found in a bedroom, Mia walked off by herself. The grounds, in any other circumstances, would have been beautiful. There was a miniature mountain just beyond the grounds and a gazebo-topped deck, its top too low to be white. There'd be no skiing in Vail, either. Maybe no skiing — other than for transportation — ever again.

She sat in a chair, looking up at the mountain.

She leaned forward with her elbows on her knees.

Then, after a few moments' contemplation, she put her face in her hands and quietly began to weep.

She was startled by a hand on her shoulder. It was soft and gentle. She looked up expecting to see Carol, but saw Hollis instead. Which wasn't cool at all, because she hadn't so much as sniffed it in before turning. She felt wet-faced, snot-nosed, and far, *far* too feminine for the likes of this.

"Hey," he said.

"Hey." *Snort.* She hadn't even grabbed any damn tissues, because she hadn't known she'd fall apart.

"Pool's nice. You should join us. When ... You know."

"When I'm done falling apart?" She sniffed again, tried on a wry, not-at-all-a-smile smile, then had to wipe her face with her hand. It was all so gross. She could feel him looking at her, not liking the vulnerability at all.

"Yeah," he said. "That."

"Are you going to make fun of me?"

"Absolutely. But maybe later."

He sat. The chairs were almost close enough to touch.

They looked at the mountain together. Sunset had come and gone. Night was so much darker now.

"Tell you a secret?" Hollis said.

"What?"

"Promise not to tell?"

"Depends what it is."

"I did the same thing," he said, rolling his hand at her general state: the tears, the snot, the surety that everything was over and nothing would be kind or nice or wonderful again, "last night."

"Pussy," she said.

"Only it was worse. Because we were in that gross house last night, with the cum stains on the ceiling. How do you even *hit* the ceiling? Shit, Mia. You think *this* is bad? Try doing it while looking up at some guy's stalactites. I was sure the sun would never rise again. And honestly, I wasn't sure I wanted it to."

Mia looked into the distance, glancing sidelong at Hollis only when he was looking away.

"That's really, really gross," she said.

"Tell me about it."

"I think so much less of you now."

"That's okay. I felt that way about you the first time we had sex, and you made that weird noise like you were clearing your throat."

"I don't do that."

"Then it was Thomas, peeking in and working his pole while we went at it."

Mia crossed her legs and sat back. Strangely, she felt better.

"I woke up anyway," Hollis said. "It helped that you were there, by then. Because the thing is, no matter how bad a picture I could make in my head, I realized the more I thought about it that I'd never be on my own to face it. Life sucks, doll. But at least it doesn't have to suck alone."

"That's cheesy as hell," she said. But, she realized, it was also true.

"We're just a few hours from Vail," he said.

She pulled a blanket from the floor. With the sun down, it was getting chilly. Duly bundled, she said, "Yeah."

"Good or bad?" he said.

"Depends if the aliens care that you're there. But you heard Carol. Brendan's little branch of the human part of that network got erased when he did, and that means that even if the aliens still want to track you, no human is."

"Does it bother you?" he said. "Going into what Carol thinks might soon be some sort of alien city with a guy who's got a target on his head?"

"I don't think it's a target. Not anymore. More like a tag. They'll just know who you are, like a person of interest."

"And *that* doesn't bother you," Hollis said.

"Nah. We're almost to Vail and we haven't seen any more people walking around brainless. Some people playing music like they used to, but it's different now. If there are no more zombies and we're still alive, that's enough."

"If *we're* still alive?" Hollis said. "Or 'I'?"

Mia reached out from under her blanked, turned onto her hip, and took his right hand in both of hers.

"We," she said.

He looked down. "I'm not really the hand-holding type," he told her.

And Mia said, "Neither am I."

43

Hollis, walking the streets of Heaven's Veil and looking up at the enormous pyramid of the blue glass Apex, didn't notice the patrol pulling up beside him until it actually stopped.

But then someone cleared his throat and Hollis turned to see an Indian man in military uniform. Hollis's pulse quickened at the sight, but it was just instinct kicking in. For three years in Vail (and then, after the conversion, in the newly minted "Heaven's Veil"), they'd been safe — and, Hollis supposed, as content as a person could be these days. They were above ground; they were in a capital instead of in the outlands; they had electricity and clean water. So they had to cow-tow a little now and then. It was still better than the alternative.

"Hollis Palmer?"

"Yeah?"

"Step in," he said, holding the door wide. Then he added, "Please."

But Hollis, still bristling even after years of alien rule no matter what velvet lining they tried to use to disguise it, felt his old self kick in, distrustful of authority.

"Who the hell are you?" he asked. Military, sure. But this guy looked highly decorated. Palace guard, even.

"I'm Captain Raj Patel. I work just under Viceroy Dempsey."

Ah. Yes. Hollis thought he looked familiar. What Captain Raj wasn't sharing was that he was also the viceroy's son-in-law. Hollis kept as far from city politics as possible, but it was hard to avoid the juiciest news, like who was the biggest nepotism-placed, power-hungry assbag ... stuff like that.

"What if I don't wanna come with you?" Hollis asked. He was still trying to puzzle out Patel's tone. The man had a reputation around Heaven's Veil of being a supreme dickhead — the kind of despot's dingleberry who'd stop someone beneath him just to demand they lick his boots clean. Everything he was doing now, on the other hand, was quiet — polite, even. If he pushed, maybe he could figure it out. Although normally, refusing a "request" like this was just asking for a kick in the teeth.

Patel pushed the door open farther, to show that he already had a passenger inside the van-sized vehicle.

Mia.

"Please," Patel repeated.

Hollis looked at Mia for help, but she only shrugged. She wasn't restrained, though, and seemed untraumatized and unharmed. Still, the implication — Raj being Raj after all — was clear. So he got in and sat beside Mia. He wouldn't take her hand, though. Doing that felt like a sign of weakness. They'd lived for years as respected members of the city, and as far as Hollis knew none of the authorities even knew there was an underground inside the city, let alone their part in it. They were just an ordinary husband and wife, doers of necessary deeds and even kept up tithes at the temple. He'd left his reputation behind, and kept his attitude in check.

The ride was short. Patel said nothing more and Hollis, unwilling to show concern, asked nothing. Still, Patel watched them both. He especially watched Mia — something that made Hollis want to demand to know just what the hell he thought he was staring at. But Hollis was wiser than he'd been in the old days, and a little less hot on the trigger. Up near 40, a guy learned to wait and see what happened before reacting violently to it. That's what grownups did, Mia kept insisting.

They pulled through the palace gate, past the guard house, and into the circular drive. On the lawn, fucking with the rest of the guards, Hollis saw someone else he recognized: the viceroy's ex-wife Heather. He'd met her once or twice. She was obnoxious, vulgar, offensive, and had no sense of boundaries. Hollis liked her a lot.

"Why are we here?" Hollis asked when they pulled to a stop.

But Patel only opened the door and, without exiting himself, said, "They're expecting you."

Hollis and Mia stepped out, avoiding a strong urge to trade curious glances. They walked to the enormous front doors as if they had every reason and right to be there (on their terms, not the viceroy's) and were wondering whether they should knock when the door opened. Behind it was a servant, accompanying the lady of the house. Hollis knew, but had not met, this one, too. The viceroy's current wife was very different from his ex, though both lived on the grounds in what struck Hollis as a weird triangle.

Where Heather was rude and raw, Piper Dempsey was sweet and quiet. She greeted them both warmly and then, without any explanation as to the reason for their visit, took them through wide marble hallways replete with pillars. Enormous, muscular, powder-white titans stood guard here and there, placid and even nodding with pleasant smiles as they passed.

"He's just finishing a call," Mrs. Dempsey told them, but opened the office doors they'd reached anyway. They saw the viceroy talking, apparently to nobody, as he paced the floor in an old-world charcoal suit. Hollis looked at Mrs. Dempsey for an okay, and when she nodded, stepped onto the lush carpet inside.

The big oak doors closed behind them.

Now, Hollis did look to Mia. They'd never been on palace grounds before ... let alone inside it ... let alone in Viceroy Dempsey's personal office.

Dempsey saw them, raised a businesslike finger, and then concluded his business with the unseen person. Then he tapped a device and turned to face them.

"Sorry about that," he said. He came forward and extended a hand. Mia and then Hollis shook it, Hollis noting that Dempsey had exactly the right amount of white cuff showing beneath his jacket, exactly the right distance above the fold of his wrist. "Meyer Dempsey."

"I think we all know who you are," Hollis said.

Dempsey ignored Hollis's informality and the way he and Mia both failed to introduce themselves. He'd started it by introducing himself as "Meyer Dempsey" instead of "Viceroy Dempsey." But then again, that didn't surprise Hollis. Dempsey struck him as a man who frowned at pomp and circumstance. Hollis, like a lot of the world, had known Dempsey's name and reputation before the aliens had come. He made an unusual viceroy. The Meyer Dempsey who'd been famous as a producer before he'd been famous as one of the Nine was known for being direct and so to-the-point as to appear cold. He'd intimidated pretty much everyone who'd ever worked with him, but Hollis, reading about him, had thought his reputed manner refreshing. There was enough fluff and bullshit in the world already.

"I'll get right to it," Dempsey said, taking a chair opposite those he offered to Hollis and Mia — and, of course, dominating it. "You were active in Austin before the occupation. Is that correct?"

Active? Hollis wasn't sure what that meant. But Mia answered for both of them.

"We were both in Austin, yes."

"And I believe you knew Brendan Banks."

This was moving too fast. Hollis tried to keep up, to keep his distant cool.

"Yeah."

"Were you aware that Banks was part of a pilot program that predated the establishment of the capitals?"

"What program, exactly?" Hollis asked.

"A sort of law enforcement. But of a very primitive kind."

"You mean he was flagged to be a outlands warlord," Mia said.

"Precisely."

"Yeah," Hollis said. "We knew that."

"Do you know why it never happened? Why his appointment never came to fruition?"

"Because he died."

Dempsey nodded. "In a rather dramatic way. We know

he was on-site at a building that our hosts detonated using one of their incendiaries."

"That's a lot of fancy words to say his bosses blew his ass up." Then, taking a risk but not caring, Hollis added. "Well. *Your* bosses."

Dempsey was unfazed. "Astral intelligence now suggests that the site of that facility was corrupted by a computer virus."

It took Hollis a moment. He knew that most of the world referred to the aliens as "Astrals" and had for years, but to him it still referred to that stupid phone app. To that stupid attache case he'd spent weeks and pints of blood chasing.

"Is that so?" Hollis said.

"Furthermore, intelligence suggests that the two of you were in the area at the time." He looked at Hollis, then. "Well, *you*, anyway, Mr. Palmer. The Astrals have had their eye on you for quite some time."

Ah. Yes. The target-slash-tag that alien cube thing had put out onto the alien network when he'd touched it. That hadn't been a thorn in his shoe for a while now, but it always came back.

"Interesting," Hollis said.

"You, Mrs. Palmer, interest our hosts for a different reason."

"Also interesting," Hollis said, answering before Mia could.

Dempsey seemed to consider, then shifted in his chair.

"I'll be blunt," he said. "What any Astral sees, all of them see. Divinity has records, and I have access to most of those records."

"All they untie your nuts to let you see of them, huh?" Hollis said. Mia stared at him; that was a nudge too far.

But Dempsey rolled on. "We know the two of you were

there, when they destroyed the building housing a proto-type intelligence based on information from the old Astral phone app. We know you were involved, though from where I'm standing, our hosts let you go. They've followed you since, and until now that tracking has been fairly useless. But there are ripples on our intra-city network, and my people think it's due to a worm. Or the remnants of one. I'd like to know what you know about it. And I'd like to know, *if* something was loosed on my city's network, who made it."

Hollis felt his heart race, but he knew this song and dance. He'd faced enough scumbags to know how this worked — and how to tell someone was blustering to get a person to crack. If Dempsey knew they were connected to Canned Heat (which, it seemed, hadn't fizzled entirely after all), he'd have led with a direct accusation backed by proof. God knew Raj Patel would have loved to string them up if they knew enough to justify the time, just for the love of beating it out of them.

But they knew nothing, and this, he tried to tell Mia without a telling glance.

"I'll let you know if I hear anything," Hollis said.

Dempsey stared at them for a very long time. A *very* long time, in total silence.

But then he stood, immaculately tailored pre-invasion suit falling perfectly into place.

"Well then," he said. "It was a pleasure meeting you."

Then, to Hollis's immense shock, he extended his hand again, and again shook both of their hands. Hollis muttered a goodbye, as did Mia.

Before he handed them back over to Patel for dispatch to the streets, he stopped one final time.

"I hope you continue to enjoy your stay in Heaven's Veil,"

he said, nodding at each of them in turn. "If you ever need anything, don't hesitate to ask."

"Uh ... okay."

"And in the meantime," Dempsey said, "we'll be watching you."

When, ten minutes later, they were back in their own neighborhood and alone again, Mia seemed shaken. So Hollis took her hips in both his hands, looked her in the eye, and said, "I'll be watching you."

She laughed, nervous.

"When you shower, I'll be watching you. When you bathe, I'll be watching you."

"Those are the same basic thing," she said.

"When you change clothes, I'll be watching you. And whenever you drop something and bend over to retrieve it with your ass facing me, I'll be watching you."

That broke the ice, and with the mood at least somewhat broken, they rounded the corner and went inside their assigned residence.

But that night and every night thereafter when Mia slept early, Hollis went to the window and looked up — at the Apex pyramid, and the mothership hovering forever above the capital.

We'll be watching you.

For now, it meant nothing. They had nothing at all. For now, they were safe.

For now.

WHAT TO READ NEXT

Did you know you can get the entire 7-Book *Invasion* Box Set for one conveniently low price? Or read it for free if you are a Kindle Unlimited Member.

Get the complete Invasion Box Set

A QUICK FAVOR

If you enjoyed this book would you please consider writing a review of it on your favorite bookselling site so other readers can enjoy it too? Just a couple of sentences would be fantastic.

Thanks!

Johnny B. Truant

ABOUT THE AUTHORS

Avery Blake doesn't want you to know where she lives, or what she does. She travels the world, moving from place to place quickly to ensure she can't be tracked. It's safer that way.

When she's not looking over her shoulder, you can find her in the corner of a cafe, facing the exit, typing as fast as she can.

* * *

Johnny B. Truant is co-owner of the Sterling & Stone Story Studio, an IP powerhouse focusing on books and adaptations for film and television. It's the best job in the world, and he spends his days creating cool stuff with partners Sean Platt and David W. Wright, as well as more than 20 gifted storytellers.

Johnny is the bestselling author of over 100 books under various pen names, including the Fat Vampire and Invasion series. On the nonfiction side, he's also co-author of the indie publishing mainstay Write. Publish. Repeat. and co-host of the weekly Story Studio Podcast.

Originally from Ohio, Johnny and his family now live in Austin, Texas, where he's finally surrounded by creative types as weird as he is.

ALSO BY SEAN PLATT

The Dead World Series

Dead Zero

Dead City

Dead Nation

Dead Planet

Empty Nest

The Beam Series

The Beam Season One

The Beam Season Two

The Beam Season Three

Robot Proletariat Series

En3my

Robot Proletariat

The Infinite Loop

The Hard Reset

Cascade Failure

Reboot

The Tomorrow Gene Series

Null Identity

The Tomorrow Gene

The Tomorrow Clone

The Eden Experiment

Karma Police Series

Jumper

Karma Police

The Collectors

Deviant

The Fall

Homecoming

Yesterday's Gone

October's Gone

Yesterday's Gone Season One

Yesterday's Gone Season Two

Yesterday's Gone Season Three

Yesterday's Gone Season Four

Yesterday's Gone Season Five

Yesterday's Gone Season Six

Tomorrow's Gone

Tomorrow's Gone Season One

Tomorrow's Gone Season Two

Tomorrow's Gone Season Three

Available Darkness

Darkness Itself

Available Darkness Book One

Available Darkness Book Two

Available Darkness Book Three

WhiteSpace

WhiteSpace Season One

WhiteSpace Season Two

WhiteSpace Season Three

Stand Alone Novels

Burnout

The Island

Crash

Emily's List

Pattern Black

Devil May Care

The Secret Within

ALSO BY JOHNNY B. TRUANT

The Dead World Series

Dead Zero

Dead City

Dead Nation

Dead Planet

Empty Nest

The Fat Vampire Series

Fat Vampire

Fat Vampire 2: Tastes Like Chicken

Fat Vampire 3: All You Can Eat

Fat Vampire 4: Harder, Better, Fatter, Stronger

Fat Vampire 5: Fatpocaplypse

Fat Vampire 6: Survival of the Fattest

The Fat Vampire Chronicles

The Vampire Maurice

Anarchy and Blood

Vampires in the White City

The Beam Series

The Beam Season One

The Beam Season Two

The Beam Season Three

Robot Proletariat Series

En3my

Robot Proletariat

The Infinite Loop

The Hard Reset

Cascade Failure

Reboot

The Invasion Series

Longshot

Invasion

Contact

Colonization

Annihilation

Judgment

Extinction

Resurrection

The Tomorrow Gene Series

Null Identity

The Tomorrow Gene

The Tomorrow Clone

The Eden Experiment

Stand Alone Novels

Pretty Killer

Pattern Black

Burnout

The Target

The Island

Devil May Care

www.ingramcontent.com/pod-product-compliance
Lightning Source LLC
Chambersburg PA
CBHW010535100726
47903CB00011B/3011